Izzy and Eve

Also by Neal Drinnan

Fiction
Glove Puppet
Pussy's Bow
Quill

Nonfiction
The Rough Guide to Gay and Lesbian Australia

Izzy and Eve

An Erotic Thriller

Neal Drinnan

Green Candy Press

Izzy and Eve by Neal Drinnan
ISBN 1-931160-46-5
Published by Green Candy Press
www.greencandypress.com

Cover and interior design: Ian Phillips

Printed in Canada by Transcontinental Printing Inc.
Massively distributed by P.G.W.

For lovers and friends, past, future and ever present

One can't forever stand on the shore; at some point, filled with indecision, skepticism, reservation and doubt, you either jump in or concede that life is forever elsewhere.
—Arthur Miller

The road of excess leads to the palace of wisdom.
—William Blake

Beggar's Belief

Beggars we are and beggars we'll be.
If Daddy's not working, there'll be nothing for tea
if Mother's not happy, then Daddy gets none
and here ends our history, the yarn never spun.

If baby is hungry and rocks all alone
and conjures up visions from nether-a-zone
then life will be humble and time will be brief
because she has a secret that beggars belief.

Sinners we are and sinners we'll be
if Israel's not Zion, who then is He?
If Jordan's an angel who's fallen from grace
then tell me who God is and show me His face.

Prologue

EVANGELINE

Promiscuous. The word rustles through my mind like a cheap taffeta evening dress or a cruel, Chinese whisper at a debutante's ball. It chases and chastens me as I slip from barroom to brothel, from hostess to whore.

The things I want are not safe things to have. In that regard I am similar to Israel. Age or wisdom haven't helped either, though I'd hoped they might. I've waited so long for something resembling emotional maturity and while I may have developed some perspective, it only serves to compound matters. You'd think by now we'd both have developed some sense in ourselves, an ordered behavioral code or some moderation to our compulsions. Israel says in the most philosophical of tones that he looks forward to being dead and I suppose I do as well but for vastly different reasons. He feels his existence was fêted whereas I think of mine more as fated.

I've the pills for Mondays and Tuesdays, and things to take for Bluesdays. Getting off the pills can kill you—or can be worse than dying because the monsters gather strength from their confinement. In the end they invariably escape. I suppose I always knew they would. And I've long suspected it would happen when I was on my own.

Israel was everything and nothing. He's everywhere and nowhere and if I'm not mistaken, I'm losing my mind.

Part I

The Gilgal

ISRAEL

Firstly, a few housekeeping details so we can get down to business. The place is a city, as big as you like. Millions of us live here in various states of composure and disarray. Like all huge cities, it's a cruel, incontinent place where excess and need bleed into one another. Most people are too ambitious, too nervous or just too damned tired to be kind anymore and I'm tired too: tired of waiting for it all to change. Each of us is no more to the other than a static buzz, a blip on the radar. Of course it's always the ones you think that about, the ones you accidentally injure or cross, who turn up again. Oops. And you're left with your foot in your mouth or worse. It's always just when you think there is no rhyme or reason, no coherence or cohesion to it all, that it proves you wrong and you're left with egg all over your face.

Somewhere along the way, here, in this crazed republic, we lost our absurd collective notions of national identity and good riddance to them I say. I never much liked our dominant culture anyhow. Now, I can barely even remember what it was.

Evangeline and I live in a small two-story house in a district known as the Gilgal. It's populated with artists, migrants, itinerants and whores. Our postal zone code defies all demographic rationalizations and our statistics on everything from health to finance are utterly skewed when compared with the rest of the nation. It's the part of town where round pegs don't have to fit in square holes.

The Gilgal is cluttered with Chinese rooming houses where residents concoct strange, stinking potions at all hours. Cooking smells and dog shit smells combine to create the signature fragrance of the precinct. Herbalists occupy attics, while advertising agencies take the basements. The cobbled lanes that run like clotted arteries behind our abodes were once used by night-men who emptied the festering latrines under the discreet cloak of darkness. Now, the same lanes attract alcoholics, drug addicts, pigeons and feral cats. Nothing's changed, yet there's a magic to the mire.

A few doors away from us stands a mosque with a rather fetching if somewhat incongruous minaret imported from the arid states of the Middle East. It is from here that the Muadhadhin calls the city's taxi drivers and rug merchants to prayer five times a day. Opposite us is an ancient hotel that functions lately as a backpacker hostel for the world's young adventurers: youthful zealots of hedonism, hell-bent on self-destruction and spontaneous seduction. Reckless punters who party all night long to songs from their homelands. Every evening they fornicate, excitedly and variously mixing the pollen of nations, and eventually lay themselves out cold with lager, cider and cheap alcoholic soda. We've found them curled on our doorstep in the wee small hours, shamed by sober Muslims on their way to dawn prayer or being shooed and beaten savagely with brooms by the district's Chinese landladies. Party, party, party, that's all these globetrotters think about. And why shouldn't they? Weren't we just the same?

There's an abundance of restaurants in the neighborhood, bars both chic and seedy, noodle factories, tattoo parlors, discount clothing warehouses, churches with bells that ring out their archaic piety whenever they please and last but not least, more brothels than you could fantasize in your wildest, wettest dreams. With a few hundred bucks in your pocket you could vanish for days in this part of town and many people do. The highlife turns quickly to lowlife and some of us never quite surface again.

In summer the heat is shockingly oppressive. In winter, the cold can kill you in a matter of hours if you don't rug up. The filth of the district mounts through the hot months then winter arrives, briskly killing off the old and the unwary. Our city is a capitalist petri dish, cleansed by an annual ice age. A place where rich and poor are able to gingerly share the streets in the milder months and suspiciously maneuver their way around each other in the cold.

The government believes that the prosperity of individuals is our primary national goal and voters have elected to share this belief for more years than I can remember. The result being that public works have gradually ground to a halt. Parks have become parched, unpleasant places to fear and avoid at night. Income taxes have dwindled while business profits soared. Private splendor and public squalor best describe the landscape of this fair but blighted city.

Years ago when property here wasn't worth a hoot or a damn, Evangeline and I bought our house and agreed to share our lives and assets as long as we both shall live—so help us God(dess). Not that she believes in God. She hardly even believes in good but as I have said to her, how can you believe in evil without believing in good? She rolls her eyes and says, "Take a look around you, Israel. Wake up and smell the *cawffee*." She has her reasons for meditating on evil. She needs it though she'd never admit as much. We've all got our problems, our hobbies, and for her evil provides both. Why not? If you live backwards, evil is what you get!

The first thing you need to know about Evangeline, is that she is not the woman other people think she is. Nor am I the man she presumes me to be. Evangeline is like no other girl I know but I guess I don't know that many girls. For some reason—I can't remember now—I don't know as many people as I used to. I always liked having lots of acquaintances; so did she, but somehow, over the years, they just fell away. I suppose it's true: what youth deemed crystal, age finds out was dew.

Evangeline is not at the brothel tonight nor is she in her workshop making medieval and Byzantine poison rings or pince-nez. No. Tonight she is going through her folder of nasties—never a good sign—but I always join her for it. She needs the support and me, I need the context.

Evangeline, or Eve as I sometimes call her (because she was my first—and last), is not a prostitute. She's a receptionist at the brothel down our road. It's been there for years. The Gilgal has mixed zoning which means you can open a cathouse or a cattery with similarly minimal amounts of bureaucracy. The brothel is opposite the Chinese mini-mart and a curiously named, and seriously not-recommended, take-out food shop called Gypsy Grits. You can pick the brothels by the clichéd red lights or the huge street numbers printed in sans-serif gold or burgundy over the awnings. Many are just known by their street number though some have more obviously suggestive names like Saigon Boy, which predictably enough offers homosexual men a smorgasbord of illegally imported Thai delicacies. There's *La Maison de Margeurite*, which specializes in the transportation of transgendered immigrants and there's the vulgarly named *La Vue Longtime*, which is popular with exotica-seeking businessmen on their way home to other more respectable precincts.

Occasionally religious groups picket the streets: mostly just a few ruddy-faced Bible-quoting men with outdated suits smelling of mothballs or prim middle-aged ladies with lips pursed like assholes, clutching cheap vinyl handbags. The women look like they have degrees in flower arranging and tea making yet they carry expensive digital cameras to photograph and document the vehicle registration plates of brothel "clients." They are not at all happy about the random, explicit things that go on between people's legs in this neck of the woods so they like to expose the hapless brothel patrons on the "page of shame" which they dutifully take out monthly in the worst of our tabloid newspapers. On one recent occasion of protest, Juanita, a big Hispanic gender-mess from *Maison de Margeurite* was out on the balcony showing the protesters her huge breast implants. She was shaking them to the sound of Caribbean music from inside when she honed in on some wizened old codger from the church. She danced about in a lurid lemon-colored negligee of shocking transparency with matching knickers proudly showcasing the thick mattress of black pubic hair beneath them.

"Hey *hombre,* you come upstairs; Juanita, she waiting, she take care of you *meester.*" Then she began fondling her breasts. "These— you see?—the doctor, he make nice and big for you baby." Then she plunged her fingers down into her pants. "But down here he make special—he make not-so-big-at-all." Evangeline and I were nearly busting a gut as we lugged our groceries past the scene but this old guy looked ready to have a coronary, especially when she waved a threatening, orange acrylic talon at him. "Juanita—she got her eye on you honey!"

You have to ignore the church folk in the Gilgal just like you ignore the drunks and addicts unless of course you're as fucked up as they are. If you walk from our house to City Central Station, you'll likely be accosted by Seventh Day Adventists or Mormons, or encounter the seemingly serene, almost transcendental woman who remains in a permanent state of religious ecstasy. Her cheeks pink and her eyes alight, she sings like a lark at sunrise from atop the station mailbox. She has handwritten fliers and recordings of her a capella song that you can buy for next to nothing, though no one ever does:

I'm going over Jordan, I'm going over there.
He's waiting there to see me,
to right this Earthly snare.

No longer will I stumble and nevermore I'll fall
and as an angel timeless,
shall I through the ages call.

In Heaven's fine interior, beyond the laws of Rome
there we'll meet forever,
He's come for to carry me home.

She's the only one who truly fascinates me; she actually sounds like an angel and nights in the Gilgal can get very dark. I know her song by heart. Everyone does. This one song is all she ever sings. Perhaps she's truly been "saved" though her faith does seem stuck in a groove. There's got to be more to enlightenment than crappy gospels and zealotry. She either did too much acid in her youth or has already moved over into the other world. She's crazy all right, but she's serene. Serenity is a scarce commodity around here. Like Juanita's breasts or the moist seductive environs beneath her negligee, in this part of the world you can never be sure if anything is for real. One minute you're listening to an angel promising paradise; the next, some kid on a skateboard whooshes past wearing a T-shirt that says *Jesus was a liar and a cunt*. Who are you going to believe?

Evangeline is a cynic. I know that's cruel to say but she's got good reason. Don't get me wrong! When she's up, she's right up there. And she can be very funny too, like she was the day when we passed some Mormons deep in theological discussion and one said to the other,

"Oh, I'm sure the Lord has a sense of humor," and she interrupted and said, "Of course *She* does. Do you want to hear a joke?"

The two were slightly dumbstruck but nodded nonetheless while nervously eyeing us.

"Well, here goes. What did the Seventh Day Adventist say to the Mormon who had taken over his street corner?"

"I dunno," ventured the braver of the two.

"Shove off brother, you're cramping my *style*."

The two looked at each other and frowned glumly. "Hey lady, we don't get it."

"Well it's simple you sillies. Who's ever seen a Mormon *or* a Seventh Day Adventist street preacher with any *style*." She was off in gales of laughter, her outlandish jewelry and blood-colored lipstick marking her out as a witch to these guardians of Zion. I felt awful taking the piss out of those poor guys but I couldn't resist doing a cartoon about it the following week. As for the Mormons, poor lambs, they're probably still scratching their heads.

The brothel where Evangeline works is at 755 Beasley Lane. Code name Seven-Five-Five and I know what you're thinking. Sure, sure she's a receptionist—aren't they all? But with Evangeline it's different. She just helps out some nights when Rahab, Magdelaine or Mai aren't around. Hers is a principled bordello, owned by a progressive collective of libertine women. Don't ask me what goes on in there, it's not my scene if you get my drift. I've been in once, quite impressive it was, too; rather like a Bedouin's tent: candles, oils, Turkish delight on the coffee tables and warm draughts of honeyed liqueurs ready to be sipped by bemused workaday punters in suits. "Byzantine bedlam," she sometimes calls it. "Totally wicked, fancy putting Ali Baba's cave so close to the mosque." But the women who own 755 did their demographics, they had a business plan and the bank even loaned money on the enterprise. "Filthy bastards, bankers," I can hear Evangeline mutter as she scoffs a mouthful of Turkish delight.

Evangeline never entertains the clients herself. Well, almost never. There is one who comes now and again, some dark prince from the Middle East. To hear her speak you'd think it was Lawrence of Arabia himself. So powerful is he, that the madam can lure her around there even when she's not working. "The sheik is here," she whispers in hallowed tones when one of us answers the phone. "Tell Evangeline he's in the Al-Ghaydah room, *waiting.*" She never says much about him, but he brings her gifts; rare expensive imported liqueurs, bizarre stones in Arabesque settings and exquisite boxes filled with pills and potions that are only vaguely reminiscent of things we've taken here in the past. Their effects always differ but they never disappoint. He won't touch them himself but he loves to see what they do to her. Ideally I imagine the prince to be young, handsome and disgracefully rich, but I suspect in reality he's merely the latter. Whatever the case Eve has projected some set of attributes onto him that allow him the rare privilege of accessing her almost anytime he calls. Her bitter feminist platitudes seem to all but disappear whenever he's in town and she's always at a loss to understand why he's chosen her. "There are girls years younger and much skinnier. I suppose I'm just Little Miss Personality."

Mostly Evangeline hates the Arabs who colorfully gather in our street after prayer times. Some are friendly and nod pleasantly as they pass in their robes of Koranic splendor or pristine white. I've even chatted to the Imam about parking and the council's abandoned cherry picker, but not Evangeline. She'll have none of it.

"Get enough of them in the country and we'll be dragged back five hundred years, kept barefoot and pregnant, banished in Purdah, strapped to pyres like witches or slaughtered like cows in dowry disputes. They want women to be slaves. I'm not going to nod to them like you do in your sycophantic way."

"Sycophantic! Excuse me, I bet the sheik is a Muslim."

"Even if he is, I'm merely his whore. You think I'm all starry-eyed about him but I'm only a courtesan. I know that. He knows that. *Genitals can meet in places where minds never could*, isn't that one of yours Izzy?"

"He makes you cum, doesn't he? That's what it is. You can fuck him stone-cold sober and the fireworks still go off."

"There's more to it than that!"

I don't inquire further. I rather like the romance of it all. I'm tempted to go and spy on him as he emerges from the brothel and disappears into the chauffeur-driven limo that hovers in the street like an incandescent cigar for however long he takes to complete his business. But there are some fantasies I'd rather leave intact.

Evangeline's real money comes from the jewelry: Pointed medieval cones fashioned out of sterling silver, pewter, platinum or gold. Metallic flourishes both beautiful and dangerous forged with anvils in our own back shed. Sharp-tipped delicacies that beautify hands as well as making them a menace. Savage rebukes for wandering paws or evil eyes. Several exclusive shops around the city buy her work, even a department store downtown. Her creations are rare and desirable enough that she can please herself about who she sells to and if her bills aren't paid on time, her customers never get another chance. She'd rather starve than kowtow to big business.

If she's well enough, stable enough, she'll put on one of her figure-hugging dresses, a brooch, several of her favorite rings—even nail varnish if her nails haven't been destroyed through her work—and set forth for her clients' shops, armed with a velvet-lined case displaying a month's worth of painstaking work. When she's feeling hale and hearty she could sell steak to a vegan, her confident fingers picking out one piece at a time and illuminating it with faux-history and lies.

"Queen Christina of Sweden was adorned with a ring just like this on her wedding night. It had a crust of Siberian diamonds and cold Scandinavian emeralds around the crown. Legend had it that if she scratched her lover with the diamonds and they were stained by the blood, he would betray her with another woman. As you can see, these stones are all red because of course he did."

The truth was she had an excess of red jasper and alexandrite and the gentle pink hues were more suggestive of coconut ice than blood but she wasn't one to let truth stand in the way of a good story. While her buyers could at least prove the quality of her materials if they wanted to, it suited them to believe the tales and pass on her unlikely myths to their customers. Her work radiates a most brilliant light but Evangeline spends much of her life in darkness. For my part I can only try to illuminate it but I'm not God so in a relationship as codependent as ours, I have to face the possibility that I might be part of the problem.

When she starts with the folder of clippings, I go to her. Her face becomes cold and intense as she concentrates on newsprint and photographs. Her fingers gently touch the ink then press against the image. She says she can feel what happened to these unfortunate victims, always women.

Today in the color section of the newspaper is a story entitled *Whatever happened to the Milkshake Girl?* It's the grim tale of Lydia Darlington, who disappeared a year ago. Lydia was a promising model with a shady past and a weakness for cocaine. The picture shows her sucking on a fluorescent green milkshake from a clear plastic bag. She's wearing a pink camisole with one of the straps playfully falling off her shoulder. Her hair is teased up wildly, her belly button boasts a silver ring and her cheekbones cut through all the bullshit.

"She's dead," says Eve as she intuits her psychic version of the story. "Dead within hours of the disappearance. She didn't expect to be killed—didn't realize the stakes were that high. She was using too much coke. She couldn't read situations properly." According to the article, Lydia had just been offered a modelling job in Japan when she disappeared. She'd been working as an escort for some dodgy Eastern Bloc couple who were pretending to run a theatrical agency. Things were going well, her life was looking up. She knew she was leaving town and started pocketing more than her share of the loot. No case had ever really come of it but to read the article you'd wonder why not. Our city specializes in these unsolved crimes and I read them as compulsively as Evangeline. It's just that I don't keep them and go over and over them the way she does. As if they were all pieces from some macabre jigsaw that will one day resolve itself.

Eve continues to murmur her psychic appraisal: "They *own* the girls, these assholes. Lydia didn't understand that. She thought the job was just a fill-in until better things came her way. When they did, she got cocky—cavalier. Careless. She was showing them she was more than a pretty face, more than pussy. That was her mistake. She decided the money was really hers. A bump of coke, dreams of fame, a touch of attitude. For a minute she *was* Cinderella, the IT girl. But oh, yuck. That pimp and his lackey…drugs…a boat in the estuaries, nasty, vigorous struggle." Her fingers jump off the page as if they'd been burnt. "Ooh she had some strength! They didn't figure on a fight like that! 'Drown ya bitch,' I can hear him saying. It's ugly, but not as bad as some. Legs, strappy high heels coming loose, panties tearing on the edge of the boat. Bubbles, struggle, a floating mess of bleached hair." She sighs. "They put weights on her and you know what that estuary is like for sharks and bottom-feeders at that time of year. They'll never recover the body."

Eve shakes her head. "It's always the same with these downwardly mobile middle-class girls. They don't understand how little worth a woman has in the underworld. They think it's a game— that they are special, smart or pretty enough to survive it—but there are always more where they came from." She nods sagely like a gypsy who's just read a crystal ball. "They're just broads. Dumb, disposable broads to these guys."

I don't know whether Eve really has the psychic ability to see beneath the surface of these stories but as so few of the mysteries are ever solved, I give her the benefit of the doubt. Even the broad-sheets love to feature these tales. They have grab lines like *To Kill a Model, Pretty Girl: Pretty Dead* or *Welcome to the Kingdom of Vanishing Beauties*. Evangeline collects them all and her folder bulges with the yellowing clippings and their faded snapshots of smiling, missing, dead girls. All of them victims of male cruelty and the dark alchemies of a gender war no one seems to understand.

Boys disappear too in similarly sordid ways but it's the girls that remain close to Evangeline's heart. And it's strange because in the real world, her own world, she doesn't seem to like women that much but when they vanish, or make the headlines, they turn into poor lost angels, flawless and beatified—while men prove time and time again to be nothing more than monsters and thugs.

EVANGELINE

We're not *proper* people, Israel and me. I suppose that's why we live in the Gilgal with all the art-trash, immigrants and rebels. We've been here so long I don't feel like a rebel but I suppose that's what I am. We don't organize our finances cleverly, or keep up with décor trends. We always hoped to renovate but our stars have never quite risen high enough for us to afford it. We haven't got short-term and long-term goals or families to keep us tethered to normality. We don't have pension plans or lifetime health coverage and we seldom even vote because there are only two parties to choose from. One's as corrupt as the other. You're damned if you do, damned if you don't. Democracy seems a farce to us these days and I wonder now if it's even a possibility. I mean if the gentle folk are too ensnared by ennui to be bothered to vote why wouldn't the bullies just take over? But politics aside, we do have our creativity and a history to bind us.

Neal Drinnan

Israel says we choose our lives, allocate ourselves certain challenges and if we're lucky we find a soul mate. He's supposed to be mine if I were to believe in such things, which I don't. This particular theory emerged during his Buddhist phase, which gave way to Tao/Tantra and now seems to have moved on to his more proactive S/M activities. The latest thing he believes is that he can get closer to liberating his soul by defiling his body and given the state he's come home in from time to time, I can only hope he's succeeding. Much as I love his fiery energy and his perennial quest of the spirit, I tend to be more your sedentary, secular girl. He maintains that my lesson for this life is faith to which I say, "And I suppose you're to be my shabby shaman?" I've argued until I'm blue in the face that I find human existence far too banal to have ever *chosen* it and if I'm to have a so-called *choice* when I die, I would *not* choose to come back. But there's no telling Izzy that. He plows through his books on spiritual awakening, even talks to the Imam at the mosque to "glean a Muslim perspective." "You want a Muslim perspective?" I say. "Well try being locked in the house all day under a burka. Try not showing your face in public or being stoned to death in the backyard because your dowry is too meagre or because you took a shine to the milkman."

"Shoosh shoosh," he says, "you're getting all mixed up. It's the Hindus who do the dowry killings and they'd probably immolate you. The Muslim husband offers the woman a dowry and they'd likely as not behead you as stone you these days. Besides, none of that happens here. This is a modern country."

Of course that's exactly where he's wrong and that's why I keep my scrapbook of atrocities. Only last year a woman in one precinct of this very city was murdered by her own father because she refused to marry. "Pride," he said and it makes my blood boil that these people are even allowed to continue such traditions as arranged marriage in this country. Why, just yesterday we were at the greengrocer's that is owned by an Islamic couple. The wife works behind the counter as well as trying to manage the three kids at her feet. This harried, rather haggard-looking corporate executive came in with a fistful of car keys and a Volvo parked illegally outside. She must have been pushing forty and was obviously throwing together a dinner for someone. She looked disdainfully at the wilted rocket and spinach: "I'm in quite a rush—do you have anything better?" The woman at the counter shook her head but smiled at the woman's pregnant belly. "You have many children?" The woman looked annoyed by the question. "No, this is my first." By then she was inspecting the tomatoes.

"Oh, is your first? Is a boy, yes?"

"No, I mean we don't know. We didn't *want* to know." She selected two tomatoes with an expression of irritation.

"Ah, boy is good!"

"We'll be happy with either," she muttered as she rifled through her bag for coins.

"Girl is pretty but boy, boy is better. Your husband, I think *he* want a boy. A boy make him happy."

"Jesus Christ." I heard her groan and between gritted teeth she said, "This fucking country." Her clever makeup hadn't endured the day any better than she had and as Israel and I watched her dump the shopping in the car, I turned to him. "There are the choices for oppression. Husband or job."

"Ah yes, they don't put five big zeros in the six-figure salary for nothing," he answered as the little girl looked warily at us from behind her mother's skirts. "You two have children?" the woman asked Israel. "Just inner ones," he smiled. She bagged our vegetables and smiled nervously. "Inahwan is nice name I think. Boy or girl?"

Israel will always have some pacifying argument for everything. He thinks of faith as a sanctuary whereas I think of it as a fool's paradise. Mostly I don't ask and he doesn't tell with all his S/M stuff. I don't get to meet his partners in crime and he's never met "the sheik," and we like it that way. I know he'll be home when he's hungry and he knows I'll be there when he comes.

For men the world is a smorgasbord, they can access and sample whatever they like. Israel in his tireless Siddharthian way doesn't see the inequality. Men generally don't and while women may seem to have the monopoly on certain wiles (which are all but useless with fags) men have an ignorant, clumsy optimism that allows them to ride roughshod and oblivious over the better part of human suffering. Izzy likes to quote people, I remember him quoting Joni Mitchell from an old scratched vinyl record that he still plays, something about us all being chickens scratching for immortality. I quote Mae West at him: "You're not too bright—I like that in a man," and while I don't share many of his beliefs, I think he probably knows he's the brightest star that ever shone on my horizon. It doesn't pay to let any man, even in a platonic relationship like ours, think he's too indispensable.

ISRAEL

Cuss 'n' Holler is a coffee shop a few doors away. I go there because the coffee's great and I know Vi, the woman who owns it. She's always good for a laugh. It's often crowded and today I sat next to a table where this big fat woman was smoking. You're not supposed to smoke in cafes these days. She was one of those defiant types, a loud bossy chick with arty black-rimmed glasses, red lipstick and heaps of black flowing clothes. The sort who would either love you or hate you from the word *go*, the fag hag type who everyone is scared of because she's so forceful, confident and demanding. The sort of person you know will be a hopeless bundle of insecurities when she gets behind the locked door of home. "The endomorph type," my Feldenkrais teacher would have called her. I hate myself for thinking that—I don't like getting into his categorizations about people and I gave up on Feldenkrais with all its intelligent movement and spinal empowerment years ago. Not because I didn't think it worked but because my teacher had all these theories about people and body types; ectomorphs, mesomorphs and endomorphs. According to him, endomorphs were self-loathing control freaks who wanted the whole world to change to fit their view of things. *It is not I who argue with the world but the world that argues with me,* which from a Buddhist perspective sounds like a fair cop. Apparently endomorphs want to contract the world down to match their mean, fearful view of it rather than expand to meet its infinite possibilities. "That is their covenant," he would pronounce with a rather absurd flourish as if people could be rounded up and dismissed in a single categorical epithet. It just goes to show the sorts of things you are vulnerable to taking in on the massage table. And here am I making a judgment about this woman I don't know using criteria I don't even accept. I looked *endomorph* up in the dictionary and it offers two definitions: one is a mineral enclosed within another and the second is an animal that lives and finds food in the internal organs of another, not a very pleasant thing to be called really, is it? The worst of it was when he realized you weren't going to argue with him. He'd feed you more and more of these theories about stuff, like how one in a hundred people is an alien and how alien girls have multiple clitorises and possibly more than one uterus and alien boys can have multiple orgasms and self-lubricating assholes. I'd drift off because his massage was always good but I had to stop and think because I know how to have multiple orgasms myself using ancient eastern methods. I did once fuck a self-lubricating boy who I thought came from Scandinavia. I didn't share my possible close encounter with my teacher though. In fact he talked so much you couldn't get a word in edgeways. Finally he just got to be too much. It turned out he was one of those people who didn't believe the Holocaust happened and whether his theories on this came out because my name is Israel and he thought I was Jewish ('fraid not), I don't know, but bait me he did because I stormed out of there one day saying, "You can't just create a scale of humanity to suit your own ends—I know what you're playing at and I don't like it one bit. Either we're all damned or we're all saved—end of story." I gave him my money and left. Probably I'll end up a hunchback but I'm no Nazi.

The problem with that endomorph thing is that sometimes I've thought that way about Evangeline—that she lives off some part of me—and then I think of myself that way but not with her, with the other people, people she doesn't really know about. There is stuff she wouldn't want to know about me. Stuff you mightn't want to know either. The funny thing is, if you find these things out, it's more likely to be because of her than because of me. Someone else always has to clean up the mess and I'm a messy pup.

EVANGELINE

The metals I use are very costly and I have to pay for them up front: gold, sterling silver, pewter and on occasion platinum. I'm not that keen on rose gold, it's too soft and generally I only use gold to add embellishments to the silver, a tiny coarse crown around a Plantagenet finger horn or a raffish twist to a Byzantine semi-precious setting. It's fiddly work and time consuming. That's why my work is expensive. That's why it's only in the best shops in town. The brothel I work in, that's just for mad money; groceries, frocks and booze. I like scotch, Izzy likes bourbon. The effect is the same and our bottles diminish at comparative rates except that he is not usually on antidepressants so he can afford to overdo it. When I do, the result can be pretty ugly, or so I'm told. Fortunately for me I seldom remember my forays into alcoholic oblivion.

I've just finished work for the day; I've locked my materials away in the safe. There are busses passing out front, which is always a strange sight in a street as narrow as ours. You'd wonder they could get into the streets at all and I'm sure there's supposed to be some bylaw forbidding vehicles over a certain size from using them. Still, every weekend they come, loaded with women from the precincts. They come to shop at all the rag trade manufacturing outlets that occupy the Gilgal. Places with names like Gilgal Garment Seconds, Mean Business, or the Big Girl's Bonanza where racks and racks of larger-sized clothes "for the fuller figure" stretch off into the fluorescent never-never. Together the women pick through piles of acrylic tents with sequined "features" on them in the ten-dollar bins then haul their bounty over to Manchester Madness or Rebock, Stock & Barrel to see what's cheap there. They wear name tags: *Merle, Shauna, Cassandra, Jacqueline*—I can see them passing now flushed with the thrill of the spend. They'll get home tonight, look at the rubbish they've bought and realize they could have done just as well in their local mall. But it gets them out I suppose and they do get to sip nasty, acidic sparkling wine on the coach for free.

A lot of those women are the same age as me. It makes me shudder, their little double chins, their quick 'n' pretty makeup jobs and the middle-aged gestures they're fighting against yet unable to hide. I can hear the coach driver, "All aboard girls. Come on Shauna, back on the bus darlin' and be sure 'n' ride up front where I can get a look atcha doll." The bus driver's a sleazy-looking fifty-year-old man who never noticed that somewhere in the last twenty years his flirtations became grotesque. And why should he when the women still giggle like schoolgirls at a hockey match or grannies who hoped their luck might have changed. It's only a matter of a few years before these "girls" are wearing cardigans over their shoulders and stuffing handkerchiefs up their sleeves; it's only a few years *since* they were hanging around the Gilgal and Latin District, shimmying into nightclubs on high heels, shopping for discount husbands. Now they come back for the clearance sales and their husbands come back for the whores. Everyone gets what he wants and life goes on. She gets a size-16 mother-of-the-bride dress for fifty bucks and he gets sixteen-year-old-pussy for five times that.

I'm cynical I know, but not without a sense of humor.

ISRAEL

I'm not good on chronology, you'll have to excuse me, but both she and I are creatures haunted by nostalgia. Silently at some distant point in the past we agreed to see each other as we'd want others, strangers, to see us. I know that's not terribly mature but I suspect a sustained immaturity is also part of our pact. "I won't see what's wrong with you if you don't notice what's flawed in me." It's a game everyone plays to some extent. The end result (apart from delusion) is a rather fluid notion of the self. But suffering seems to be a fair indication that something might be amiss. Not self-inflicted pain *a la* my forays into masochism but episodic periods of torment such as those visited upon and suffered by Evangeline.

I could choose for instance to descend into a narrative reverie of our trip to Venice many years ago. We were young, laughing at antiquity with all its pretty ruin as if we were outside of it. Beyond its grasp. We then went to Paris where we escaped the July heat in the dank catacombs. We spent hours among the stacked skeletons Napoleon had placed there when he emptied cemeteries to build art galleries and other more utilitarian monuments to himself. We smiled benignly at a French sign that proclaimed in direst Gothic script:

Laugh fair mortals,
while ye may
the sun still shines
on this your day
but winter beckons
as it surely must
so soon your bones
will outnumber us.

Izzy and Eve

Who would have taken mortality seriously then? Not Eve on *Canale Grande*, always up for another glass of fine wine or even a plastic cup of cheap Chianti. Her breasts heaved under thin cotton dresses and her billowing hair shone like honey while an Adriatic breeze caressed her cheek. My reflection in her sunglasses and hers in mine. But I'm not going to launch into "Those Were the Days My Friend." Everyone started young and got old. It's the oldest gag in the book, boring as bat-shit and not something for which you get any pity.

I could tell you about a more seedy and jaded Hawaiian holiday we took ten years later on a bunch of mileage points I gathered in my brief moment of corporatism. She'd put on a bit more weight, a bit more makeup. I'd lost half my hair and half my brain cells. We were a different pair than those wet-behind-the-ears simps on the steps of *San Marco*.

What did she say on the plane? "I feel like Elizabeth Taylor when she came out of Betty Ford." I said I felt like nothing at all but that wasn't true. That's how I feel now. Sometimes that's a good thing, sometimes not so good. The problem with the world, this hard-edged material world, is that we're really only perfectly geared to it for about twenty years. We get help for the first fifteen, the next twenty are a relative walk in the park but after that we get baggage, emotional and physical. Coughs persist, fat spreads and backs ache. Is it an injustice or do we deserve every one of those mounting handicaps?

We neither of us care about the affairs of the world anymore. Me, because they no longer seem real to me, and Evangeline because she is unable to cope with them. She determinedly avoids news programs on the television and even the horror stories she collects usually come from the color weekend section of the newspaper. She skips the front pages.

"I spent years, Izzy, *years*, fretting and agonizing over starving children, the environment, the stark horror and injustice of the world. I'd watch the TV or read the paper and feel like I was a live fish that had just been scaled and left out in the sun. My flesh would crawl when I realized I was one of these creatures—and whatever lyricists might tell you to the contrary, the female of the species is *not* more deadly than the male. Then one day, I think I was about thirty, I just decided not to play anymore: Bombs, wars, natural disasters. I don't want to know—I can't afford to know or take them on board. They cost me too much!"

Me, on the other hand, I tend to stick to reading those articles about people whose lives and careers have taken off splendidly: women who manage to have two children, a corporate directorship, several honorary fellowships, a sensational wardrobe and entertaining tips for those less fortunate. I could never be one of these people myself you must understand, I'm far too lazy, other people's power and competition intimidates me terribly and life is far too brief for me to bother with acquisitions, yet I read them nonetheless so I can at least maintain the illusion that the worldly struggle is a worthy one. The papers run these articles in the same issues as Eve's disappearing-girl-act stories. One city resident finds her way down to the murky depths of the estuaries while another enjoys three hundred and sixty degree river views. It's the way of the world after all.

EVANGELINE

If you know the city as I do, you know not to go into Gethsemane Park after dark. Both Israel and I have been mugged there and the muggings are usually done by teenagers. The teenagers mostly come from the Causeway or the nearby housing projects that are hotbeds of social strife though if you're an egalitarian, you're not meant to say that. The muggers were also members of the Haseeshi people who are the indigenous people of this area and one certainly isn't supposed to mention that. It seems the more often a social symptom manifests itself in the Gilgal or the city, the less polite or correct it is to mention it in the company of liberals. Now don't get me wrong! If the Haseeshi youths had wanted to retaliate against all the monstrous injustices dealt them in the past, they could have slit both our throats from ear to ear, disembowelled us and left our innards hanging from the trees and still not made a mark on the carnival of atrocities waged against them over the centuries. But that's not the point. The point is that it is no wiser to go through the park at night on your own than it was for Snow White or Red Riding Hood to wander off into the woods. The politics and injustices of the past don't enter the daily decisions I make in order to avoid injury or incident.

Israel says the outcome of every decision is in suspension until you act. He thinks that anyone's behavior at the moment of an attack can profoundly influence the outcome of a situation. While I handed my purse over without a second thought and retrieved it (*sans* money) a short way down the path, Israel maintains he managed to stop them from taking his cash. Exactly how he went about that I'm still at a loss to explain. I don't like confrontation and I'm awfully fearful of violence. He would probably maintain that I'm obsessed by it. Would women be violent towards men if it were they who had the physical strength? Who can say? In the short term at least, it seems that men want different things from women and are prepared to use different ploys to get them. I no longer understand gender. It seems like some arbitrary commodity purchased in a church thrift shop and handed out by clueless charity workers.

ISRAEL

In this city it is not hard to fall between the cracks in the pavement. Many do and there are plenty of exciting distractions to occupy you on the journey down. I've spent years "plumbing the depths" as Eve often calls it but quite aside from pleasure, there are other benefits I seek. To live as an ascetic, to deny the self its appetite for sensuality may very well yield the same results as a total immersion in the senses. This is the theory I'm testing when I venture out in the evening to play with Torsten and Gustav. They have created a secret kingdom beneath their house, an entire basement invisible to the outside world that is equipped with every possible device needed to bring about physical and mental disassociation from the self. They are explorers, as Torsten says, they like to "push boundaries." Gustav doesn't say a lot but I know he likes to push too. It's usually him who's being pushed by Torsten to take me to the next level. I've seen some extreme things at that level: black sheep, ravens, blood-red sunsets, mysterious caped figures and even Jesus himself who turned into Satan before my very eyes and then winked at me. "Is good, is good ya?" urges Torsten in his thick German accent. Sometimes I can't answer him. It is intense, expanding, revealing, it may even be enlightening but is it good? I couldn't say just yet.

The demimonde of this city offers many alternatives both in its range of social reprobates and in venues. The great concession wrought by the rampant capitalism is the ultimate inevitability of decadence but even the word *decadence* may be a misnomer. There are groups of people you could hang out with who are constantly inebriated on one substance or another, or at least that's how it seems. "Israel try this, it's new." They give me things that help me see them and the world in a different light. The aftereffects unfortunately also make me see Evangeline or myself at odd and shocking new angles too. That's quite simply the price you must pay for stealing heavenly thunder.

My work is boring me these days. I draw cartoons, often for those adult men's magazines you probably thought went out years ago. Those sexist illustrations that seem to have belonged to males from another generation all my life. Eve hates a lot of the cartoons but she will have a chuckle at them from time to time. Last week I did this picture of a woman with huge breasts, huge hips, a luxuriant pussy and a pinhead. She was standing naked in front of a man and the caption read, *I want someone who is going to love me for my brains not just my body.* As soon as I'd done it I realized I could do a similar one for a gay magazine so I did a guy with a huge cock, huge muscles and a pinhead, then used exactly the same caption again. Sexism can often translate very conveniently from heterosexism to homosexism. That's fine with me if it means twice the cash.

We don't watch the news; Evangeline can't cope with it and lately I've found the stories have no relevance to me. We have agreed to confine ourselves to our bare media essentials, which tends to mean movie channels, DVDs, a few sitcoms and music videos though even music film clips seem more about reinforcing youth and conspicuous consumption than art. When Evangeline is getting depressed she can't even watch the Nature Channel. The other day when I came downstairs she was frozen in front of the screen as a lion tore the throat from a gazelle or some similarly elegant creature. *Nature is neither cruel nor kind, merely an archaic script for survival: a savage, if poetic system of balance, order and chance...* The narrator's voice droned on without expression and Evangeline muttered, "Everything devours everything, the strong slay the weak and on it goes infernally, eternally. Cruelty is victory and we are a part of this!" I noticed then that for the next two hours she was hypnotized by the Home Shopping Network. There is safety and sanity in banality, I could almost hear her muttering as a synthetic-looking woman with a deeply insincere voice dangled nasty gold necklaces in front of the camera. "I'm going out, darling," I say to her. She barely seems to hear me. Her gaze is unbroken, her finger remains poised over the remote control. It is not unknown for her to be still sitting in that exact position when I return, sometimes twelve hours later. When this occurs, I know things are bad.

EVANGELINE

Sometimes I get mixed signals from the articles in the newspapers. Like today my fingers are running over the face of another model. This one was found at the bottom of a cliff near the seaport: Twenty-two, promising career. Handsome boyfriend. Money in the bank—the usual story. And the police closed the book on it months ago. "Suicide," they said but surprise surprise, now they're not so sure about that. They think the boyfriend might be the culprit. There's the possibility he was actually on with a phenomenally wealthy male solicitor who found reasons to dispatch the model himself. As my finger runs over the ink I get the feeling there is someone missing. There is someone else involved and the journalist hasn't uncovered this fact. "*Someone else helped throw her from the cliff,*" I say but of course no one else is home. Israel is out. He's always out and I need to get my act together. Seriously. I pour a scotch. Perhaps after two have burned their way into my gullet I'll have the courage to leave the house, visit Bar None, see who's there and have a laugh with Curtis. Israel and I used to do that all the time, it seemed perfect. Something's changed lately and I can't get a handle on it. I look to Israel for help, or at least substance these days but he's not there. It's like something has snapped inside him and he no longer inhabits the same world as I do. I go back over the past again and again to see if I can work out how we got to this exact point. I look at photos, party videos, letters from lovers and things don't add up. One plus one never equalled two.

We have both had lovers in the past. Many. I always managed to scare mine off and I'm sure Israel helped me do it. I was guilty of saying things I shouldn't have to some of his beaus, things that may have contributed to the demise of those relationships too. I remember doing things of which I'm not particularly proud. I'd answer the phone and the voice would say, "Is Israel there?" I'd say, "Pierre! No he's not, but I'm sure he'll be very pleased to hear from you." I'd intone it suggestively knowing full well it wasn't Pierre but Caleb or whomever and the voice would say, "This is Caleb, you remember from the other night. We met—Evangeline, isn't it?"

"Oh yeah," I'd say, "Sorry, you sound just like Pierre," and I wouldn't need to say any more because the suspicions about what type of man Israel is would be planted. The thing that infuriates me is that he'd be a total slut for months then meet some man who was *different*. He'd get all moony over this guy and suddenly act like he's the quiet monogamous type. I know the truth and because we try to be honest with each other, it is my job to remind him and anyone who comes into his orbit exactly what sort of person he is. If I've sacrificed all the traditional possibilities of heterosexual life for a life with Israel, I'm not going to up and have it threatened by some five-minute affair that at the end of the day won't make anyone happier. Erotic passion is a beast that must be fed but we both know it never lasts. And so the Calebs, the Pierres, the Walters and the Stratoses of this world come and go.

Unfortunately the same can't be said for the Torstens and Gustavs who seem to have taken an unhealthy interest in him of late. They lurk like wolves in the shadows at the edge of the woods, always eager to take another piece of him once they've lured him into the darkness.

You'd think age and vanity would settle men down eventually but things only seem to get worse and dirtier, for him at least. I don't know where he goes or what they do together but when he comes home sometimes he looks as pale as a ghost and smells like hell. I don't like to sound like anyone's mother but I never liked the look of those Germans from the first moment I set eyes on them. They're shifty, misogynistic and I wouldn't trust them as far as I could *sling* them.

In truth, I preferred that awful period when he took to going over to the pub across the road, drinking with the much younger back-packers. He'd delight these lads by drawing caricatures for them. Perhaps it was his hunger for their youth or nostalgia for our own years of carefree travel. But there was always someone there, a young Spaniard, German or Israeli whom he could get drunk with, momentarily befriend, and lure over to our place with the promise of pot or more liquor. I'd be half asleep when they came crashing and laughing through the door and I'd try to block my ears when the raucous camaraderie turned into dangerous seduction or when these handsome young straight boys with broken English got wise to the game. Sure, some of them played, their voices becoming whispers then something else altogether. Sometimes Israel got what he wanted but other times it was a terrible, terrible mistake. I'd lie nervously waiting to hear the breaking of a glass, an accented voice raised in rage or the sickening echo of a blow to Israel's face. Then a fight and the slamming front door as the exotic stranger made his hasty retreat. And Israel would be left muttering drunkenly to himself: "If you don't like the heat, sunshine, then get out of the kitchen," or "There's plenty more where you came from fella." He'd climb the well-worn stairs, flop onto his bed and I'd say nothing about the shiny black bruise that surrounded his eye the next day. A woman's silence speaks volumes. Any girl knows that.

ISRAEL

When Evangeline takes a shine to someone in the platonic sense she becomes like an adolescent with a new best friend: totally infatuated for about five minutes. She'll be hanging around at Bar None and meet some man or woman. They'll get totally hammered then she'll drag them home for more drinks and they'll be yadda-yadda, rah-rah-rahing until daylight. From there, there are two possible scenarios. One is that next time she sees that person, she'll virtually snub them or pretend not to recognize them. Or she might begin to court them and socialize heavily with them for a month or two. It'll be "Marisa this," "Marisa that." "Izzy, you should come out with us sometime, Marisa is so much fun. She's just amazing and knows some fantastic people. GOD and can she drink me under the table." I doubted this final declaration would be true but I would say nothing. Then, all of a sudden it would stop as quickly as it began. Something would have happened and she wouldn't see Marisa or whoever the friend *du jour* was again. No explanation, no nothing and when I asked her, she'd just screw her face up as if she'd swallowed some nasty medicine. I don't join in her new friendships because I know they won't last but maybe I should have at some time. Just so I could see what happened—see where it all goes wrong.

With men it's a little different. They also come to her drunk and bleary with desire but they come to a different Evangeline. The one she becomes after countless alcoholic beverages is a demure affectionate creature but as capricious as the devil Herself. She'll be real sweet but as she gets to know them, she'll start pushing the wrong buttons. Fucking with their heads. They might get a second date, occasionally a third but few ever make it to the fourth or fifth. The wise ones work that out. Once she came home drunk with a black eye and I said, "Who did that to you?"

"Never mind," she said and began to giggle like a little girl.

"You should ring the police," I begged.

"Yeah, right."

"Well who did it then?" She wasn't listening, just absentmindedly hitting her sleeve as if in punishment. "Who did it?"

"Evangeline was very naughty and the bad man hit her."

"For God's sake, Eve!"

"I deserved it."

"What nonsense, what happened?" Suddenly she went deathly serious and looked me square in the eye.

"Listen Israel, I'm a big girl, old enough to know the rules, I deserved it. Believe me, I *really* did!"

I would have pursued it further but something in her expression told me not to. We never mentioned it again.

She plays tricks on men. She always has. She acts the way she thinks they want her to. Then, when she feels she's suckered them in good and proper, she starts punishing them for believing her in the first place. "To grow up female in our society is to grow up as a creature of secondary value. A discount item in the gender sale. You can ticket yourself as low as you wanna go. You really can." Evangeline loves these dire little prognoses on the human condition. Something hurt her once and she seems to nurture the pain as if it was a fine thing, worthy of cultivation. She would harvest this pain one day if she could and I shuddered to think what crops it might yield. Her games with men amused her enormously when she was young and pretty and could easily mimic what she thought it was they wanted. Now it seems to have a momentum of its own. She couldn't stop if she wanted too and it is sad as well because there aren't as many players as there once were and her gruesome charade is becoming a parody.

Somewhere in our history we tacitly agreed that romantic love was an illusion, a commodity peddled to us via the machinations of capitalistic endeavor. We never said we would no longer attempt it. We never make any promises at all. But if one of us is to miss out on something, it seems implicit that the other must follow. Our dysfunctional emotional setup may be no better than the romantic hetero-illusions thrown our way by movies and magazines but at least it is our own creation. Whether it be fine or foul is for others to decide.

Tonight in Anchors Aweigh, candles were burning brightly by what appears to be a shrine at the back of the club. I don't like to look at the photos on the back wall because I know one of the guys pictured there. Jordan and I had been together a few times and I had felt like I was getting hooked, on him or silt I couldn't tell. I'd been hungering in the pit of my stomach to see him again. Aching for his fragility and fragrant, fey, fatal lust.

We had just about taken each other apart in an orgy of silt last month. Naked in the desert, the sand felt like satin on our skin. Coyotes howled like moonstruck demons while we bathed in some kind of miraculous light, a rare illumination, and I couldn't tell whether it came from within or without. I held him like he was dying, his body bathed in sweat, saliva and other more sophisticated fluids we had made. Fluids neither of us had seen the likes of before. My mind was so wild I couldn't work out whether we had just been born, or had just died.

"If this is what it's like, I want to be there," he whispered.

"I know baby, I know." He was weaker than me, even more strung out, and fear and desperation crossed his face. "I'm not gonna make it, you know. I'm gonna lose my beautiful Haseeshi man and end up in Hell."

"No you're not."

"Oh I am. This can't be the right path. It's a diversion."

"You think the path should be pain? You think you gotta hurt more?"

I put my hand in him again and he whimpered. I adored this man and would carry him myself if I had to. I rocked him in my arms and shot him up with insulin.

"He's coming Israel, maybe just beyond that mountain. He's coming for us all and I'm afraid of where he's going to take me. I'm not so strong you know, and not a soul knows we're out here. You and me, exposed to the elements. Miles and miles from home."

I tried to reassure him but even I wasn't convinced. "If you look in the distance, Jordan, you can see your window light flickering, I can see mine. Can you see your man waiting, steam from the kettle, food on the stove?"

His face brightened. "Anton," he cried. He looked up at me and stroked my face as if I was Anton. "I'll never leave you." And as he said it I couldn't tell whether he was saying it to Anton or to me. In the far-off city I saw other lights and someone else waiting. Curtains rippled

in the breeze and she stood, arms akimbo, looking out over a city. A
city that could hide a thousand secrets and obscure a million souls.

"Public bravado and private terror," I heard her mumble as she
turned away.

Now his face shines out from the shrine with all the other prime
cuts. Some have religious memorabilia pinned to them: St. Andrew,
patron saint of travel; St. Jude, patron saint of desperate remedies;
Catholic prayer cards; Sacred Hearts and a few rolled up Haseeshi
prayers in black ink on roughly cut papyrus amidst clumps of dead
flowers congealed with wax. Nothing but notes on where they were
last seen or with whom. People have added arrows to some with
information that might be helpful, others have contributed drunken,
obscene scrawls: *A dud fuck this one, You call this a prime cut?*
Mountains of melted wax collect beneath the pictures and none of
the bar staff attempt to clean it. It's as if the wax itself has become
sacred. I light a candle beneath Jordan and wonder if he was right.
His picture has been here for days. I go to write something but stop
myself. It's not for me to interfere now. I turn to leave but decide to
use the bathroom first. Inside the dim, fluorescent lights glow purple. They've put them in to stop junkies shooting up in there. The
toilets in Anchors are dank and terrible, they hark back eighty years
to when men's rooms were cold mausoleums of ceramic and steel.
Water drips coldly and indiscriminately from rusty brown pipes as
the music from outside booms eerily through the walls. One light is
out anyway as I push my way into the cubicle. My heart doubles its
rate and I nearly crap myself when the door slams shut behind me.
I turn to face a tall dark figure.

"Who the fuck...?" I realize it's Giovanni. He virtually lives in
these toilets. Someone has carved *Giovanni's Room* into the wall.
Who knows it may even have been him who scrawled it.

"No Giovanni, I don't want my cock sucked and I don't want

drugs. I'm way beyond that now."

"Maybe you do if you wanna find you pretty friend."

"Evangeline?"

"No her, she *pretty ugly.*" He cackles at his joke. "You pretty man what got him some Haseeshi boyfriend."

"What do you know, Giovanni?"

"Me, huh. Me know lotta stuff you don't wanna know. You better buy some silt or that girl o' yours gonna be in big trouble."

"Are you threatening me?"

"Hey I jus know what's good for you, *baby.* I hear you talking to him. That's what you call him, '*baby,*' that diabetic little ho. 'You gonna make it baby,' I hear you say. Him sweating and moaning like Jesus on the cross and you got your hand inside him. You big man, you gonna save his ass? Now that I wanna see! So if you know wha's good for you, Israel, you'll buy some tonight, you put it somewhere safe. Otherwise, that girl, she ain't never gonna find you. And *fratello,* you got a long trip ahead o' you."

I did what he said, I don't know why, I'd had a gutful of the stuff and it was fucking with my head big-time, but as soon as I had it in my hand, he vanished, humming a tune. It took me a minute to figure but it was, "…going over Jordan, I'm going over there." How on earth had he seen us? We'd been in a place without others or at least I thought we had. Now I was more than a little scared. For Jordan, for Evangeline and of course always for myself.

Sometimes I work in the courtyard out back. It has a large tree overhanging it. Trees are scarce commodities in the Gilgal. It is not uncommon to find a chimpanzee by the name of Tibby Leister hanging from its boughs. He's the boy next door. Poor kid—it's probably the only tree he's ever climbed and something in his monkey-like gestures tells me he needs a wider acreage for his child-hood. Tibby is ten years old and has the look of *Dennis the Menace* about him. I half expect him to have a slingshot dangling from his baggy shorts and a missing front tooth. He asked me to do a picture of him once and his mother framed it and hung it above his bed. That was five years ago and I don't think he likes it anymore. I'd better do another, I suppose. He's alternately watching me draw and staring into the murky little pond in our yard, chewing on some sort of candy. "Here's trouble with a capital *T*," I say.

"You still got any goldfish in that pond?"

We don't, we haven't had any since last summer. "Nope," I say, "they've gone to live with Jesus. He's looking after them now."

He snorts. "They never went to live with Jesus. That gray cat got them, that's what I reckon."

"Well, sometimes when you are a goldfish, you have to pass through the stomach of a cat before you get to Jesus."

"No way." Tibby loves it when I string him along like this.

"It's true. If camels have to pass through the eye of a needle, why shouldn't a fish have to pass through the belly of a cat?"

"You're crazy. My dad went to live with Jesus in La-la land. That's what Ma reckons."

"He went in *search* of Jesus, or the next best thing. There's a difference." He considers this for a moment.

"Hey, how come you and that lady don't have no kids?"

"THAT LADY!" I say. "You know very well what her name is."

"So how come you don't?"

"Because we're too busy and we want to spend our money on other things." *What a cop-out*, I think to myself.

"Like what?"

"Like hats and bags, food and liquor." He thinks for a while.

"Why do you want bags?"

"For to carry things home."

"He has come for to carry me home," sings Tibby in a theatrical imitation of the woman at the station.

Izzy and Eve

"Maybe I need money to buy her tapes too."

I've stopped drawing now because I was just about to draw tits, pussy and cock. I'd better not in front of the kid. He knows what I'm drawing and is quite prepared to wait as long as it takes to see the rude bits.

"No one buys her tapes. Mum reckons she's not right in the head."

"Who is right in the head?" He doesn't know of course.

"So why you need bags?"

"For shopping and stuff."

"They give you bags with shopping."

"Not smart bags."

"You're weird. How long you and her lived here anyhow?" Suddenly he sounds like an interrogating cop from a TV show.

"Forever."

"No way."

"Well since before you were born, which is forever to you isn't it?" He thinks on that awhile.

"So doesn't *she* want any babies?"

"What *Evangeline* wants and what she gets are often two very different things. She'd have to get them from someplace other than me anyway." He lets that one go.

"You don't even have a car."

"Nope, I guess we're not much good, are we? No kids, no car just a house full of hats, bags, liquor and food."

"Got anything good to eat—and you know what I'm talkin'?"

"Maybe we got, maybe we don't got," I drawl in my best gangster-speak.

I've always loved Tibby though kids can get irritating when you are trying to work. His mother is quite cultured and very well spoken yet for some reason Tibby always sounds as if he is a young hooligan raised in the gutters of the Causeway. Apparently he gets it from the television. His mother says he suffers from Gilgal gutter mouth. I can see their back door open and out she comes, still dressed in a conservative business suit. She's a lawyer and she and her partner bought her house a few years after we bought ours. The difference however is that she's spent loads on tarting hers up.

"Is he making a nuisance of himself, Israel?"

"No more than usual. I'll get the rifle out and shoot him down like a clay pigeon if he gets on my nerves, Mary." She laughs.

"Where's Evangeline?"

Now this is classic Mary, this scenario. She will be wanting to go down to the shops or something and if she could be sure Eve was home, she would ask if we could look after Tibby for half an hour. If Eve's not here she'll make out it is too much of an imposition for me to do it "especially while I'm working." Mary is an intelligent woman, a nice woman but I am a homosexual. With homosexuals and children, well, you just never know do you? I try to make it as difficult as possible for her because the subtext to all this is deeply offensive to me even though I will never let on.

"Do you want to speak to her? You could see her at Seven-Five-Five if she's not still upstairs."

"No, arrr, it's all right. I just needed to go to the supermarket and if she was in…" There is no way Mary would go around to the brothel looking for her, the whole inference is about something else, but I love setting up these non sequiturs to complicate people's pathetic subterfuges.

"I can look after Tibby, you go and do your shopping." Tibby is now hanging from a bough upside down like a sloth. His face is bright red and he's making faces at his mother that she can't see from where she stands. It's hard for her to get around it once I've offered so firmly.

"Tibby Leister, I want you to stay in the yard until I get back do you hear and you are not to go into Evangeline and Israel's because

Izzy and Eve

Izzy's working, okay?" She smiles at me and I smile back. I wonder what she is like defending or prosecuting or whatever she does. I hope I never find out.

He's nodding and rocking at the same time having taken up the pose of an ocelot. As soon as her car is out of the lane he drops into our yard. "Can we look in your cupboards then?" *We* means *he*. I tell him there are potato crisps in the pantry and some ice cream in the freezer. Tibby likes to dip the potato crisps into the ice cream. It's disgusting and his mother won't let him do it but Eve and I do. Sometimes he watches TV with Eve and eats a whole tub. He knows and we know that we must keep schtum about this to Mary or there will be no more visits and Tibby thinks it is excellent value hanging out at our place.

EVANGELINE

A man was recently tried and convicted of seven charges of first-degree murder. The story was in the paper this week. The headline was *Express Lane to Murder* and there was a bleak, hand-drawn illustration of a shopping cart filled with women's limp bodies heading towards the *8 Items or Less* checkout.

Apparently this murderer would wander the aisles of the supermarket and ram his own cart into that of a passing woman. If she said "Watch out," or "Look where you're going, buster," she was fine. But if she apologized, as many women are apt to do, he would follow her home and murder her brutally. It turned out that the man's father had brutalized him as a child and his own mother was too passive to ever try intervening on his behalf; thus, he became a psychopath and murdered seven women to punish his weak mother. I looked at the illustration and realized it was one of Israel's.

"When did you do this drawing Izzy?"

"Last week."

"You never told me this story."

Neal Drinnan

"I figured you'd sniff it out for yourself soon enough. Besides, there's nothing for you to solve is there? It's in the bag, as it were."

"I think it's disgusting having a cartoon like that with a story like this."

"Not easy either, you try drawing seven bodies in a shopping cart without it looking humorous. They paid lots for it, I'd rather be doing drawings for major newspapers than smut rags."

"What's the difference? I can only count twelve legs."

"That's because he cut the legs off that one up in Hillcrest Province. I do my research properly I'll have you know, Eve."

"Yuk, yuk, yuk."

Israel's birthstones are turquoise and lapis lazuli so I'm making him a special ring for his birthday using both. Sometimes I wonder why I ever started making jewelry. Was it the metals or the stones, the anvil or the mallet? Perhaps it was the soldering iron, so phallic and lethal. One thing I do know is that sometimes when I work, I become so engrossed that hours vanish, entire afternoons, and I don't have to speak with anyone or smile at those brothel creepers.

We had dinner together last night, Israel and I. We talked about things, life. He said the idea of life was better than the reality. Finally—something we both agreed on. He's never attempted suicide. I have. They say if you really want to do it you don't give yourself any second chances. I would never do the pills and booze thing again. Next time it would be a stranger who found me, perhaps at the bottom of a cliff, perhaps washed up on the beach. It feels so strange moving through this world in a temporary shell, finding a hill that you ran up with ease just a few years ago is suddenly a chore. Sometimes I fancy us living in the country, I imagine the pace to be less depleting but in the country you have to know everyone. Everyone knows who you sleep with, what you eat and how much you drink, who needs that? In the city even most of your neighbors don't know your name and both Izzy and I prefer things that way. Our appetites are such that they favor a certain anonymity.

I want to believe some of the things Israel believes in; I have a name that supposedly inspires faith but I act against it. Israel is the promised land and I'm the ship that is sailed to reach it. That's what he's said before when he's feeling bright about things. *Yeah, the* Titanic, I thought to myself, and I can't follow his belief system. I can't believe that we'd choose to be murdered like those girls who fill newspapers and shopping trolleys. The Mormon church barks at my heels, a milder Protestantism barks at his and I find a world that requires eternal beliefs in order to suffer ephemeral existence too disappointing. Sometimes, just to bear what lies ahead seems too daunting even to consider.

There was a time when we both hungered for the world, for suc-cess. A time when Israel would schmooze whomever he had to in order for his pictures to appear and I would beat the pavements to interest clients in my jewels. We both had exhibits in galleries, were included in collections and endured a million air kisses but there are always people who schmooze harder, who are hungrier and this is a city where tenacity is often rewarded more lavishly than talent. I didn't cling tenaciously enough. It seems this is the world he has eschewed and I suppose I'd like to as well. We get enough business to live on. So why want more? My problem is that I can't see a world beyond it. I can't imagine a place where everyone isn't so self-serving. Even Israel says the world is both a cosmic adventure and a dimen-sional crisis. However you look at it, the situation is not soluble. The world is as it is and it does not agree with me.

Tibby Leister is always full of questions. I let him sit with me while I work and his innocence can be a tonic though some of the rubbish he likes to eat would turn your stomach. I wish I'd had a child sometimes but it always scared me too much and now, well it's too late. He doesn't quite understand about Izzy being gay and he runs riot in the house looking for embarrassing things to question me about. He found an unwashed dildo once a few years ago that he brought into the lounge while his mother and I were talking. "Look! It's got cha-cha on it," he said as I snatched it and threw it into the washing machine, out of harm's way.

"How come you and him don't have the same room? Is it true that what you want and what you get are very different things, Evangeline? Can you only have babies with someone you love or can anyone do it with you?"

"Questions, questions," I say. "You love your mum don't you?"

"Sometimes. When she's not in a snit."

"Well, people don't have babies with their mums, at least not in this part of the world."

He screws up his nose. "That's a different type of love."

"Well, Tibby, you tell me what the other sort is and I'll give you some more crisps."

He's already had one packet and I won't let him have any more ice cream in case he's ill or his mother has me for child abuse. I'm beginning to feel like the witch in "Hansel and Gretel," fattening up the little boy who no doubt will be good enough to be eaten by someone else one day.

He giggles. "I can't say because it's rude isn't it?"

"Promise I won't get offended."

"Well, it's when you get a stiffy."

"Is that all?"

"And some other stuff too, like being all mushy and that."

"Stiffies and mushies, sounds pretty messy to me."

"Yeah, well I wouldn't know, I'm only ten."

"But not for long Tibby, not for long." I drop the silver into an anodizing bath and he fishes it out after the appropriate amount of time. He loves these processes and I make something special for him every birthday. The time will come when he'll fly the roost and hopefully he'll keep the things I made for him. He means more to me than he knows. I quiz him on the things I've taught him.

"How many birthstones do you have, Tibby?"

"Three, which is more than anyone else born any other month on the calendar."

"And what might they be?"

"Peridot, sardonyx or carnelian."

"And what sign does that make you?"

"A Leo the lion *roarrrr*."

"And name three blue stones for me."

"Azurite, labradorite *woof woof* and lapis lazuli."

"And what other color might you find labradorite in?"

"None."

"No, it comes in one other color."

"Uh-uh…because it comes in white and that is not a color—gotcha!"

"All right, go and get some more rubbish from the cupboard then."

Mary doesn't know what to make of me, she never has. Years ago before she had Tibby and before Buggalugs left her for some tart in an ashram, she'd come and drink with us, smoke pot and generally whoop it up. Now she's like another person. She knows I work at the brothel but she doesn't know in what capacity. I think she's scared we're a bad influence on Tibby but she doesn't have a lot of choice given that she's on her own. She's watched over the years as Izzy gets more tattooed, pierced and generally more extreme looking and hasn't a clue what to think of it. She's gone from a blushing hippy to a power bitch and if I hadn't seen it with my own eyes I wouldn't believe it. I like Tibby far more than I like her these days; in more ways than one he really is the child I never had and sometimes he says he wishes he could live with us. I feel sorry for Mary, but of course he doesn't mean it.

ISRAEL

The first thing you have to work through with S/M is the concept that you are not your body. It's imperative that you lose that sense of your body as your self. It is merely a gateway to the chakras. When I'm blindfolded and hanging in suspension, I am powerless and every sensation is multiplied tenfold. The clamps on my nipples, the cockring, the weights on my scrotum, all the way to intensely challenging penetration: it goes way beyond being a sexual thing. Suddenly the universe inside my head seems as big as the one outside of me. It is through these activities I can experience how outer space is replicated by inner space. A lot of people don't understand it. I don't talk to Evangeline about it and I don't vocalize the experience to my partners but they all seem to know, in their own ways, exactly what is going on.

Something is happening to me that I can't explain. It's like something I've always wanted but I sense a certain danger. Losing the self is what it's all about but I seem to have taken a radically different path from various Buddhists to whose way I once aspired. The voice in my head that comes and goes assures me I'm heading in the right direction but I get a bit sentimental about my body from time to time. It's getting wrecked and it's not what it was but I still have an attachment to it. Granted I don't strut around like I used to and I'm kind of bored by worldly limitations but my body is a serious habit and I am a creature of routine.

This time it's awe inspiring. I see a medieval village where everyone seems to be wearing Evangeline's jewelry. The streets are cobbled, the colors vivid. The sky wears a rich purple cloak, it's the color of the warm nights close to summer solstice yet the mountains have

Izzy and Eve

shrouds of cool autumnal mist clinging to them like mink stoles. I know there is magic and wonder here, and it has nothing to do with my body but everything to do with my mind. It is something I've created and I'm keen to be there again but I am concerned about the cost.

As Torsten bids me farewell, he can see from the expression on my face where I've been. "Is *guden* ya? Bavaria?" he says. I don't know how he knows it was Bavaria but I guess that's exactly where it felt like I'd been. Was it his hand that sent me to his home in the days of yore? Was that the connection between he who was serving and he who was being served? Would Chi send me to the Orient or Black Marvin to Darkest Africa? What was I playing with here and what was in these brown crystals I used to facilitate all this stuff?

A clammy fog has descended over the Causeway. It can be dangerous at night and the poorer Haseeshi prowl this area like junkyard dogs so I hail a cab, laughing at the absurdity of "danger" after what I've just done. I feel like I've been turned inside out.

I fish in my pocket to make sure I have enough for the journey and hope I don't smell too off. They really should get showers in that joint. The cabbie recognizes the club, knows I must be a bit of a freak. "So what is it you guys do in there?" I look at his dark Haseeshi eyes in the rearview mirror. "Anything at all driver, anything your heart desires and your body can stand." The car gains speed, the night streets bleed off into a blanket of darkness and the mist hangs ominously low over shabby residential towers and squalid low-rent shanties. I feel a strange new sense of liberty as the city about me continues its demise.

EVANGELINE

I had a most unusual and lurid dream last night. I felt transported to some village in olden times where women wore pointed conical hats as they do in fairy tales and many wore my rings. I searched for Israel, sure that he was just around the next corner. I was searching for him

46

but everywhere there were distractions, temptations. Fascinating stalls, alehouses with fragrant mulled wines—there for the taking— and thickly set Teutonic men keen to lure me down one of the many tiny streets in order to find their way beneath my abundant skirts. I drank some wine and felt greatly affected by it. I knew that the burly man at the bar would follow me down the cobbled lane and I knew I wouldn't mind. It was cool and private down there. My heart tripped with excitement. I was a perfect whore—just perfect—utterly shameless. When he found me loitering in the darkness he never spoke a word. He smiled, pulled gruffly at my blouse and bared my breasts. He hoisted me onto a barrel and busied himself like a violinist beneath my skirts striking rare and brilliant chords that left me gasping. I was lost in the thrill of it and then he took me like the whore I was. I'd never felt so penetrated, so "plumbed" as Izzy would say. I felt myself flushing from the fill of him, shocked by his size. "Guden ya, Bavaria?" he whispered, his breath tinged with sauerkraut. And I whimpered that it was so. And he filled me and filled me with deep approving grunts until I hadn't the breath for any more then he left me open and glowing under a purple twilight, the likes of which I'd never seen before. I wondered as I sat there if there would be others following him and if so how many? I'd never imagined spontaneous sex could be so fine, was this why Izzy loved those dark clubs? I felt as if such sex was perfectly normal and wholesome yet I awoke in my bed to a world where of course it wasn't. Oh, but in olden Bavaria, where people proudly wore my rings and I was free to be the village tart with ease and joy. Well, that seemed to be another story.

Israel didn't come home last night or this morning. His bed is untouched. I'm feeling much better. I swear the dream perked me up. I've no idea where it came from but I'll happily take some more of those.

I put on my suit, varnish my nails, select a few favorite pieces of

jewelry to wear. Then I phone my best clients to let them know I've
fresh wares to sell them. I ride the train to First Century Avenue and
take the trolley car to Dark Lane. Dark Lane is a charming little
eighteenth-century shopping strip filled with mystics, bohos and
antique shops. It's so narrow the eaves from each side of the lane
are almost touching. There are antiquarian bookshops where the
proprietors look older than the books and musty galleries selling
ancient portraits of the Haseeshi. There are bric-a-brac and crystal
stores and there is Gothic Mist where Fiora Bijoux sells some of the
loveliest and most elaborate jewelry in the city.

"Evangeline my love!" Her swollen purple lips brush both my
cheeks.

"I have freshly ground coffee for you and petit fours from *Maison
Latin*. What treasures do you bring for me?"

"I've been feeling rather Bavarian lately. Did you know that the
whores in the days of Fredrick III were paid in jewelry as wars
between the regions at the time rendered currency worthless?
When his soldiers had taken over provinces and castles as far afield
as Burgundy, they discovered vaults of jewelry that had been hoarded
by Pope Eugene IV and his Vatican cohorts for centuries. For them,
the eternal *qui vive* and the misfortunes of war were easily forgotten
in the arms of courtesans. So they pillaged all the lolly, spent most
of it on wine and harlots, some they gambled, and I suppose the
rest, they must have squandered." Fiora screeches with laughter
and claps her hands. "Such tales you have, Evangeline."

"I've copied a collection I saw in an exhibition there a few years
ago. I think you'll like them." And without further ado and only a
few more spectacular impromptu lies, I open my case while Fiora
quivers in delight and anticipation.

"Of course when the Hapsburg fortunes were liberated, so were
a good many of the women. With all that hard currency going
around, being a whore seems to have been the most canny choice."

Fiora buys fourteen pieces. If I can sell all thirty I should be set for a month. I seldom make appointments and I virtually handpick my customers. I like quirky little shops that have a certain plush velvety glamour to them but I adore Carlo Monenzo's, which is very sleek and modern. There every designer has his or her own display. Carlo showcases all the city's finest designers and he made each of us write out our signature in white plaster: Cory Lee, Desma Cox, Constance Spry and just simply *Evangeline* in my best copperplate.

"Where have you been hiding, scrumptious?" he says when I walk in. "Three pieces of your work are all I have left and they are *weeping* for company. I have to rub the tears from them daily." He launches into an absurd little routine, comforting one of the rings as if it was an infant. But he's right, my case does look decidedly under stocked.

"Well, Monsieur Monenzo, you had better buy up big today because you never know when this girl will be in your part of town."

"You have come to me first *bien sur?*"

"Of course Carlo, I always show you first, darling." Quickly I regret lying. He'll probably go past Fiora's just to see if she has pieces he hasn't seen. *Ah vay*, what can you do if *zay all vant my jewels zey'll have to take vhat zey're given*.

On the trolley home I see a woman wearing one of my rings; it's a garnet and ammonite cluster in a kind of lotus flower setting. I was doing a lot of Oriental stuff back when I made that. I love it when I see someone I don't know wearing a piece but it has only happened about three times. Her ring would be eight years old. Israel had me do him one at the same time using black pearls. He'd bought some in the coastal provinces back when you could still get them quite easily and he gave me a couple as well for earrings. I turned them into droplets on long Gothic poles with marquisette insets.

The carriage moves onto the aqueduct, an old bridge that leads back into the Gilgal. It's one of the highest in the city, nearly three hundred years old. I look out the window and I think I see Israel shivering on the walkway. As we enter the tunnel I apply some more lipstick in the black reflective glass. What's wrong with me? Why do I see Israel everywhere? Why am I always looking for him?

ISRAEL

There are certain darknesses that won't or mustn't have light shone into them. A confessional, a sex venue, the haunted house at a funfair, a nightclub or an opium den. All these places would lose their mystique, mystery, appeal and romance if they were to be seen under the glare of a fluoro' or the rays of the sun. There are thousands of people in the Gilgal who only come out after dark. Vampires, we always called them. Lured as they are by the delicious or false promises of nighttime. None of them are too keen to be scrutinized under the full light of the sun and even in their nocturnal hours, many seek out the darkest corners of bars and clubs.

For some folk, Heaven would be nothing but light: full of how-do-you-dos, lacy collars and gurgling baptismal fonts. They'd want cheery, rosy-cheeked rectors with wives who bake mountains of cakes. There'd be legions of perpetual virgins smelling of soap on the arms of decent chaps with eternally good intentions but I rather hope it's something you can create for yourself. I'd have seedy bars with constantly flickering neon, martinis that always stay cold, grotty old empty warehouses that no one has any intention of turning into residential lofts or historic shopping precincts and ancient churches in semiruin where lost angelic boys and girls kneel, scantily clad, waiting by a font that has sprung from the altar. It would be nighttime for as long as you pleased and on each corner reckless beauties would hover, illuminated only by their cigarettes. In my Heaven all gifts would be squandered because they could never run out and beneath the street bravado and dirty talk of those consigned, there'd be a joy in knowing at long last that being the *wrong* sort of person was right after all.

Now, in the darkness I have sought, I can't see what is coming and I hope I'm prepared but it is Evangeline I worry most about. It was always Evangeline I have worried about because there are some journeys we can't make together and faith cannot be taught, it must be known. I see more lights. I feel a flash of pain, I know she's thinking of me and I see her staring from the train window. Her gaze is empty. Her eyes have no spark.

EVANGELINE

It's started pouring with rain and the weather's become suddenly colder. That's how the season changes here. People are wandering around with that shocked look they always have when summer shifts into fall. A melancholy has descended as I struggle with my key in the lock. Something feels wrong and I have a growing sense of dread. "Izzy," I call as I put my case down. But there is no answer. I go upstairs to his room. His bed is still how it was this morning and I know he hasn't been home. The answering machine blinks sullenly in the hall; I play it hoping it will be him with one of his epic tales of debauchery, another lost night in his underworld of depravity and his quest for the grail. But it's not him, just Mary wanting to know if I can look after Tibby, some editor wanting one of Izzy's cartoons and that creepy Torsten with some obscure reference to Bavaria. What is it with Bavaria at the moment? I switch on the television and watch a gardening show. I had thought my mood was improving but now it has darkened again. I gather the cushions from the outdoor furniture. Already they are soaked. I put them away for the winter then lock the doors as another night descends.

Before I know it, Tibby's out front, knocking with an armful of toy cars and electronic gadgets. I'd rather not have him tonight but I'd also rather not be alone. "Where's Israel?" he asks and I don't know. I open the paper, not sure why I even bought it. Today the headlines are about a couple who were found murdered after what appears to have been a home invasion or an aggravated burglary. They were trussed like turkeys and had plastic bags taped over their heads in order to suffocate them, it makes me feel ill to read it. Tibby is playing with his cars on the stairs as my fingers run over the text. The couple had been in a hard-core residential action group that was seeking to stop another god-awful mutimillion-dollar apartment development in the Cartesian Precinct. The Cartesian Precinct is where a lot of the Haseeshi live, but now they have been priced out of the area and the government is no longer prepared to make housing concessions for them based on their mistreatment in the past. This happens time and time again in this city and if I've learned one thing in all my years here, it's that people who come between wealth and its expansion all come to the same end. Worse still, none of the murderous development henchmen ever get caught. I have pages of similar stories and one of my own. On the social pages you can see the smiling millionaires sipping their champagne. On the front page you can see their victims, trussed up like turkeys or being dredged from the bottom of the river. The developers don't kill them themselves of course but there are plenty of guns for hire in this town. Plenty of lumbering thugs who don't seem to care one iota for human life.

"When will Israel be home?" whines Tibby

"I don't know!" I realize I've snapped at him. "Sorry Tibby." I ruffle his auburn hair. The man on the television drones on about autumn garden tasks, safeguards against frost damage, squirrels gathering nuts. Tibby asks if we can watch something else because this is dead boring. I look through the rain-slicked window and think about going nuts myself. I pour a drink to sip while I put on some spaghetti, the only thing Tibby seems to eat for supper and the only thing I could stomach. And I get angry at Israel because he really should ring when he's gone this long. He's just not fair sometimes.

ISRAEL

The curtains are still open even though it's dark. She's sitting on the couch while Tibby Leister makes a motorway of the coffee table. I won't mind missing the winter. I never liked it that much. I can tell by the way she stares at the screen that she's troubled, she'll stare at it all night. She's still going to need my help but things are going to be different from now on. It has to be that way.

EVANGELINE

I'm walking along the balcony of one of those grand hotels in Nice or Cannes only this is much better than the shabby ones we stayed in. This one is in its full heyday—and my shoes are a pair of those sexy little slip-on mules I used to wear when I was younger. "Wear your slutty slip-ons," Israel would say when we were holidaying abroad. I'd laugh because so many gay men liked to play at dressing up dolls when they were children and most of them hang on to at least one girlfriend so they can continue to play with real dolls when they are men. I'm on my way to a very swank hotel room. There is no sound but the clatter of my shoes across the marble. The elaborate Baroque double doors swing open as if by magic and Israel is on the huge bed in a smoking jacket, wielding a champagne flute and looking breathtakingly young. "Everything old is new again poppet," he says handing me a glass and preparing to charge them. I look at the mirrors that line the walls, and I see that I too have changed. I realize, for the first time, that in dreams we have no age. "Shall I ring down to room service? Have them send us the freshest batch of boys from the provinces and we'll eat oysters off their smooth bellies?"

I'm speechless. "What are you up to Izzy?"

"You'll see, you'll see!" And then the doorbell rings but it's not in the hotel, it's the front door. It's Mary come to pick up Tibby and I've been asleep for half an hour on the couch.

"Look at the mess you've made of Evangeline's floor."

I look around to see what she means before realizing she's talking about our usual mess. "He had nothing to do with it Mary, believe me."

"Thanks for giving him some supper." She hands me a bottle of scotch in gratitude, though now I have a taste for champagne and oysters. "Where's Israel?" she inquires.

"Where Palestine used to be," I reply. She laughs. "Oh, you know Izzy, why come home while there's flickering neon bars still open and men loitering on street corners," I go on glibly even as my concern mounts. Mary laughs uncertainly and I realize the coarseness Israel and I have always loved is no longer appropriate for a woman my age. Am I supposed to have changed like Mary? What would I become? I wipe the thought from my mind. They go, leaving me alone, and worry mounts and mounts. I've never been strong enough as "one" so I take a sleeping pill, pour another scotch and put all things from my mind.

"Where are we going?" I'm with Israel, in the woods it seems. European woods certainly. He's wearing lederhosen and me, I'm in a lace-up Heidi dress carrying a basket like some absurd Germanic parody. There are spotted toadstools, the birds and the animals seem quite friendly. I feel like Snow White.

"Come with me," he whispers with an almost lusty urgency.

"Where?" I ask, a little annoyed by all the secrecy.

"To this house, it's swell. You can eat it."

I'm tripping along behind him and the woods are growing darker, why do they always have to grow darker in fairy tales? The toadstools look more toxic, the birds more ferocious. On we run and I'm thinking aren't we supposed to tie bits of string to trees or drop bread crumbs in case we get lost, when all of a sudden, there before us is a gingerbread house. I get it. We're Hansel and Gretel.

"Eve, look at this house. We can eat the whole damn thing, even inside." And he vanishes through the icing-frosted front door.

"No Israel, you can't! You mustn't go in! There's a witch in there." But he's gone and I'm alone. I edge closer to the cottage. I hear the twigs breaking underfoot. I hear my own breath, my heartbeat thumping in my ears. I'm almost at the blurred, frosted window-pane, which smells of barley sugar. Through it I can just make something out. It's Israel, trussed like a turkey, suspended in a sling. A wicked witch whose face I can't make out is attending to him in some profoundly indecent way and then, through his torture, he sees me through the pane.

"Go away Eve, there's nothing you can do. It's too late."

I don't want to leave him. She's putting a plastic bag over his head and then I glimpse the witch's face. It is so ugly, so hideous, I'm afraid to stay. So I run like Snow White through the dark, dangerous woods. Ravens shriek while wolves growl carnivorously, just out of sight. A tisket, a tasket, I've lost my little basket and my dress catches on snags. The moss underfoot is slippery and cold. I'm disoriented, I know I'm lost, then I slip and fall, awakening breathlessly on the couch.

It's four a.m. and still he's not home. He always rings, *always*. I feel something awful has happened. I get up from the couch and climb the stairs to his room. His window is open, the curtains wet. I lie on his bed, the cold quilt over me. I can smell him on the linen and eventually I fall into a groggy sleep there.

"Is that Torsten?" I shout into the phone.

"No, is Gustav."

"Gustav, it is Evangeline. I'm looking for Israel." There's some sort of commotion on the other end because Gustav obviously has a language problem.

"Hello, ya is Torsten."

I repeat the question.

"No, not for two days. He left the club, I think before it closes. We see him go."

"Which club?" He is quiet. "Which club Torsten? I am worried about him, he hasn't been home!"

"Is called…Gutz."

"Where is it, what is their number?"

"Is not…ahh. This is not club for woman, you understand. Is men only."

"I don't care if it's for dog-fuckers only. I have to find out where he is."

Torsten reluctantly gives me the address. He doesn't know the phone number and it is not the sort of place likely to be listed in the directory.

"What were you guys doing with him?" I ask perhaps too accusingly. And it seems Torsten can't answer. I wonder if he thinks I'm a possessive girlfriend or some deluded broad who doesn't realize Israel's queer. I don't know where to begin searching and I don't know enough of his acquaintants.

I don't like visiting the Causeway. It's far worse than the Gilgal. As I walk along Creeper Street towards the lane where Gutz supposedly is, grubby Haseeshi children pester me for coins. I give them candy that I'd bought for this very reason but some of them are so nimble fingered, you can lose your watch or purse without even feeling it. I should have taken a cab and made it wait.

There is nothing on the door to indicate what sort of club it is. Just the word *GUTZ* in faded red paint, a single broken red bulb suspended above it. I buzz the intercom. Two Haseeshi women are gossiping in their yards nearby, they point at me, laughing. "Don't think you'll get much joy in there, love," says one as they both collapse into fits of giggles.

"Yeah," comes a gruff voice on the intercom.

"Look I need to talk to someone in there, my...housemate has disappeared and I know this was the last place he was seen. Can I show you a photo in case you recognize him?"

"Sorry darlin', no women in here."

"Well, would it be too much to ask for *you* to come out and see *me*?"

"I'm holding the fort here doll, it's kinda difficult."

"Please! It will take thirty seconds."

There is silence. I don't know whether he is ignoring me or on his way. I hang around the entrance looking ridiculous in a smart black dress and sunglasses. Eventually the door opens a fraction, a pasty-faced man shot through with countless piercings emerges and he is clearly distressed by the daylight. I show him a picture of Israel. It's a headshot taken at the last party we had twelve months earlier. He looks, or rather squints at it.

"We get a lot of men through, it's pretty dark in there. I don't take much notice. Maybe I've seen him around."

"His name is Israel, you'd remember a name like that."

"Don't ask names in here, darlin', besides most of 'em sign in with an alias: Dick, Rod, Pokemon," he laughs. "What you see is what you get."

"Sounds more like what you *don't* see is what you get." He's shaking his head at the photo. He is about to go inside but I still want to ask him more questions.

"What *sort* of club is this?" I manage before he can get away.

"A men's club."

"I know that. Is it a regular men's sex club though?"

"It's a sex club. Men have sex here."

"What I need to know is, what is different about *this* club, what special needs does it serve? Why would he have come all the way to the Causeway when there are plenty of perfectly filthy clubs in the Gilgal where we live?"

He's opened the door wider now, and a fetid, masculine odor drifts from within reminding me of unwashed socks and locker rooms.

"That's something you'll have to ask him, doll, it's not a chick kind of thing if you can get your head around that." And with no further ado, he vanishes inside. I feel flushed with humiliation, the indignity of it. The women continue pegging up laundry but stare pityingly at me as I wander back down the lane clutching the photo of his smiling face, gripping my bag for fear of snatchers. I feel stupid and desperate but as I reach Creeper Street again, my heel catches in a grate and my shoe is pulled loose. As I bend, my eyes catch sight of a business card in the gutter. I don't know why I pick it up, but I do, and on the back is something I can't make out, scrawled in Israel's writing. The rain has blurred it but the card itself is printed: *Torsten and Gustav, 37 Collier Place, The Escarpment.* I put it in my purse because I hadn't previously known where they lived. A trolley approaches so I climb aboard, pleased to escape. I hate the Causeway. Israel never used to go there.

ISRAEL

I want to leave something for her. There's a half-finished drawing on my desk of a dog peeing on one of the tower blocks that have caused so much consternation in the Latin and Cartesian Precincts and in Evangeline's life. In the next frame the dog says, *"On second thoughts,"* and goes back and takes a crap on it as well. That would not be an appropriate gift. The pressure to move on is increasing so I make up my mind that I will do everything in my power to light the way. My lingering in the shadows like this may be her undoing but I'm hoping it can also show her the path that I've found, or am hop-

ing to find. This city and all its burnt offerings are not as easy to
escape as I had hoped and even the filthy rain that washes litter
down the storm-water drains seems to be urging me on lest I too be
washed out to sea.

EVANGELINE

"Curtis, a whisky sour please, you precious saint."

"How ya doin' angel-puss?" he says polishing a cocktail glass.
"Haven't seen you and Iz-ray-el for the longest time. You two chillin
been hidin' out or something?"

"Not really. Izzy does seem to have disappeared though. I'm very
concerned."

"Now sugar, don' you worry none about that ol' piece o' trash.
He's like a bad penny, he'll jus' keep showin' up again and again."

I try to smile, wishing it was true. Curtis and Israel had a brief
affair about a million years ago and some nights when Israel stays
at Bar None until closing time, the two will continue drinking.
Curtis will end up in Izzy's bed again, and the two of them will be
cackling away like a couple of old drunks until the wee hours. I
don't even know whether they have sex anymore. Israel is convinced he is getting too old to bring strangers home and actually
face them in the morning. He prefers anonymous places where
the lighting is dim and more inclined to flatter the maturer gentlemen. "Let love be a fantasy and lust be a mystery," he'd often
say. I'd envy him sometimes because he could live that way.
Women can't go to places like Gutz—and after seeing it, why would
they want to? For me lust's like one of those melancholy Joni
Mitchell songs where desire grows with each drink and an ugly
stranger becomes handsome. The fire is ignited with liquor, for a
few hours the whole world basks in its glow, then, unless I've
obliterated myself with pills I'll wake at four in the morning to the
blackness and the darkness and a stranger who's lost the magical

light he seemed to possess only hours before.

"You're not looking too happy Evie baby, w'as wrong?" Curtis is sitting down at the bar opposite me. His brown skin is still as smooth as it has always been but in the last few years he's developed a lightning bolt of white through his frizzy black hair. Israel always teased him about it being dyed that color so he could become Lightning Bolt Curtis but Curtis maintains that the shock of being fucked by a white man with a dick as small as Israel's just sent him white overnight.

"My momma took one look at me and said 'Curtis, for shame. Your pappy done get that same stripe and he got it from messin' with a white woman,' and I said, 'So that's how I got it, that wasn't no dick that was a white woman's clit, and all the time I was thinking Israel's a man with a tiny pecker but he's just one mean ugly chick with a big clit!' "

God have we had some laughs with Curtis, he's got to be my favorite barman. Right now, he's waiting for me to answer.

"He's never stayed away this long before, not without calling, and he's been getting into some kind of weird scenes. Curtis, have you ever been to Gutz?"

He stands up, puts his hand on his hip and waves an accusing finger at me.

"Now 'zactly what type o' girl do you think I am, Evangeline?"

"Well, I have wondered… It's just a sex club isn't it?"

"Not *just* a sex club, they got some heavy shit going down in there and I do mean *shit*."

"Like what for God's sake? I feel like I've stumbled across some sort of secret fraternity—it's an S/M club right? I'm a big girl, women give birth to things that are bigger than fists for Chrissake. I can cope you know." My glass is empty. "Another of the same please, Curtis."

"Not jus' S/M, they into all this astro travellin' stuff. They handballin' each other an' talkin' to God, they's takin' drugs I ain't even heard of. I never been there, I hate the Causeway—I'm not yella enough for the Haseeshi and not white enough for the honkies. Only place I belong's right here in Bar None and the tips are lousy." I pushed my dollar change back across the bar.

"Do you know Torsten and Gustav?"

"I done told you, I ain't seen Izzy or none of his crazy-ass friends in weeks but if you see him tell him it's about time I turned *his* hair white if they ain't already done it for him at Gutz."

I wonder if a gang of Haseeshi youths might have done something to him. It is dangerous in the Causeway. I gulp thinking about where the aqueduct runs into it just down from Creeper Street and how many bodies have been discreetly dispatched that way in the past. I walk by 755 but can't be bothered going in today even though they owe me money. The sheik's supposed to be in town next week but I never hold my breath for him. I get to our house, it looks empty and forlorn. Summer is over, Izzy is nowhere and I'm a little fuzzy from Curtis's generous double shots.

There are no messages on the machine but I can see Tibby out back in the tree. "Hey Tibby, seen Israel?"

"I saw him upstairs." He's swinging upside down from the tree as is his way and my heart leaps a thousand feet. I run up the stairs to look in both our rooms. He's nowhere to be found, his room looks untouched. I dash back to the courtyard.

"When did you see him Tibby, when was he here?"

"Oh, I dunno, just a while ago."

"An hour ago? Half an hour?"

"I guess."

"What did he say to you?"

"Nothing."

"What, he ignored you?"

"No, he was upstairs. I just saw him in the window. He was staring out. Then I looked again and he was gone."

"Did he wave?"

"No, don't reckon he saw me. He looked kinda weird. Spaced out."

"And you didn't see him go out or hear the front door?"

"Nope. Nothin'."

I notice Tibby's holding something in his hand. A piece of rolled up paper. The sort of expensive parchment Israel does his work on.

"What's that?"

"Nothing."

I grab it from his hand and unroll it. I gasp. There on the paper is a drawing of that awful gingerbread house I'd visited in my dream, only now it looks harmless and sweet. There was no mistaking it was one of his pictures. My heart begins thumping at an alarming rate. I feel sick.

"Where did you get this, Tibby?"

"Nowhere."

"Where did you get it?" I'm shouting and I know I shouldn't. He's getting frightened.

"I just found it out here on the table."

"When Tibby? Today, yesterday? It's *very*, *very* important. Was it out here in the courtyard today?"

"Yeah, just lying on the table. It was going to get wet in the rain so I rolled it up."

The back door opens next door and Mary comes out, drawn no doubt by my raised voice. "What's up, is he wrecking the joint again?"

"He said he saw Israel upstairs." My mind is racing because Israel doesn't have a key to the security grille on the front door. He'd lost it a week ago and would have needed mine to have a new one cut. When I came in the security grille was locked. I shouldn't have locked it in case he came home but I hadn't thought.

"Are you absolutely sure you saw him?" I realize I'm a little hysterical, Mary is becoming concerned.

"I'm sure if Tibby says he saw Israel then he saw him. Now come on mister, inside, it's time for your bath. Are you okay, Evangeline?" Tibby is hurriedly climbing back over the fence.

"He couldn't have got in, he doesn't have a key to the grille. He would have had to get a locksmith. He hasn't touched a thing inside...and Tibby found this on the table out here."

Mary looks at the drawing and smiles. "Well there you go, it's definitely his drawing. Perhaps he found the key and didn't tell you."

That seems unlikely given where he'd said he lost it but there's no point telling her that. As it is, I am looking more and more unstable with each passing moment. I can see the pity in Mary's eyes. "You-poor-fag-hag-waiting-around-for-some-stupid-old-homo-who-never-grew-up-and-has-no-sense-of-responsibility."

"I better get his lordship some supper. I'm sure he'll turn up."

I want to tell her about the drawing, which she casts her eyes over curiously. "That's not Israel's usual subject matter is it? Not a tit or an ass to be seen. Did he do it for Tibby?"

"Tibby says he never spoke to him. Just saw him up in the bedroom window looking spaced out."

"He still uses a lot of drugs, doesn't he Evangeline?"

I shrug. "What's a lot of drugs these days? Sleeping pills, depression pills, pills for hard-ons, mood enhancers, jet lag pills, beta-blockers?" I leave it there. She's always been happy to take anything the doctor prescribed and she's too nervous to get up in court without beta-blockers. I'm fond of Mary to an extent but it's worth reminding her from time to time that she's not been without her own moments of serious neurosis.

Mary can tell I've been drinking. She asks if I want to come in for dinner but I know she doesn't really want me there. I've raised my voice at the golden boy, I've shown my true colors; all right, I'm a neurotic, so sue me Mary!

She vanishes inside and switches the light off. It's getting dark early now and I'm standing in the cold with the picture hanging pathetically from my hand. I look up at my window and imagine seeing him there. I will it to be so and then I feel furious. *What in the name of Christ is he trying to do to me?* Tears are springing from my eyes and I go indoors before the sobbing starts. *I love you, Israel. Wherever you are please, please come back.* An emptiness opens inside of me. No one else is out of his mind with worry so why am I? I can't eat a thing tonight. Not one single thing. I pour some of the scotch Mary gave me and kick off my shoes; my feet look awful. For a moment I forget my age. Sometimes that happens to me and I can't believe that sometime in the last millennium, I've slipped over forty. "Everything old is new again." That's what he said. Why does that keep coming into my mind?

Part II

In Purda

"Can you believe we have to call him Mr. Tait? I mean what a tosser. 'Yes, Mr. Tait'; 'No, Mr. Tait'; 'Three bags full of different-colored shite, Mr. Tait.'"

Evangeline has just rushed through the door in her usual after-work delirium, thrown her bag onto one of the ugly old beanbags we keep meaning to get rid of, kicked her pointy stilettoes under the couch and slumped in a heap.

"I hate it Israel! Working in that place is driving me nuts—they're still using typewriters, can you believe? *Mr.* Tait doesn't think computers are necessary at this stage in the business's development and he certainly doesn't want staff wasting time on them. He's absolutely convinced that games will be the scourge of the modern workplace, that all us twittering administrative assistants will be utterly unhinged by them. To hear him talk we'd do nothing all day except play Space Invaders or Pacman or something."

I tell Evangeline that she is already *utterly* unhinged.

"God, I would never have gone into this stupid mortgage if I'd known I'd have to go and get a job like this. Me, a typist! Look what you've made me do Israel, I'd rather be a whore. And I've got to go to college tonight when all I really want is to get smashed with you and some of our pals."

"I've got to finish this Dirty Nurse Lushboosie and Dr. Dick cartoon for *Waz* mag."

Eve looks over my shoulder and wrinkles up her nose. "Why does Dr. Dick have to have such a huge dick?"

"Because he *is* Dr. Dick after all."

"I can't believe a gay man could get so involved in doing these straight porn cartoons." She glances at the picture again. "Just how many layers of outer labia do you think a woman has?" Eve is staring at the obscene penetration scenes in which Nurse Lushboosie is making all sorts of indecipherable WAH, CLUCK, THWACK and UNG noises while Dr. Dick almost splits her in two.

"It's disgusting. And I hope he washed his schlong after fucking her in the ass. She could get a nasty infection if he goes straight back in her pussy after being up there."

"Nurse Lushboosie doesn't get infections. You can do anything you want to her and she'll always be ready for another filthy round."

"She's a dirty slut and something should be done about him, maybe do an episode where he faces a malpractice suit?"

"Perfect! He can accompany the judge into *her* chambers for the *deliberations* and he'll sort her out good and proper then she can reemerge in court dripping, dishevelled and ready to declare a mistrial!"

"They're chauvinistic nightmares those rags you draw for. Men like Dr. Dick are why girls like me won't go to a male doctor."

"You just wait and see the next installment where Dr. Dick meets Mighty Matron Multicunt. *How will our steadfast hero satisfy the unquenchable, the insatiable, the unimaginable lust of Mighty Matron Multicunt? She's got double the holes for twice the action. Stay tuned and watch this space…*"

"Can't wait. But enough about you, lets talk about me for a minute. I know I'm just an office girl right now with nothing but a set of tits and some high heels to make my way in the world but one day Israel, my jewelry will be the talk of the continent—collected by museums—and when that happens Mr. Tait can go and get Nurse Lushboosied for all I care. Now Israel, did you read how that development company, Quakers or something, want to put up those condos right where the Haseeshi Community Center is? The new government's not going to do a thing about stopping it. The councillors can't even perform their secret handshake, their palms are so greasy."

"I know, the papers are full of it. That fuck-wit of a congressman, Luckett, said after three centuries of the Haseeshi milking the coffers of this fine nation he's not going to continue to throw good money after bad. Can you believe he actually said that on television?"

"I'll believe anything about that asshole." Evangeline tosses her hair back and starts kneading the beanbag with her fingers.

"Well, Mr. Tosspot Tait just got the contract for those condos and I feel it's my duty to personally sabotage the project, so if you do a poster Izzy, I can run them off at work while Mr. Tait's not around. He says we are not to let our personal feelings about the Haseeshi *problem*—that's what he calls it—interfere with the task at hand. He doesn't like us *girls* to wear *slacks* at work. That's what he said, mind you there are no restrictions on cleavage. I can't wait until the last man of his generation expires. Boy will I roll out the ticker tape that day."

"All right, let's stop those condos. Power to the people and all that crap! You can be our Mata Hari working from inside. Tait & Simkiss my ass."

"Groovy."

Back when we first bought the house, we both had a little bit of family money that would have been wasted on God-knows-what if we hadn't sought our own piece of real estate. Evangeline was doing her jewelry design course at night school and working during the day. I was drawing a lot of nonsense for these outrageous comics that seemed to be simultaneously the most subversive and the most reactionary passion of the nation then and we were trying to cover rising interest rates as the new government began its unshakeable reign. We hoped then it wouldn't last and I guess we still had some fight in us. But when Eve got sacked from that job after it became apparent that she was involved in the Haseeshi support project and the condos looked like going up anyway, something shut down inside her.

"This country is a shit-hole," she said one night when she'd got another more suitable job working at an upmarket jewelry store called the Crystal Palace. Let's go to Venice. We have just enough money and I've sold some pieces for less than I suspect they're worth but it's a start."

And we did. Evangeline was a chameleon in those days: a quantum feminist who played by her own rules. Pretending to be the exact sort of woman she wasn't. Fuelled by Germaine Greer and inspired by Marilyn Monroe. She was a force to be reckoned with. She dyed her hair blonde, wore low-cut tops, teetered on high heels but was an enemy of the patriarchy and increasingly, an enemy of the state. To make things worse, she had a look that betrayed her victims. She wasn't model beautiful or anything but she could parody the girls who were numb to feminism, and she always seemed to get what she wanted. To this day I wouldn't know if she enjoyed fucking all the men she did. I can only assume so, why else would she have done it? It's not like they'd held a gun to her head, usually. But in the end it was me she wanted to be with. Israel and Evangeline.

"I fucked that Italian boy Israel and I let him buy me dinner and he had a lovely big cock that feels like it's still in there, but I won't see him again. Can you say you're my boyfriend or something? He'll back off then, you know how territorial these Latin boys are. I don't want to talk to him when he rings." And I would do like she said though I probably shouldn't have and on we'd go, to the next city, the next hotel. The Izzy and Eve roadshow. All aboard for the ride. No safety belts, no harnesses and certainly no net to break our fall.

"What are we Israel, forty-two? I forget these days."

"Fortysomething is all you need to say." And she'd stare off distractedly into the distance. "You're invisible after forty my mother used to say."

And I'd say, "I always wanted to be invisible as a kid," but of course I knew that was not what she meant. Neither of us wanted *that* sort of invisibility but in the darker places of this rotten town, there are mirrors I can look into. Deep pools of longing that Evangeline can't share.

"We've got each other Izzy and our grubby little *liaisons de nuit*. Will that do you until we're old?"

"Of course, Evangeline. Of course it will."

After she'd been fired from Tait & Simkiss for "illegally" copying documents on the firm's equipment and acting against the interests of their clients, Evangeline continued her fight to stop Quaker Pty. Ltd. from developing their condominiums on the ancient Haseeshi site. She wasn't ordinarily an activist or a zealot but on this single issue she became quite driven. Partly I'm sure because she came to despise Mr. Tait for being the patronizing, patriarchal bastard he was but also because in the course of her administrative work she stumbled upon some legal anomalies in the planning application. At the time, congress was busily working on ways to make it easier for developers to rid themselves of the tedious encumbrances and restrictions that had previously slowed them in pursuing their ultimate goals.

Why wait for a future—
When it can happen right away?

Izzy and Eve

That was the slogan. Right was right and white was right. The campaigns had cost millions and the government's advertising agency had hired fifty different choirs from across the land to join in song as an aerial camera showed our cities by day and night growing in wealth and strength. These scenes were overlaid with images of smiling children in brand-new schools running to meet their exultant mothers, smiling doctors in gleaming hospitals surrounded by state of the art equipment, grinning Haseeshi children painting bright pictures of native birds and neatly dressed businessmen smiling and shaking hands with politicians as they quietly secured the deals that would forge our nation's future in a brave new millennium. What a crock it all was, what a stinking loathsome crock. For all the talk of an Age of Aquarius, the future became nothing more than a marketing concept for a fresh generation of ambitious and acquisitive prospectors. They were grand days for some, full of brave promises if you believed a word of it, which I didn't. I knew the world was merely an exercise in all these things, and I'd already grown weary of it. I'd fallen out of step with the endeavors of mankind.

Evangeline? Well perhaps then there was still an ember of optimism burning somewhere inside her, perhaps she still thought the world might somehow redeem itself. So, in her youthful verve, she took her own small part in helping the Haseeshi by using the information she had stumbled upon to prove that there were legal technicalities being breached in the planning permit and that these had been deliberately overlooked. They were mostly to do with a three-hundred-year-old document allowing the Haseeshi to continually occupy a certain percentage of the city's central region. Therein they were free to conduct their own enterprises. Using what was left of the public court system, she and a group of lobbyists had an injunction brought against Quaker Pty. Ltd. She had threatening phone calls at home and at the Crystal Palace. She was almost hit by a car on Parkway Boulevard and she suspected she was being followed. Then one night changed her forever.

EVANGELINE

There's a bag over my head when I come to, my head aches, my mouth is taped, my wrists are cuffed. I'm starting to remember that something very bad has happened to me. My feet have no shoes and I'd worn my favorite pair to work today. I'm thinking about what I wore but I'm groggy and we're moving in some sort of vehicle. I wore my gray tube skirt, my white Krista de Veille blouse, and a cropped bolero jacket with buttons shaped like perfume bottles. I don't have my bag either and it was an original '60s patent leather Christian Dior.

The sack over my head feels like the hoods they used to put on the condemned in the past before hanging them and I wonder where you would buy such a bag nowadays? We have little drawstring red velvet gift ones with gold *C.P.* monograms on them for jewelry at work but nothing big enough to cover a human head. And I wonder if, when they used these bags for hangings in the past, it was done so the spectators couldn't see the expression on your face when your neck broke or while you were choking. I read somewhere that it can take up to ten minutes to choke someone to death. I expect that would have been the thrill for them in the old days. With the bags, well you'd just have to be satisfied with watching the legs twitch and dance about and for those who thrilled to that sort of entertainment, it wouldn't be the same as getting to see the victims' faces in full mortal torment would it?

They're hauling me from the car now, I feel the chill of the air outside. It's dawning on me that I am in this situation because of the Haseeshi community center. They're walking me somewhere, perhaps a park because there is damp grass underfoot. Then, as they throw me to the ground, I feel two of the buttons on my blouse pop.

Someone, a man, kneels beside me; he says, "Evangeline. Can you hear me?"

I nod because I can't speak though I wonder if it is better that they think I'm still unconscious. The man's voice is very calm, very controlled. Evil.

"I think you know why we're here Evangeline. I think you are aware of the trouble you've been causing over at city hall, can you hear what I'm saying?" I'm nodding vigorously inside my bag, wondering if they'll lynch me like the settlers used to do with the Haseeshi, then leave me swinging outside the community center or in Gethsemane Park as a lesson to all.

"Evangeline, we're reasonable people but we are *business*people do you understand that?" I nod again.

"Good, now we're getting somewhere. What I need you to understand is that in business, on the scale at which we operate, obstructions such as the one you and those Haseeshi parasites have brought about are very *very* costly to our venture. I'll explain this to you so you'll understand why we are concerned enough to have brought you to this meeting, tonight."

As if on cue, two men grab me then drag me into a lake or pond. It's freezing and they hold me under until I take in water through my nose. They haul me back out but I can't cough it up because of the tape over my mouth, I think they must have forgotten about the tape in which case I might choke anyway. I'm insane with the panic of my breathlessness and just at the moment I think I'm going to pass out or die, they hold me upside down so the water runs out my nose. They're professionals these men.

"Okay Evangeline, you're a smart girl and an attractive one. Not a true stunner, not really inspiring enough for a fellow to swing for and hell, when it comes to broads, I've got to say I've seen better tits but this isn't really about your tits is it, darlin'?" I don't move.

"I SAID IS IT—DARLING?" I shake my head. "Good, atta girl. We want to make good 'n' sure you haven't nodded off on us. So as I was saying, when a group of chaps invest fifty million dollars in a project then borrow considerably more in order to realize their dreams, you'll understand when they get a little upset when someone bars their way. I think you'll understand it even better if I explain that every day this project is held up by you, it costs us ninety thousand dollars in interest alone. That's quite a lot of money don't you agree, Evangeline?" I nod even though I feel like being sick. I'm trying not to vomit because if I do, it will probably kill me.

"Ninety thousand dollars is more money than you've ever had isn't it?"

I nod.

"And that's every day. Have *you* ever had anyone offer to spend that much on you every day Evangeline?"

I shake my head.

"I didn't think so. Even the prettiest girls don't have allowances like that to spend do they? So you might be starting to understand why *we* don't want to be spending that sort of money on you. HELL, we're not even sticking it to you, bitch! Believe it or not, Evangeline, we're gentlemen and before we adjourn this meeting let me point out that our development will be able to house sixteen hundred and fifty people where currently the area merely services two or three hundred itinerants, who, as part of the deal, will be given a new residential location in the Causeway where they will be free to drink their liquor and take their heroin and crack. So are we in agreement Evangeline that this has been a fruitful meeting for all parties involved?"

I nod again.

"Good. Now, we're just going to give you a little injection and we'll be on our way."

I feel a tourniquet around my arm. Adrenalin rushes through me and I wonder what agonizing poison they are about to fill me with. I feel the needle pierce the vein in the crook of my elbow and I vanish into an oblivion of white light.

ISRAEL

A call came from St. Barnaby's at midnight asking for Evangeline's next of kin. "She's suffered an overdose of heroin. Fortunately she was discovered in Gethsemane Park by a dog walker who called an ambulance."

"Heroin?" I said. "She doesn't use heroin."

"Well I'm afraid she did today, sir."

"But that's absurd, she doesn't go near the park at night."

"Well apparently she fell in with some Haseeshi. You can come and collect her but she will need to undergo counselling. We need the beds but she's agreed to do whatever is required to be signed out."

She was sitting up in the emergency room, staring out the window at the city lights.

"Are you all right Eve?" I said rushing to her side. She nodded, vaguely, without looking at me.

"What on earth is this about heroin?" I whispered. "And what happened to your mouth? You look like you've been kissing a prickly pear." She turned to me, her eyes dead, steely gray, but let her lashes fluttering coquettishly.

"I got in with the wrong Haseeshi crowd on the way home from work. We had some cans of beer and they took me into Gethsemane Park. I was a little drunk so I had sex with some of them. That's how I got the nasty gravel rash, they're not big on shaving. Then one of them said he had a bag of heroin and would I like to try some. I thought that might be fun so I did and that's how silly ol' me ended up in St. Barnaby's."

An orderly was looking on gob-smacked as she told the tale as if she were a Stepford wife or some lobotomized bimbo from a beauty pageant. I noticed bruises on her wrists and began to ask about them, but she held her finger to her lips to shoosh me.

"I think we should go now, Israel. There's plenty of more needy people who can use this bed. I'll tell the doctor that I don't actually think I need counselling. That heroin really didn't agree with me and once will be enough I'm sure."

She heaved herself out of the bed, put on her shoes, which had been left beside her with her handbag minus her wallet, then she slipped into the dress that I had taken in for her and threw her other outfit in the rubbish.

"I don't like that skirt or blouse anymore, too slutty." I saw bruises on her legs and wondered again what horrors had befallen her. "My days of social activism are over Izzy," she said as we rode down in the elevator, "and there aren't many girls in the world worth ninety thousand dollars a day. That much I know for a fact!" I looked at her in bewilderment. "I've decided I've been a bit quick to judge the condo development down at the Haseeshi center. Why, those condominiums will house nearly two thousand people, can you believe? I think we've been too hasty and cynical in our condemnation of the project."

EVANGELINE

Around the edges of the business card, there is a border of chains and barbed wire. The text is all in black but drops of red blood drip from the barbs. As I feel them, I realize they are embossed. Expensive. I wonder if by feeling the card I will find some clue to Israel's whereabouts but I feel nothing. I think soon I will have to pay Gustav and Torsten an unexpected visit.

It is now three days since I've seen him so at some point I must decide when to go to the police. I haven't left the house myself for over thirty-six hours and for some reason the thought terrifies me. Do I go today or tomorrow? When I feel like this the effort just to make a cup of coffee is too much and sometimes I'm not as compliant with my medication as I'd have Israel believe.

Once Izzy and I discussed disappearing people, not the dead ones but the ones who come back after years of absence. Sons and daughters who for whatever reason put their family and friends through untold grief—the dreadful process of wondering where they were and then the ultimate moment of giving them up for dead. The incredible thing is that these people turn up and everyone is so pleased to see them that they forgive them for what they have done. It is always later that terrible resentments surface. Israel and I both agreed it takes a special type of person to disappear like that, an unimaginably self-absorbed and thoughtless person—yet almost all types of people can be loved by someone. We are linked as a species by the most fragile web of connections, some of us have many but it seems I have just one and right now it has broken leaving me spiralling into space like a spider that has fallen from a web spun across an unfathomable gorge.

I take the photo I have and brave the outside world. This time I leave the security grille unlocked—just in case. The precinct headquarters is awash with half-processed people. Criminals and help-seeking citizens loiter morosely like casualties in a hospital. It is hard to know who is there by choice and who by force of some misdemeanor. There seems to be no one at the desk but in the distance, policemen and women mill about like bank clerks. They seem not to want to do any work. Finally a woman comes to the enquiry counter and I go up to speak with her. She's a frumpy-looking, no-nonsense woman. The type who could be salt-of-the-earth helpful or, just as easily, a right cow. You can never tell with her type until she opens her mouth.

"I feel a little awkward about this," I say haltingly, "but my partner disappeared three days ago and I'm very concerned about him. He doesn't vanish for days like this without a phone call."

"But he sometimes *does* disappear for days and let you know?"

"Well um, yes."

"Well honey some women really know how to pick 'em. So what is this guy, your husband, a de facto, a business partner? What are we talkin' here?"

"Well none of the above really, we've lived together for twenty years but he's gay." The woman looks me over as if this one fact explains everything and for the umpteenth time I wonder exactly what sort of woman I'm perceived as being.

"Let's just say we're close enough for me to be very concerned."

"So you have reason to think something might have happened to him?"

"I feel as if something might. I mean yes, obviously!"

"Okay, what sort of guy are we talking about? He's gay, is he promiscuous? Is he involved with drugs? Does he use rent boys? You're gonna have to fill in the blanks for me here."

I groan inwardly; the blanks were many and Israel was not going to come up smelling of roses. Israel has in fact been mired in so much stinking, sleazy business for so long I should be able to sniff him out for myself, so I try to rescue the situation.

"Israel is forty-two years old, he's done a lot in his life but he's no criminal."

"Drugs are criminal though." She regards me suspiciously, as if this fact may have eluded my attention.

"Well yes, of course, but he's no spring chicken, not really in the popular demographic for drug abuse or for sinister disappearances." I laugh stupidly. "If everyone who used drugs in the Gilgal were to be imprisoned, there wouldn't be many folk about, would there?" She stares at me like I'm an idiot.

I think about my folder, bulging with pretty faces: milkshake models; lollipop girls; the attractive, unfaithful wives of business developers; prostitutes with axes to grind and outspoken young Haseeshi activists whose deaths are routinely dismissed as drug-related suicides. I see the shopping cart in my mind again and see Israel riding up top. His leather chaps flapping free over the torn stockings and high heels of all those nervy murdered housewives who apologized because a psychopath rammed their carts.

"Look hon, I gotta be honest with you here. We got us over three thousand missing people in the database right now and to tell you the truth, our resources are stretched to the max, but if you want me to enter his photo and details for you, I can. One thing I'll tell you for free, is that in my experience, men go missing because they want to, women go 'cos they dead."

I ponder her dire evaluation of the situation, wondering if she kept a scrapbook herself. She looks like she might be a lesbian but with policewomen you could never be sure, they all seemed to have a slightly butch edge to them, tough love at best, hard bitch at worst. She passes me the MP16987 form, which I begin to complete. "Relationship to the missing person?" I proceed to *other* and think *life partner* sounds too absurd; *cohabitant and close friend of twenty years,* I write.

As I stand to one side of the counter filling out the form I hear someone addressing the policewoman. "Dierdre, can you get some more of those Haseeshi 16214s printed up? We'll need them for the weekend." I'm taken aback because the voice sounds familiar. I look up but don't recognize the face, a senior police officer approaching sixty. It was something gravelly in the way he said *Haseeshi,* perhaps he's appeared on the television. It nags at me as I fill out the form.

"Who's he?" I ask Sergeant Dierdre. She looks over her shoulder. "That's the chief commissioner no less. Likes to keep his hand in with the rank and file." He's gone now, leaving a scent of heavy, old-fashioned aftershave behind him. I have no faith in the process I've just involved myself in. No faith at all, yet it seems I must go through it none the less. I can't see that revealing too much about Izzy's habits and penchants will encourage them to stretch their resources any further so by the end of the report he ends up looking like a stable gay man in his middle years. The sort of wholesome gent one is likely to see held up by the gay community as living proof of their hard won place in a world of respectability and common decency. *Graphic artist* instead of purveyor of dirty cartoons, home-owner, et cetera. It occurs to me as I leave the building that I've never asked the police for help before, Israel and I have never been the types and by a miracle of chance, we've never been burgled. Then it occurs to me that the voice of that chief commissioner sounded similar to a voice that has given me nightmares over the years. Could it be that of my assailant many years ago? He didn't recognize me of course, I was blonde then, it was almost twenty years ago and my report is unlikely to pass before his nose so I don't expect to have any more to do with him. I can't even be sure—how could I be? And where I thought I would be chilled to the core to hear that voice, I feel nothing at all. I simply realize that what was done to me back then was done to me by the law. I'm seasoned enough not to be the least bit surprised. I have studied the wiles of this city far too thoroughly to ever be surprised by evil. It seems in the past it has buzzed around Israel and me like a carrion bird, high in the sky, circling in wait but never diving upon us except for that one terrible exception. Now I feel it descending like the winter as I push past the deserted sidewalk cafes still hoping to make a few bucks out of the last of the season's tourists. As I round the corner into the Gilgal I notice a drunk Haseeshi woman, her filthy skirt hitched up, taking a crap in the gutter. People stop and stare in shock, motorists nearly crash their cars at the disgrace of the image. "If you don't fuckin' like it then don't fuckin' look!" she screams at pedestrians. Mary's hovering nearby with Tibby who is on his way home from school. She's crimson to the core, trying to make him look the other way. He's transfixed with uninhibited fas-cination. "Why's that lady doing a poop in the gutter, Ma?"

I don't want to be with them for this little talk but I need to get past the woman as fast as I possibly can. I pretend to look in the shop windows as I go by then before I know it I'm alongside Mary and Tibby.

"Did you see that lady, Evangeline? She was pooping in the gutter—that is so gross."

"Certainly not ladylike," I say idiotically, trying to mask my own embarrassment and sense of desolation. The image of that woman could give me nightmares.

"Why wouldja do your business in the gutter?" He looks to his mother so I let her field this one. "Because she's drunk, darling, now don't go on about it. It's not very nice."

"*It's not very nice*," mimics Tibby. "Where's Israel?" he asks me.

"I don't know, Tibby." We're in the side street now with only a couple of blocks to go until we are home. Mary looks at me with concern.

"Still no sign?"

"No. I just filed a missing person report at the police station—can you believe it? I'm beside myself. The policewoman said women disappear because they've been murdered, men because they want to. It was so humiliating." I decide not to mention my fears about the policeman. Mary is likely to try and rally me into some sort of action against him. The thought of going through something like that makes me feel weak as a lamb.

"I don't know what to do."

Tibby is running a stick along the fence. "Perhaps they've come for to carry him home."

"Tibby, don't talk like that please."

"Like what? Wha' did I say wrong *now*, Jeez can't say nothin' these days."

"*Anything* Tibby, can't say anything."

"I'm the Tibster, I'm not Tibby anymore—it's a stupid name. Israel called me the Tibster and I reckon that's what I'll be. I sure hope he comes home." Tibby stops with his stick and considers things for a moment. "He's one helluva guy that Israel. Good job you two didn't have any kids if he's flown the coop."

Neither Mary nor I say anything this time. It's too exhausting to keep up with Tibby and he's already at his front fence doing a drum solo on their gate. I'm supposed to go to the brothel tonight. The thought irks me but the mortgage is due. I'll have to work harder if I'm truly on my own now.

ISRAEL

"So did they rape you?"

"No."

"You're sure?"

"Of course I'm fucking sure Israel. It wasn't that sort of attack, they were businessmen—gentlemen if I am to believe what they told me."

"Which you are not."

"Izzy try and understand. These are dangerous men, powerful men and I have just learnt what that means. There are powers that it is not wise to contest in this town. What they are doing might, in some perfect moral universe, be absolutely wrong but we are not living in that universe. Quite the contrary. We are living right here in the Gilgal and while much of life is shitty as can be, I'm too afraid to die right now. Christ, they might even be right. Money might actually be more important than people! Did you ever stop to think about that? Certainly people will do *anything* for it. Those hands could have done whatever they wanted to me but they showed mercy. They held my head firmly under the water. They knew exactly how long they could do it before I drowned. You know why? Because they've done that sort of thing many times before. They are professionals these guys and I am NOT. I'm a silly girl with a headful of idealistic nonsense. THEY WIN, ISRAEL!"

I paced the lounge in fury while Eve seemed to be so cool. Too cool. I knew she wasn't really, I knew beneath her callous veneer, damage was manifesting in all sorts of hideous ways. Little parts of her were breaking, coming unstuck. Her circuitry was in peril and I felt sure the results would reveal themselves in twisted and dangerous behaviors during the years to come.

"Izzy, you're not like other men. You're certainly not like these, and if you keep going with this protest it is more likely to be me than you they force to ride the big white horse into the vast technicolor oblivion next time. I am asking you to leave it alone for my sake. Can you do that? Can you do that one thing for your best friend whose life may hang in the balance? There is only one acceptable answer to this question by the way."

"Yes." What choice did I have?

"Now, I'm going to go and work at that brothel I told you about that has opened up around the corner. They've been looking for someone to do the books and manage reception. Rahab, who runs it, thought it would be great to have someone so skilled and close at hand."

Evangeline made it sound like it was a childcare center but I couldn't understand her new career path at all. Cruelly, by way of some extra sabotage on the part of her attackers, her employers at Crystal Palace had been led to believe that she was a heroin addict. We weren't exactly sure how this came about but she was dismissed when she returned to work the week after the attack. It was then she decided that she no longer wanted to be part of the mainstream workforce. Her back was to the wall.

"If I have more time to do my jewelry, I might even make more money, Israel. It makes perfect sense."

Her pragmatism made me very nervous but I couldn't say a thing.

"I'd rather know where I stood with men. I'll clean up after them when they soil the brothel sheets. I'll put on a little-girl voice for them when they ring up to make their appointments and I'll wear low-cut blouses so they can get started on their erections before the girls have even taken them upstairs. But I'll be fucked, *fucked* I tell you, if I'll ever trust one of them again."

So there I had it. The new hard and emotionally rationalized Evangeline. A new generation of woman. Enter at your own risk.

We destroyed all the posters and leaflets. We told people they'd been given the wrong number when they rang to support the Haseeshi cause and then as the condominiums rose from the ground like delinquent prophesies, Evangeline spoke about the architecture as if it was just any other crap building going up in the city. She even made me look at the finished apartments, criticizing the fittings and finishes as if we were interested young home-buyers ourselves.

"I'd want the east-facing ones," she said when we'd gone on our absurd inspection. "You can imagine how hot those west-facing rooms would get in the summer. At least they give you blinds with them, even if they are hideous and would break in five minutes flat."

The realty agent listened curiously as people always did when Evangeline chattered on in her inimitable way. "I couldn't live with an electric cooker," she said dismissively as we went through the kitchen. I just wanted to get out of the place. The apartments were so not us, yet it seemed Evangeline needed to territorialize them, like a cat. It was as if she'd already put down the deposit a year earlier that night in the park.

"Thank you," she said curtly to the agent. I said nothing. For me it was as if anyone who had anything to do with the development, from the architects to the realtors, were all personally responsible for what had happened to Eve.

She took a card from the agent and slipped it into her bag.

"They're not really what we had in mind. A little too stark and modern for us."

EVANGELINE

Pornography doesn't bother me per se, in fact I quite like some of the gay stuff Izzy used to collect, which is a little disturbing as there is really no place for me to go with it. It's not as if I can actually have any of the sex I'm witnessing, so it can be quite a conundrum for me, as a woman. What disturbs me at the brothel, and I'm surprised they allow it, is that in the Scandinavian room there is a large-screen television that johns can rent to watch porn on while they're having sex with one of the girls. As I'm on the front desk it falls to me to switch on the screen and put on a DVD. I have a small monitor under the front counter so I can watch it to make sure it hasn't finished before the client has. I don't know where they got *Cat on a Hot Teen Roof* from, but the lead actress in it disturbs me greatly. For a start she never shuts up. She hisses and yowls the whole way through just like the cats in heat that keep us awake at night in the lanes behind our house. She must be on some extreme hallucinogen or a barrelful of crystal meth in order to carry on as she does. She seems barely human. She also does the double penetration act, which I find too much to watch myself. That delicate fret of flesh between the two orifices seems so fragile and forlorn in the shots, my heart would go out to her was she not making such an absurd racket. None of the girls like working to that movie either. The johns adore it but it gives the punters too many ideas and the noise of it is intolerable. I hate it; it makes an animal out of a girl. They request it when they request the Scandinavian room and I've made an executive decision to tell them the DVD has been scratched and won't play. They have to make do with *The Sultan's Whore,* which has the double whammy but not all the other nonsense that goes along with it.

It's quiet tonight. The weather turning this week hasn't helped and only Catriana and Mai are on. No blondes tonight, which has already taken one punter elsewhere.

"There are some wigs out the back," I say to Catriana. Mai is Chinese so she wouldn't fool anyone, though Suni is also Asian and has done quite well on her nights since she bleached her hair a silvery white.

"No way, I hate fucking in a wig," she says as she drags an Epilator over her petite ankles. "You think the wig's gonna come off all the time, it itches like crazy and of course I'm still not *blonde* in the right places."

I ring home to check if there are any messages or if by some miracle he might be there. There's another message from Torsten, for me this time. I dial the number.

"Hello, Torsten, this is Evangeline."

"Ah, have you seen Israel?"

"No. I have gone to the police. It will be five days tomorrow since he disappeared. What happened at Gutz the other night? I found your card outside."

"Gutz, ah, for different people, different things happen." *Jesus*, these guys are impenetrable in any way but the most literal.

"I can imagine. But what did Israel *do*, what did he say?"

"He'd had too much he said."

"Too much *what* Torsten? Too much drugs, too much sex, too much to drink?"

"I think yes."

It's useless. I'll have to try and speak to him in person. I'm finishing at ten so I tell him I'm coming over later. This doesn't suit him as he has *friends* around. It doesn't seem likely that I'm about to be one of his friends.

"Is bad about Israel, yes."

"Yes it is very bad, Torsten. I'll come tomorrow at midday."

I hang up before he can argue. I don't like him at all.

ISRAEL

There's no use in my going back to the Gilgal or to the house anymore. The houses all seem like cottages in fairy tales with their lights twinkling from inside. People scurry home faster now winter

Izzy and Eve

is upon them and I too seem to be gathered up with the leaves as they rustle along the streets in search of bonfires to smoke in or gutters to block. Each person is a story I could follow. A frail web of disappointments and joys, of lies and truths and my heart grows heavy with the magnitude of it all. The world looks like a set: *Oliver*, *Moulin Rouge*, *The Wizard of Oz*. I wonder if the joys can ever make up for the sorrows. I suppose the fact that people keep going suggests they might. I look at the shopping bags people carry with cans of soup for their supper, bread for their breakfast and flowers for their table. Islands moving closer and then apart. Auras and energy which, if I blur my vision, become quite surreal. It's like I've turned a pair of binoculars around the wrong way. What once was close, now seems a mile away. The cars, the bikes and pedestrians. Shifting tectonic plates each of them. Kind or bitter, it's hard to tell. Yet any one might let you love them or befriend them if you played your cards right. Push the right buttons and they could lay themselves out naked before you. Surrender themselves to your power, put aside their shopping, forget the flowers and canned soup, offer themselves up and try their luck again. *Maybe this time I'll be lucky*. I know that line, it's from a movie. What was it? *Cabaret*. And that is just what it is like. Maybe you'll get lucky and he'll stay, maybe he won't. Maybe I will. Maybe not.

The woman at the station still sings as loud as ever, though her cheeks are flushed ruddy from the cold or is she suddenly older? I can't seem to tell how old people are anymore so I watch the trains moving in and out of the platforms, wishing I could speed them up as they do in films where their movement is jerky and caricatured. I wish the lights of the city could appear as they do in those postcard photographs that use time-lapse photography. The grit of the city obscured by long trails of light, the trolley cars gaily painted as they trundle above the Causeway on the ancient aqueduct. I see Evangeline's staring from the window, nervously twisting her rings and I remember the long taxi ride that cut through the darkness with sharp red lines and delivered me to this new beginning. To a life of which Evangeline cannot be a part, yet one she will know of soon enough.

EVANGELINE

The wind rattles a loose tile on the roof as I descend into a turbulent sleep. I dream of the religious woman on the mailbox only her song is not the same. She seems to sing more earnestly, more urgently, to ward off the cold, or perhaps to ward off demons.

I can't walk but I can fly.
My heart won't beat yet I won't die.
I loved you then yet love you more
as winter knocks upon your door.

At the rate the weather is changing there's likely to be snow a month before fall's even done. There were gale warnings on the estuaries yesterday and this morning the paper claims a body has been found there: "The unidentified body of a man in his late thirties," it said and I wonder if they can tell the age right off. I never read those crime novels so I'm not sure. There is a color picture of a body bag being loaded into an ambulance. My heart is in my mouth as my fingers run over the image. I feel nothing, or at least nothing that equates with Israel. I sense violence, I can tell this is a murder, not a boating accident, but I can't tell a lot of things anymore. My frequencies are blocked. I phone the missing persons line to see if I can find out anything more and after I've been transferred several times I learn that the body has been dead for at least a fortnight. It cannot be him and I feel relieved. There is a grim joke that goes about from time to time that if you're fool enough to go fishing in the estuary, you're more likely to catch a person than a fish; it's also said that the fish at least get to eat several of us before we eat one of them.

I think about the missing boy stories I've read in the past but bypassed for my collection. The murdered boys are usually young and pretty like the girls, drugs seem often to be involved as well. Beauty and youth certainly seem to raise the murder stakes on people but then there was a killer some years back who specialized in grandmothers, and another who was murdering welfare recipients in some appalling but ingenious manner in order to collect their checks. What could anyone want with middle-aged men? Perhaps their wallets are the fullest but no one carries much cash these days, you'd be an idiot if you did. I feel heavy with the horror of it. I wonder if Israel has fallen prey to a new murder demographic. I suppose gay men, for whatever reasons, have always been high risk in whatever they do and isn't it always those who live at the loudest volume who are at greatest risk of being switched off? I must stop thinking about death.

I pull my angora coat out of the closet. It's a dark, dark purple and I must have had it for six winters now. It smells a little dusty from hanging there since last spring. It's cold enough for a hat too but even my plainest one seems too jaunty for the way I feel right now. I don't need the card to remember Torsten and Gustav's address, they live only a mile or so away. I decide to walk.

Their place is located on the Escarpment, an area in which the houses appear to cling to a cliff face. Many are wooden and painted brightly but some are stone and seem to almost burrow into rock. Torsten and Gustav live in one of the stone ones with a deceptively small frontage. I ring the bell and a dog barks from inside. Gustav opens the door but only nods. He leads me into a lounge room where I presume I am to wait for Torsten, who has a better grasp of English.

The room is what I would have expected. Black leather furniture, large framed photographs of near-naked men with impossibly perfect physiques and improbable swellings beneath their jockstraps.

The type of images you can buy for fifty dollars in any tourist shop in the gay district. And a few Tom of Finland prints. Black rubber coasters are neatly stacked on a coffee table next to a pile of perfectly arranged men's magazines covering every topic from bodybuilding to cars. Any trace of anything that might be considered feminine has been studiously avoided. I feel like I'm in a surgery waiting room except that a large German shepherd has wandered in and is sniffing curiously at my crotch.

"Different isn't it, pooch?" I say. "Bet you don't get many of them in here?"

The dog doesn't answer but gives me a lick of surreptitious approval, then Torsten arrives.

"Poor Israel," he says. "Things are bad right now I think."

"What do you mean?" I say.

He shows me the paper that I have already seen.

"It's not Israel," I say. "I've already phoned. That body is two weeks old."

"Ah, but this is one of many."

"Why do you say that?"

"Same age, gay men. Someone is killing who does not like us."

"Since when?"

"Maybe three months now men disappear. This one is first to be found."

"But how do you know this man was gay? They do not even know who he *is* yet."

Torsten waves at me dismissively, as if I am a fool. "He will be, you wait."

"We can't wait, Torsten, and I don't expect much help from the cops."

"Police don't care. They want us dead." He drags his hand over his neck in a throat-cutting gesture to add to the drama.

He says it with such bile that I think he's overreacting. While it wouldn't surprise me if they didn't care particularly whether gays *lived*, I do think it's a bit strong to suggest they actually want people to be murdered. Still what would I know given that it may have been one of the very same police who nearly murdered me?

"So you really have no idea what happened to Israel after Gutz?"

"No."

"Did he seem to be okay when he left?" This was all I had to go on now.

"I think he was, he walked, he talked. He said so long."

"Did he come here often?"

"Sometimes."

"What did you...*do* here?"

Torsten takes an exasperated breath and gestures for me to follow him. We walk through the house, passing through the kitchen where Gustav appears to be cooking some sort of goulash. At least that's what I hope it is. I climb after Torsten down a spiral staircase to what is obviously their pride and joy: their basement, which has been cut straight into the cliff face, is full of leather paraphernalia. More than I've ever seen. Whips, harnesses, cages, slings and racks as well as a punishing array of dildos and faux surgical implements that set even my heart into a racing panic. I pretend confidence as I walk around the room, as if I were a dominatrix surveying the apparatus. I even pick up a cat-o'-nine-tails as well as an implement I suspect might be some special type of proctoscope—I drop it quickly. Everything seems to gleam as if hours have been spent shining the implements and polishing the leather. Even as I wander around I notice Torsten buffing up a stirrup with a silver cloth. It occurs to me that they are as proud of this room as teenage boys are of their cars. There's even an area with a shower, toilet and douche hose. On the wall, manifesto style in sombre black lettering, are *The House Rules* in *Deutsch und Inglese*. As I scan it quickly I realize Torsten himself has done the translating, with lines like *If the glove fits where it*, to which someone else has added *is* between *where* and *it*.

Another line says *If you have distended bowel tell Gustav*. And I'm not sure whether this is because Gustav needed to be warned of such things in advance or because it was something he was especially fascinated by. I would laugh except they obviously don't think this is at all funny. How could two men who would have to be well in their forties build their entire life around *this*? And what do they do for jobs for Chrissake? Houses on the Escarpment don't come cheap and renovations like theirs would have cost plenty. In fact they may even have overcapitalized by adding this chamber of horrors.

"So Torsten, with all *this* at home why would you go to Gutz?"

He shrugs casually. "There are others there. Others who maybe we don't want in our home."

Jesus. I shudder as the dog sniffs me again then moves on to some polished leather. It's time to go, so I ask him to call me if he hears anything. He says he will and I suppose I believe him. Still I think about Gutz and wish there was someone else I knew who I could send in there. Perhaps Curtis might go when he realizes how serious it has all become.

Why would they want to have sex with people they weren't prepared to have in their home? Perhaps I'm more naive than I thought or perhaps this aspect of physical exploration falls into a different realm of experience altogether.

ISRAEL

The church will tell you a lot of things. It takes a discerning mind and steady hand to separate the truth from the garbage. When I say *church* I mean any of them, Jewish, Hindu, Islamic, Christian, the whole screaming cacophony of tradition, fundamentalism and dogma. Established religion seems to have as much to do with faith as apples have to do with bananas. Of course you get your Yiddish wisdom, your Islamic proverbs, your pithy Christian aphorisms and your cryptic Buddhist metaphors—but never having been a joiner of anything, my faith lets me float freely. I figure if humanity is as fucked as it is, then God must be a bit gaga too. For every flicker of light I bring to Evangeline, she can cast a shadow of doubt.

So I live explicitly, though not explicitly by any of their rules but there are some things I wonder if you can change irrecoverably. Like sex. When you make sex the vehicle for exploring more extreme and visceral aspects of being, do you run the risk of it never being synonymous with love again? I don't know what sort of a mess Eve's made of it in her head. For her it's like a combat sport. For me it's like a parallel landscape where animals can't be tamed, where the most savage congress can yield the most intimate mental imagery and vice versa. What choice do I have as an outcast of conventional sexual morality but to seek a raw new terrain? An opportunity lost can be wisdom gained. To have lived through ostracism and pestilence is character building but once the fear of the vile body has been overcome where does that leave you—or me—or her?

I look at my hands and think of the things they have done. I imagine them reaching Heavenward to touch God's outstretched fingers as if in a Michelangelo painting. I'm confident I could reach them but I'm scared, in the same way I used to be of electric fences. I'm scared if I touch them I'll be transformed into a different type of energy. I know it will be awesome but I'm not convinced I'm ready yet. I notice there is no ring on my hand though I can't remember ever taking it off. I often removed it, of course, so as not to injure others, but I'm always fastidious about keeping it somewhere safe. It was my most precious possession, now it has gone. My hands look perfect, there's not even the tan mark I usually have beneath my ring at the end of summer.

I think about my bedroom, my large square pillows and the small coal fire I lit there in winter sometimes. I think about my desk and all the sticks of charcoal and pencils. There's a window that looks over the street and if I close my eyes I can see the Tibster kicking a soccer ball around on the street below which means his mother must be up the road at the market or something. She wouldn't let him play ball in the road. He looks up at my window and frowns. He takes some chalk from his pocket then draws a line across six other lines already on the wall opposite our house. He looks up again and I think maybe I see a tear but then my vision is not so good anymore.

EVANGELINE

"What are you looking at, Tibby?"

"Just at Israel's window."

"Did you see something?"

He hesitates before giving the ball a hefty kick that sends it under a passing car.

"I never saw nothin' lady." He's imitating a movie gangster again. He takes the chalk and circles the strikes on the wall.

"Seven days and I ain't seen a damned thing."

It's been a week and Tibby has been counting the days like a prisoner in a jail cell.

"But you saw him last week didn't you? That day you found the picture?"

"Reckon I imagined that, lady. Reckon there ain't no room for ghosts in this gringo town."

"But you *thought* you saw him didn't you? I didn't mean to be cross, Tibby."

He doesn't answer. He retrieves his ball, which missed the wheels of the vehicle, and he's bouncing it, circling me like a star basketball player.

"If I could grow to six foot eight, I could get paid a million dollars a year for playing basketball and I wouldn't even have to try to play good."

"Is that so?"

I've just photocopied one hundred posters to put in bars. I feel such dread at the prospect of stepping out tonight with tape and scissors in order to stick them up but it must be done.

Tibby suddenly launches into what appears to be a magician's act. "Nothin' up my sleeve!" And he produces Israel's ring.

"My God Tibby, where did you find that?"

"In the back garden. Under the table. That's hematite, isn't it?" Tibby is fingering the two small saddles of silvery-gray stone that sit either side of the black pearl.

He puts it in my hand. I close my fist around it eager to feel if there is any energy and I get a blast which nearly makes my head explode. A series of images so fast I'd need to feel it again at one hundredth of the speed to make any sense of it. I open my eyes to see Tibby staring at me.

"You all right, Evangeline?"

"I think so." I look at Tibby, it looks as if he's about to cry.

"Sweetie, what's up?"

"He's not coming back is he Goddam it?"

I put my arm around him just as I think he's about to crumple but he suddenly squirms from my grasp in anger then kicks the ball without even looking, straight into his mother's car that is cruising along in search of a space. She's looking at me as if I've done something terrible again to upset him—the crazy woman next door. He leaves the ball and runs off around the corner as a gust of wind pulls several of my posters from beneath my arm. Mary catches one as she gets out of the car and considers which situation to deal with first. She looks at the poster but I can't read her expression.

"What was that all about?" she asks accusingly. I feel a flush of anger that I try to diffuse.

"He's upset about Israel." I try to save another poster as the wind takes two more skipping down the street to the ends of the earth. I point to the chalk marks.

"He's been striking off the days since Izzy went. He realized it's been a week today. He's angry."

Mary seems relieved. She seems to believe me.

"Poor Tibby, Israel has been the only real adult male in his life." She says it as if this were an unfortunate and disappointing turn of events.

"I guess we have to take what we're given, Mary." I almost stop there but go on because she never appreciated how fond Israel was of Tibby. "They spent at least an hour a day together, more time than a lot of fathers spend with their kids…" and certainly more time than Tibby's dad ever spent with him, I thought, though I spared her that.

"Well he definitely learnt to draw breasts better than most of his contemporaries." She smiles begrudgingly.

"Israel adored him, Mary. I don't know why you were always so suspicious when his own father…" I stop myself.

"Probably *because* of his own father. Probably because his own father left me with barely enough love or resources to bring him up at all much less the way I'd hoped to. What a stupid empty-headed creature I must have been back then." She looks off into the distance waiting for me to reassure her.

"You got into law Mary, there must have been something useful going on up there." Suddenly I realize how similar our situations are. I wonder if I can ever get back with Mary to where we used to be when she and Joshua would sit with us in the lounge drinking wine, smoking joints, listening to music. In those halcyon days, back before I…interfered. Joshua always had some new thing we *had* to listen to, something he'd recorded or bought. Everyone had to be right there with him. "You'll love this, it's awesome," he'd say and sometimes it was, but mostly it wasn't. Mary was too Catholic to have an abortion and Joshua was too insubstantial to stay around when the responsibilities presented by Tibby looked likely to infringe upon the vagaries of his flaky existence.

"He's been in childcare since he was eight months old and I don't really even know where Joshua is now." Mary looks at me with resignation.

"You know where *he* is don't you?" I ask.

"Israel?"

"No, Joshua."

"Oh, in some ashram in India. I stopped answering his letters two years ago. Now he doesn't even write me, which is a relief because the letters were so full of theosophical gobbledygook that they just infuriated me. The last few I sent were all exactly the same: 'Your son is now six…seven…eight…and can't remember what you look like. He gets photos out all the time because I won't have them up anymore and when it's his birthday he mopes around the mailbox for days waiting for a card or present that never comes. You've broken his heart so work that out at your spiritual focus forums or whatever it is you have there.'"

I'm surprised to hear all this because Mary and I hadn't spoken of Joshua in ages. I guess I knew he was the one responsible for hardening her so much to the world and I suppose Israel's spiritual mumbo jumbo mixed in with his pornographic drawings made him look even worse than Joshua.

"Look what Tibby found in the courtyard."

I show her the ring.

"I think he's seen Israel."

"What, today?"

"Maybe, and the other day. He says there's no such thing as ghosts. I don't know what he meant."

"I suppose children see things we can't."

"I think he's…gone, Mary."

"You can't know for sure, Evangeline." But that is where she's wrong. There was something in what I felt from that ring that told me I wasn't going to find him in this neighborhood. I start to sob quietly and Mary takes me inside.

The Latin District is always busy on Friday nights. It's already too chilly for some of the buskers but the fire-eaters are still out, so is the organ grinder with his mangy monkey. The monkey wears a little striped sweater that Mrs. Organ Grinder knitted and those two attractions alone keep the Latin circus tenaciously alive as days grow colder. The dwindling funds of the government's arts council actually pay for the better performers to do their stuff on weekend nights. The District attracts a lot of tourists so it is one area where public money is still spent. There are large, brightly painted murals on the buildings of joyful Haseeshi children playing by the estuary in traditional tribal costume to confirm for the visitors that we are in fact all one big happy family. Most of the land on the estuary is now privately owned and all the water frontages are restricted moorings for the owners. The artist who did the mural wasn't even Haseeshi and their flag appears nowhere in the picture. The real picture should have been of grubby urchins playing in the gutters of the Causeway but I don't suppose that would have pleased the tourists who come to buy bogus Haseeshi crafts and paintings from the cluttered, tacky stores that litter the district. They all want the *real* handmade thing but aren't prepared to part with real money so imported mass-produced rubbish from sweatshops in Asia fills the racks and sells much better.

I take a poster from my bag, stick it to a lamppost that is already covered with hastily designed advertisements for illegal raves and underground club-nights. There is another poster about a missing kitten that seems to have been scrawled by a child: *If you no where Mr. Wiskers is please ring me cos Dad ses he was probly run over.* I avoid covering that notice as well as another missing person poster for *Roger* who vanished a month ago.

They are like premature gravestones, these missing person ads. I look at Israel smiling out from his, and wonder if anyone will even recognize him from the pic. Then I have another horrible thought: if someone has taken him, that person may have the keys to the house. I can't believe I hadn't thought of that though he didn't have the grille key with him and I locked it tonight. His wallet is still at home, only his ATM card is missing. I must go to the bank and see if he's used it. We at least had the sense years ago to get power of attorney for each other. Now I just need to find the damned documents.

I walk into Crust to pin one of the posters on their notice board. As I do I see three more, all for men. I begin to imagine some dungeon filled with men, and a woman torturing them all for the misdeeds men have perpetrated upon her gender but of course it is never women who do this sort of thing.

In Blue Nile it is crowded and smoky. People look at me oddly as I tape a poster to the back wall near the pool table. The barman quickly tears it down because, I suppose, they don't want to alarm any tourists. I work my way through the more popular straight and mixed bars thinking Israel probably never came to any of them anyway. Finally I reach Stonemasons Walk where the more hard-core gay venues are located and I brace myself to deal with the doormen as I push my way into Crouch, which demands anyone over six feet tall do just that.

"Sorry darlin', it's lads only tonight."

"I know, I'm just looking for a friend."

"Aren't we all, me lovely, aren't we all? Tuesdays and Thursdays are the nights for you girls."

I suppress my rage at being dismissed as a "girl," I suppose in some parallel patriarchal universe I'd be flattered by this, "at my age." I hold out a poster pathetically, he glances over it with annoyance then seems to recognize the face.

"Izzy, I know him. Bit of a regular he is."

"How regular and how recently?" I ask with impatience.

"Oh, he must have been in a few days ago. You forget with faces, dontcha? Maybe last weekend, nice enough fellow."

"Well he's been missing for a week, do you think you've seen him this week?"

He scratches his chin. "To tell you the truth love I couldn't really say. He didn't strike me as the type to have a bird on the side."

"On the side?"

"Well he was more a lad's lad if you know what I mean."

"Of course I know what you mean, I live with him for God's sake, I'm not his *bird*."

I leave the poster, which to his credit he is actually pinning up next to the cloakroom. As I turn to walk away he looks back at me.

"None of them turn up."

"What do you mean 'them'?" I ask nervously.

"The geezers. The prime cuts."

"Who are the *geezers* for Chrissake?"

"The older ones. There's been a lot lately. The young fellas tend to turn up quickly in the estuary or down the Causeway. It's over quickly with them, the sickos have their fun, pop 'em, burst 'em or fill 'em with drugs but with your geezers you never hear a thing and it would be my considered opinion that Israel is definitely in the geezer and prime cut category."

I'm mortified by these casual theories. Then I remember that a year or so ago there'd been a particularly nasty incident at Crouch. They had a back room that was very popular and pitch black. Some psycho got in there with a switchblade and turned it into a blood-bath. A man's penis was cut off and stolen. The perpetrator escaped the club with the penis, never to be seen or heard of again. The man whose penis had been severed lived. Israel said he didn't think he would have bothered to survive such an attack himself: "That guy lost his handle on life," he said. Apparently after that they painted the room red then turned it into a video lounge nicknamed the Bloodbath. I wondered whether this doorman had been here then. The club was closed for months. When it reopened they decided to make the most of a bad lot and renamed it the Cock Robber's Inn, though everyone still calls it Crouch.

"You can go and talk to some of the lads if you want to, love." I look into the smoky temple of testosterone at the morose clusters of middle-aged men in absurd cowboy outfits. None of them seem to be having fun yet but as Israel says, "It goes beyond fun in the end. Way beyond fun." I wonder what he meant and how far beyond fun he now is. I turn to the strange doorman.

"No, I don't think I'll bother, thanks for putting the poster up."

Next I go to Anchors Aweigh. Another pub with a torrid history. It was bombed some years back by a lunatic. The irony is that on the evening the primitive homemade nail bomb exploded there was a Latin District planning meeting taking place in their function room. Two of the people killed were straight women, one a florist, the other a Haseeshi gallery owner. The bomber had been a right-to-lifer in a previous decade and the florist had been pregnant. All in all he was a very fucked-up fellow. He was jailed before the cock was robbed so it can't have been him mixed up in the other business.

Anchors Aweigh isn't infiltrated by the straight crowd on the weekends the way some of the other clubs are. Because of the bombing and the major media attention the incident attracted, straights are still too nervous to go there. The crowd is a motley crew with a broad age sweep and I'm one of only three women in there. When you've spent as much time in gay clubs as I have, you can do a head count of women in about ten seconds flat, all three of us probably invisible to the rest of the drinkers but I like to know where I stand in these dives. I move towards the back wall and to my horror there is an entire pinup board of missing men, a shrine almost: Jason, Kyle, Gulliver, Christobel, Karl, Jordan… All quite good-looking judging from the photos. For a second I can almost hear Izzy saying *Couldn't you have used that photo from Christmas instead of the one you chose?* I tear off some tape and stick it up.

"Welcome to the club." I turn to my left to see a man standing alone with a beer. He offers me a melancholy smile. He would have been beautiful once but now a worried intensity seems to have etched itself deep into his face. I'd put him at around forty, at least half Haseeshi. His accent, definitely provincial.

"That's mine there," he points to a neat-looking man with perfect teeth in a photo just beneath Israel's.

"Hah, Jordan is next to Israel."

"What?" I say, a little confused.

"Well it's like a map. My partner's name is…was Jordan. Yours is Israel. How strange. How long's he been gone?"

"A week today," I answer.

"Mine's over two months." He points to Christobel. "That guy they dredged up in the estuary. They think it's Christobel. A reject."

"A reject?"

"Yeah, Christobel was as camp as a row of pink tents. Did drag shows—had a gutter mouth like you've never heard. I think Christobel probably had bipolar disorder or Tourette's or something. Anyway he's the first to turn up so they're saying he's been rejected. I think it's unconnected myself. You wanna drink?"

"I think I'd better. Scotch thanks, on the rocks."

I stare at the pictures, the candles and the prayers in disbelief. I had no idea something like this has been going on. Israel must have known but he never said a thing. Even Curtis hadn't mentioned it. I sit on a stool and put my bag of posters down then reach over and touch the photo of Jordan. Again I feel an explosion pass through my fingertips but nothing coherent. He returns with my drink.

"Prime cuts, that's what everyone's calling them."

"Prime cuts? Why?"

"All men in their prime. The youngest is thirty-three. How old's Israel?"

"Forty-two."

"Well that's the oldest I know of. Whoever it is doesn't like 'em young, and he doesn't seem to take many Haseeshi, though we go missing all the time—that's another story. They've mostly been healthy but Jordon was diabetic, he probably only had a couple of insulin shots with him so I pretty much buried him in my mind after a week."

I feel like I've been existing on another planet for the past six months. We introduce ourselves. His name is Anton and despite his Haseeshi blood, he has curiously blue eyes.

"The police didn't even say anything specifically about this epidemic of disappearances when I reported it."

"Funny that."

"Why though, why funny? You don't think *they're* behind it do you?"

"Can't see why they would be particularly. You'd think they'd at least pretend to make an effort but I suppose motiveless crimes are just too much work. Why go looking for middle-aged queens when front-page models are vanishing at a rate of knots?"

I don't suppose anything should shock or surprise me but the idea of an actual systematic genocide of men in their prime seems absurd. Anton gets up to go to the restroom. A man who had been hovering in the corner brushes past me and nearly knocks my drink over. I think he's about to steal it, and I grab it defensively.

"Clean but dirty, that's the way they go," he says. I don't see his face, he moves too swiftly. All I see is a long leather coat sweeping behind him, the sort that would have been very expensive a few years back. He vanishes into the crowd by the bar. His breath smelt fetid.

Cocksucker breath is the term that perversely springs to mind though I'm not sure why. Anton takes a while and comes back looking pale.

"What's up?" I say.

"Some graffiti in the cubicle. It says *Going over Jordan, Gone over there.* There's also a very crude picture of a man lying on the ground with a syringe in his arm. Too weird."

"What do you think that means?" I ask.

"No idea. Don't much know what anything means right now. So many things seem connected to all this but nothing adds up to diddly. Apart from that body, not a trace has been found of anyone."

I tell him about the guy who brushed past me.

"That'd be Giovanni. He's a fuck-up if ever there was one. He blows guys in the toilets for free drinks or drugs if you can believe it." Of course I can.

Anton broods over the writing on the wall while I fetch two more drinks.

"I hope I'm not...cramping your style."

"Jesus no. Do I look like I'm on the make? I just came to look at the board. For some reason this pub has become Prime Cut Central. Maybe because of the bomb, I dunno. But if anyone wants to talk about it, this is where they do it. Unfortunately there are now a number of ghouls who have made it their business too, a couple of journalists and this bizarre guy who's doing a PhD on the whole thing. I'll put money on the line that he'll be on the phone to you wanting an interview when he sees your poster. He'll come to your place and go through everything. He'll be especially interested in any fetish gear Israel may have had. I wouldn't talk to him. He can't help you. Was Israel into weird scenes?"

"Umm...yeah."

"Jordan too. He wanted to go places I never could, physically, I mean. So I let him have his fun. I figured he'd be home when he was hungry or wanted some vanilla love. Course with all this crap going on I got concerned and then when silt came on the scene..."

"Silt?"

"Yeah, this dangerous powder. My people used to use something like it in initiation ceremonies years ago. It's a kind of peyote or mescal and someone's been synthesizing it. I have a suspicion that all these guys who have disappeared were using it though there is no way of knowing. The kids down in the Causeway sell it but they'd mix it up with other rubbish. You ever heard of Gutz?"

"To my knowledge that's the last place Israel was before he vanished."

For a minute Anton seems distracted as Giovanni's shadowy figure slips out the door.

"Yeah, well a lot of 'em use it in there."

All of a sudden I feel very strange. My vision is changing, Anton begins to appear almost tribal before me, his eyes luminous. I wonder if he's put something in my drink and I feel afraid. It occurs to me that perhaps the cocksucker has done it. I sit on a stool to steady myself.

"Oh God, I think that guy spiked my drink. I feel very strange."

"Can you walk?"

"I'm not sure."

"Let me take you home."

I wonder if I might actually be sick. There's all this noise in my head—why would he have given me something like that? I don't think I can trust anyone to take me home.

"Come on, it'll be all right."

I don't really have a choice. Suddenly he looks like a handsome Haseeshi prince, the type the museum keeps sepia daguerreotypes of in the natural history section. The rest of the people in the bar have faded into nothingness except I think I see Giovanni lurking outside the door. He seems to have transformed into the Headless Horseman, his coat looks as though it is a huge cape. I am no longer in the world I know. I feel how I have felt in my dreams recently, the colors of everything I see are more enchanting.

"This must be silt," I say, but then I wonder, why would he waste it on me?

"I think folk develop habits fast because from what I hear it's very interesting."

"It's that all right. You look like the chief of the Routou." I laugh.

"Hah, that was the tribe of my people. There are truths to be found in that stuff but the Ancestors only let you have so much, after that it turns on you. When that turn comes, the result depends on the man."

"Or woman."

"Women weren't allowed to have it."

I push him playfully. "Women were never allowed to have anything except babies."

I'm starting to feel very good but I look back at all the missing people and I spiral down inside my mind. It's as though I'm running, looking for Israel again and snow lines the path. "I see windscreen wipers beating at the rain and a long road ahead of me. I can see this even as I see everything else about me."

"You'll be in the silt-pit then, that's what they call it," Anton whispers as he motions me gently to the door.

ISRAEL

The hunting has begun again. I suppose she'll not rest until she finds me. The trouble is I don't want to look at what she wants to see. Why would I? Things are falling into place for me but she's staring at a roomful of scattered jigsaw pieces. I reach down and turn one over. She can't make it out yet; I turn over a couple more. She can use those pieces if she wants to come closer to the truth, or at least her truth.

EVANGELINE

The water tastes like liquid diamonds, icy and sparkling, and as I drink it I can visualize it going down. A crystal cascade through a pristine wilderness, a frozen wonderland of icicles and rivulets: my body. My mind shifts again; I think of Israel and the things he was doing at Gutz, his escapades with Torsten and Gustav. I catch my breath because I am beginning to understand. If water could feel as good as it does, what might other things be like. I look over at Anton who is sitting on my couch and a blush envelops my face because for a second I actually consider launching myself at him. I want to mate with the Haseeshi and have their saffron-colored babies. He senses my dilemma. He smiles and that simple act seems to send shards of joy into every corner of the room.

"I'm too old to be doing drugs like this Anton," I murmur to cover my embarrassment.

"It's not like you chose to do it."

"No, but let me just say. I can understand what all the fuss is about. It's so primal and yet so modern at the same time."

I've no sooner said this than my visual image of the room turns into a jigsaw puzzle, a madly postmodern extravaganza shattered into all its pieces on the floor. In my mind I reach down and turn some over. It's part of a face, Israel's face, I knew it.

Part III

Purgatory

Joshua does it with guys sometimes. Mary doesn't know this but I do. Well I do *now*. He says for him it's about "exploring communication at different levels." This is essentially bullshit. It's more to do with the fact that after a few beers he's a randy bastard and as we sit in my courtyard, I'm aware that we would not be having this discussion at all if Eve or Mary were around. He's a sort of Peter Pan. I also know that he has had sex with Evangeline at least once because she told me. If it had happened since I wouldn't expect her to confide in me about it. She, after all, has her own special, intimate little projects. It's the sort of thing I expect would happen while Mary's at university in the evenings, while I'm out prospecting and Eve's good and liquored up. I can just see her in those low-heeled slip-on mules, shimmying into the courtyard on a summer night with ice and whiskey clinking in her glass, the chunky heavy-bottomed ones we bought in Italy: "Hey Josh, you wanna keep a girl company, it's way too hot inside. Looks like it's gonna be a long *scorching* summer this year."

I look across at Joshua, who is wearing those muslin hippy pants; he's very brown, probably because he sits around all day in the sun doing fuck all. They would be transparent if I threw some of my beer on them. His cock lies to the left and I'm pretty sure it is increasing in length as we talk.

"We'd be like one big happy family then wouldn't we, well except for Mary? Poor Mary."

"Whaddaya mean?"

"Man I know you've been poking Eve."

"She tell you that?"

"She doesn't have to."

"You two that in tune?"

"I know her and I know you. That's enough isn't it?"

"Hey listen, I'm really not into delineating relationships. Eve's a beautiful woman. I'm a man, chemistry—like shit—happens and some moments are fuelled by nothing but need."

"Oh Joshua, spare me the hyperbolic crap. She's one hot patootie when she gets a few drinks on board. 'Moments fuelled by need,' *puh-lease.*" I throw some beer at his groin and watch the fabric cling to his cock. "Whaddaya reckon this moment is fuelled by, big guy?" I await his response while I imagine how it would have been for him and Eve.

Eve's few drinks not only heighten her desire but they blind her to consequence and guilt and these are things I've a tendency to blinker myself from as well. Her foot still dangles in the shape of the mule that's slid onto the cobblestones. Eve leaves it that way because her foot is now the same shape as Barbie's and we know how men like that. Mary never wears heels. "She's so sensible," I can hear Eve saying and wrinkling her nose. One thing Eve could never be accused of is being *sensible.* She wears dresses made from fabrics that seem to attract the breeze and Joshua would have noticed her doing that wicked, wicked thing she does when she's putting out a call with her icy glass as she brushes it ever so softly over her nipple, moistening it with condensation and then hardening it with the cold. Eve would have noticed Joshua's eternity ring. She had forged it herself, Mary has a matching one. She would feel at moments like that as if all who wore her rings were attached by an invisible string. That at any moment she might rein them all in to her as though she were herself Mother Earth or some twisted alternative Gaia. That people could be spellbound, enchanted, beguiled and somehow hers by virtue of the fact they wear her jewelry was a plausible philosophy for my girl.

Joshua battling his demons as her coarse nipple pushed rudely at the fabric of some lightweight summer frock is something I would almost (but not quite) like to have seen. That Joshua was so insubstantial and that she could at times be such a perfect slut, meant that only Eve really had the power to thwart the inevitable. I wish I could have been *her* taking *him* inside her, I can almost feel it as she guides that great big useless thing of his into her cunt with her slender fingers. And as his turgid metaphysical nonsense mixed with her potent, magical nectars, he would feel her stealing away a fraction more of what little worldly power he possessed. I can see them on the couch in her workshop, the seduction given over now to something more animal and Eve making one of those comments she can't help but make, as Josh's ring brushes her swinging breasts.

"Argh Joshua, what *would* Mary say?"

And I can feel the shock she must feel as all Joshua's wishy-washy esoteric platitudes fall away and she stares into the face of who Joshua really is. Someone much more brutal and self-serving than we had imagined him to be. Something dangerous and predatory, a wolf in sheep's clothing. His hand swipes the side of her face with some kind of force as he moves faster within her, his seed already burning for its release into yet another universe.

"Shut it bitch, you want this just as much as me."

And as the vigor of his thrusts and the sting of the slap mix with the hot, raw shame of her own impending orgasm, she lets him plow even deeper because in some terrible, broken, masochistic part of Evangeline, she knows that what he said was true. Just like me, she has moments when she wants the seed of every man in the world. That's a difficult and dangerous enough truth for a man to live with. But the world has always been even crueller to girls who embody such appetites. Perhaps our appetite alone was the profoundest thing we shared. Perhaps that is why we've always been peripheral to normality. Necessary evils.

"You bastard," cries Joshua as the wetness from my beer spreads and his cock lies revealed and eager to prosper with its ever beckoning expansionist policies.

"You're not seriously trying it on with me are you Josh?"

"I'm Joshing you!" He laughs at the joke.

"You don't get that hard without good reason."

"I get hard all the time man."

"Not for me you don't."

I can't have him thinking Eve and I are a free-for-all. A party to which everyone is invited.

"I've never thought of doing it with you Josh, it seems…weird. Grotesque even."

"You told me that sometimes you do five guys at once in some of those clubs. Guys you don't even know, and now you tell me that a bit of horseplay with a good buddy is weird? You guys!"

"Eve and I live in a strange universe the laws of which are complex and capricious. You've already dabbled but I wonder if you're up to it…. I'm not sure you are, Joshua baby. You've got a wife and a little 'un on the way. For me to embark on something like what I think you are suggesting would be…well it would be monstrous." I relight the joint we had been smoking earlier, offering it to him with an enigmatic smile.

"That's bullshit Israel and you know it. We're not married, I didn't want to have a baby and I've never made any promises to anyone. Mary's gonna hate me one day because I'm going to fail to live up to all the conventions she's setting up. She's going to blame me for not being the movie screen of her projections. I'm a free spirit. I'm free floating. Ain't no one gonna tie me down. She can be some hotshot lawyer and career mother if she wants to. Reckon I'm nearly done with sex anyway. Ready to move on to the next level but before I do..."

And with that, Joshua moves towards me. So close I can smell the beer where it has soaked the cloth.

"So what exactly do we have here?"

I pull his cock out and weigh it in my hand like a piece of fish.

"Interesting color variations around the foreskin and glans area. A decent nine inches is my guess—nicely proportioned scrotum with the left testicle resting slightly lower than the right. What exactly do you propose I do with this, Joshua old man?"

"Well you could put it in your fucking mouth for starters." He shoots me one of those puzzled expressions that I would later come to see often in Tibby.

"Mmmm, not sure about that Mr. Leister. I mean full compliments to the chef and all but..." I held it, examined it from several angles like a doctor, then sniffed it as if it were a glass of vintage red wine. "Mmmm, I'm getting yeast, hops, cow dung, a hint of cheese, a piquancy of sweat and testosterone... When did you last shower?"

"Cut it out Izzy, you love this sort of stuff."

"Oh yes, it's all fun and games until someone loses an eye. I'd feel like I was cheating on Evangeline—stealing her bit on the side, to say nothing of Mary." I put my hand to my mouth and in mock horror say, "What if she found out?"

Truth is I don't really get off on the straight guy thing, though thousands of fags do if you were to believe the porn industry. But I especially don't like the idea of falling prey to someone as flaky as Joshua. That being said, it's not in my nature to look a gift horse in the mouth, especially as it's braying near my own. Whatever Josh expects—I expect more, and so rather than do as he directs I force his head down on me instead. If a sexual encounter is going to take place between him and me, he's going to be the one to feel humiliated and the truth is I don't stop until I've got him into Eve's workshop and take him to the place that terrifies straight men to the very core. It's certainly not somewhere he's planned on going and I suspect not something he even enjoys but having had him in such a way, I casually finish the job by opening another couple of ice-cold beers afterwards. "Reckon we could both use one of these." This seems to bring us back into the male world we'd previously inhabited. But of course it isn't the same world anymore. I've punished him and I'm sure, in her own way, Eve has too and whatever the experts might say to the contrary, my experience suggests that men can be damaged more easily than women. Their wiring is different. When you press the wrong buttons, as so many of us do, most members of the male tribe don't even try to recover. I've done something to Josh that has been done to me a thousand times but it alters him in some way. He doesn't last long after this.

EVANGELINE

I never told Israel about the baby or the abortion. His lack of intuition about such monumental things often disappointed me. It never was actually a baby, just a bloody clump of life's thwarted possibilities and a three-day charade about why I stayed in bed. Perversely, I told Mary. I told her it was Israel's, which she believed. She thought it would be great for me to have it because, "Guess what? I'm pregnant too."

I was nearly sick. Joshua's blondness would never have looked anything like Israel's dark. I was thirty-three and had to actually think about it, Goddam it. We could have sold the house, moved away, lost contact with Mary and Josh—but I came to my senses. What would I want with a baby? Especially the baby of that scatterbrain. If it had been Israel's I would have wanted it but ours were strange, shadowy genes to inflict upon a child. We talked about having one sometimes, when we were drunk. Always when we were drunk. And I didn't suppose that in the years to come we'd be getting any more sober so I decided to keep my figure that was already developing a will of its own. Instead I watched Mary expand with Tibby as I downed some gorgeous new tranquillizers with the perennial scotch on the rocks. I mated with Joshua several times throughout the pregnancy, despising myself thoroughly while remembering Israel's line about being a moral maverick. "Someone's got to keep the bastards honest." And I'd say, "And we're the rat-catchers, aren't we Izzy?" I had my tubes tied shortly after the abortion. I figured if my descent was going to get dirtier and boozier, I didn't really need to be bothering with fertility precautions. The couplings we make after thirty-five might be a lottery but it was a lottery in which I hoped everyone would be a winner; that each player at least walked away with a little something more than what he or she brought to the table. Israel wasn't afraid of the dark side so why should I have been?

How I kept so much from Mary I'll never know. Whether the distance between us these days is because she knows what happened or just because certain betrayals create their own standoffs, I don't know. I think betrayals create undercurrents that interfere with communication and perhaps in that regard, Izzy was right: there are things we know at some other level. The problem is, if we trust our suspicions, our intuition, without ever having any real proof, it begins to drive us mad. Stark, raving, bloody mad.

It was strange watching her swell with the child while I hardened with my own deceits and loss. Josh and Israel no longer spent time together, Israel just decided he was a bore or a boor—I'm not sure which. Friendships that rely entirely on certain facts remaining undisclosed are the strangest ones of all. The idea that containing one dirty little secret can keep our tiny world from splitting apart always chastened me. I wonder: if Mary found out now, would it make any difference anymore? I'm sure she would have despised me ten years ago but now? With both men gone and a child she needs looked after, could she afford to hate me? She always thought I was "that sort of girl" anyway so I was merely acting out. Monkey hear, monkey be. Israel always said if you make judgments about people, it's tantamount to wanting them to behave according to that judgment. Once again, I don't know if I follow that line. I'd like to be allowed the burden of my own sins. I think I'm strong enough for that at least. Sin is life's travail.

ISRAEL

There are certain things I could never have explained to Evangeline. Things she wouldn't want to have known. Things that some people do with nothing but a mysterious inner directive as their guide. I call it the shift and strangely enough there is a bar in the Latin District with the same name. The shift doesn't translate too well into language. It's more a way of thinking, a way of looking at people. A way of knowing them. It is not a state that is necessarily encouraged by society at large and indeed many social moderators would tell you it was a subliminal death wish, a lack of self-esteem, a delusional response to substance abuse but it is much, much more than that.

Until you have known absolute humiliation and utter debasement, the entry to the kingdom I speak of remains barred. That Earth is but Heaven seen through a glass darkly (and now face to face) is the most exciting, multifaceted scriptural conundrum I've encountered. I can leave this shifty underground for brighter plains at any time I want but I've business here yet. As I wander the corridors of some abandoned place to which I've never been—yet know all too well—I hear the cries of another. Not a woman's but a man's and I follow the sounds to where he lies. "I'm going over to Jordan," I mutter to myself and there lies an exquisite angel of a man, his golden skin glistening, a Maltese cross illuminated on the portion of abdomen just above the pubic region. It shines like molten lava and within the glow there seems to be yet another dimension of inner space.

"It burns me so, dear God why must it burn so hot for so long? Deliver me oh Lord."

I go to his side and he looks longingly at me. "Are you HIM, are you the one to whom I must recount my fall?"

I smile. "Maybe I am. Maybe I'm not. You tell me your story and let's see where it gets us."

"Can you stop the burning, at least for a moment?"

I reach out and touch his skin, it's like liquid as my finger sinks into him. It is that very same feeling I've felt when I've previously transformed the base matter of flesh into gold, times when pure lust could melt perishing flesh into something molten and precious. The cross still remains lit but his pain is gone. Now he seems on the edge of some sort of ecstasy.

"You are HIM, you are!"

"Now you just tell me the details and I'll decide whether I am HIM. Or HE will."

"Yes, Sir. Make me whole again. Please."

I touch him again and again. His rapture spreads through my fingers, it makes my own heart glow ecstatically in my chest. The whole universe smiles as my apprenticeship begins.

EVANGELINE

When I wake, my brain seems to slosh around in its casing. I am tucked into bed still half dressed. I can't remember getting here but then I start to recall the events of the previous night. I drag myself out of bed, heading for the bathroom but as always I glance into Israel's room. Just in case. My heart leaps when I see the shape of his figure beneath the quilt. "Israel," I cry, almost leaping on top of him, only to come face-to-face with Anton, whom I had completely forgotten about.

"Sorry to disappoint you," he mutters groggily. "How is your head?"

"It's been a lot worse on plain liquor," I answer, crestfallen. "What was *that* all about?"

"You just had your first experience of silt."

"But why would someone spike my drink with such a sought after commodity? Especially someone who works so hard for it in the toilet?"

Anton sits up in bed and regards me warily as he speaks. "The Haseeshi say, and I don't know if I actually believe it myself, that there is a dimension between here and the other place that the drug can sometimes open up."

"What '*other*' place'?" It's now my turn to regard him with caution.

"We call it Dionahkesh; I guess it's the afterlife."

"Well I don't even believe such a place exists. I'm sure our minds can come up with some extraordinary fantasies given the right chemicals but I'm not the type to see ghosts. The only thing that can haunt us is our fear." I feel a shiver as I watch Anton pull himself from Israel's bedclothes. I still wonder whether I can trust him, whether it might be him who spiked my drink. Now he's poking through stuff on Israel's desk; he pulls out a page of doodles.

"Oh my God," he says. He's looking at a rough drawing of a man with a tattoo. "That Maltese cross…it's just the same as the one Jordan had, same position and everything." There's no head on the figure so I ask him whether Jordan had a dick the size of the one in the illustration.

"Umm…no, sadly."

"Yeah, well Israel never could draw those to scale. If the world could have been the way Israel imagined it, our anatomies would be drastically different from how they are and none of us would be able to carry the weight of our genders."

"I think Israel knew Jordan."

"Why?" I ask.

"It's more than just a hunch having seen this."

"I suppose but Maltese crosses you can buy off the rack in any tattoo parlor. So what are the components of this silt stuff? There must be some chemical breakdown that can be done?"

"Of course, but if it is the real thing, only tribal elders are supposed to know where it comes from. Some people say it's a fungus from the forests, others say it's in the roots of a certain cactus you can find out on the prairies and others say that the elders themselves possess the secret ingredient that needs to be added to make the shift happen. That it may in fact just be *magic*. Certainly they wouldn't be trusting the likes of Giovanni with such sacred stuff."

"So are you saying people could be half dead?"

"I don't think so. When you take it during ceremonies it's supposed to allow you to visit your ancestors; to pay your respects and learn that there is a greater home than this one."

"Nice idea. And did you do this ceremony as a young man?"

"No, the government really clamped down on initiation ceremonies. I'm half-caste so my Anglo father didn't approve of all that mumbo jumbo. But strange things have happened nonetheless. The human consciousness is fragmented into many families. Culture is not just about having a different history, it's also about having different knowledge."

"You and Israel could have talked for hours on that topic I'm sure. Faith, knowledge—he's obsessed by them."

We go downstairs and I make coffee and toast, but it turns my stomach to eat it. I watch Anton drink from his cup. His bronzed arms have thick ropey veins down them and his chest gleams, naturally hairless; it's as if only his face shows any signs of age. There's something feminine about him yet he is not effeminate. There's also something absent. I wonder if the absence is merely Jordan.

"Where could they have gone, Evangeline, and what for? Even

psychopaths have a modus operandi."

"And we're in our own halfway place. Somewhere between loss and bereavement. We're mourning but without the closure.... I can't believe I just said something so lame."

"Ha, just because some grad student tells us we're supposed to have *closure*, it don't mean we're gonna get it!"

"No, of course."

The steam from my coffee feels strangely pleasant on my face. Anton looks up from his own. "This is good." He pauses. "Do you think we could be friends?"

Something in me already loves him but my old cynicism recoils at the idea, perhaps it's the drug. Perhaps I'm frantically needy right now. I don't believe he spiked my drink, nor do I think we've had our last encounter with silt. I smile at him. "I think we need to be, don't you?" He crosses the kitchen towards me, kisses me gently on the mouth. I feel something akin to what I felt from Israel's ring, a shift in reality, both frightening and promising. I look into the yard where I see Tibby jumping from the tree into our place. He's coming to the back door. All at once I feel amazingly together, like the sort of mother who manages a million things. I cross my arms in front of me and smile out the window at him.

"Hey lady, lemme in."

"I'm thinking about it, mister."

He dangles a key ring from his hand and I freeze. They're Israel's keys.

ISRAEL

Nothing lasts for long. Even eternity is fractured into chapters that might well be managed by a cartoon fairy. She hovers above; only when her wand blazes into sparks may I turn the page. Jordan seems momentarily in stasis as a storm cloud rolls in. Thunder booms and I see the figure looming like the headless horseman. His face, as always, is in shadow but he dangles my keys like some cocky executive about to take off in his Porsche.

"I thought I'd seen the last of you, signor," I groan.

"Maybe I want come along for the ride." He tosses the keys in the air and catches them. He looks at us. "What you got there?"

"Neither staves, nor scrip, neither money; neither have we two coats apiece."

He looks at me and I see his lips curl into a humorous snarl.

"Good boy, your mumma, she teach you the Bible, your papa? Maybe he show you the road. And me, maybe I come for to carry you home." His leather coattail arcs into the wind as the keys jangle like ancient wind chimes in the humming gusts of the cosmos.

"That lady o' yours. She makin' big eyes at his boy. Big lovin' mumma eyes. Maybe those two like to take a trip together." He looks down at me where I kneel, nursing the broken figure before me. In the sky I can almost see the fingers reaching down but I know I must carry this man a way still. If I were to lift him though, it wouldn't be work, but art, Tintoretto, Caravaggio, a bloodred sky and a cry to the Gods for I'll take nothing for my journey now but that which lies before me.

"Giovanni, he got his eye on you, mister."

I've heard that line before and with it he throws down the keys. They hit Jordan on the chest and seem to sink inside him. "Giovanni!" I yell as he beats his retreat from our sacred space. "What are you doing?"

"Me? I got business with your lady. She no pretty but she dirty and I like that in a *puttana*."

He pokes his tongue out at me, a golden stud glowing at its center. "I'll be back, you gringos. I'll be back real soon."

EVANGELINE
"Where did you find them, Tibby?"

"Nowhere."

"Tell me sweetie. I won't be cross. I promise."

"I never wanted to be in this game. I'm just a kid, Goddam it."

"I know you are, Tibby. What game do you mean?"

"I'm not supposed to talk to people like *him*. You know what I'm saying? Ma says if you talk to men like that, you end up in the estuary. Reckon I'll have nightmares now."

"Oh Tibby." I put my arm around him. "What happened? Who are you talking about?"

"You won't tell Ma?"

"Of course I won't."

"Well she was kinda late picking me up yesterday see, and I'm not supposed to leave the school yard until she gets there but no teachers were watching and I had me a few nickels and dimes so I went to the store for some crisps. Well just as I'm passing the alleyway, I look down and I think I see Israel and he's walking around a corner into another alleyway. I'm so sure it's Israel I run after him. I'm yelling, 'Israel!' but he doesn't hear me. Then I turn a corner and it's a dead end see, and there's a man there but it's not Israel. It's a creepy guy, sorta dark looking and he's waving me over towards him and he's got something shiny in his hand and I go to him even though I know I shouldn't. I just wanna see what's flashing in his hand. Then, when I'm right up near him I say, 'Where's Israel, I saw him!' And he says, 'Israel where he always been, right there next to Jordan.' Then he went back out of the lane and I stayed because I was scared and when I went back to the street I found these keys near the end of the alley."

I look at Anton. He looks at me. He mouths "Giovanni" at me.

"Tibby, this is Anton," I say as he switches back to his television gangster persona.

"Jeez lady, you don't waste any time do you?"

"*Tibby!* What a thing to say!" I hold the keys in my hand and a warmth spreads through my fingers. An almost indecent warmth. I look at Anton and say with a sense of certainty, "I think our men knew each other intimately."

Tibby is hopping around in an agitated state with a frown of consternation too heavy for his age.

"The man didn't try to hurt you at all then did he?"

"No, he just gave me the creeps big-time and he could'a used some toothpaste I reckon. Seems to me like an open-and-shut case and Mr. Bad Breath is your man."

I look to Anton again; he's biting his lip, weighing up the facts.

"Yeah, we'll see. Don't be afraid, buddy, that man's not after you."

I regard Tibby, adult to adult. "And I'm not sure it is an open-and-shut case, Tibby. I'm not sure at all."

ISRAEL

I'm wondering about faith and about Jordan. He's in some sort of Hell yet he's right by me. We're in the same place but he's being punished, and he thinks I can save him. He thinks I'm Him, he can't remember me. Such a shabby savior me, still what's done is done. And you get what you get.

I think about Evangeline, or she thinks about me. Sometimes I can't tell the difference but in the distance her window seems to glow. Her house looks made of gingerbread. Inside something terrible is happening. It's so far off I can't intervene. I don't suppose I ever really could with her. I try to whisper to her that it's all just a dream. This is what I'd always hoped and now I find it is true.

EVANGELINE

I struggle through the day as my mind goes in useless circles. I wonder if Israel is actually dead or if he's just slipped away through some tear in this dimension. His theory, not mine. Of course for that to happen I'd have to believe in another dimension to begin with. Outside the weather shifts from fair to foul. I turn the heating on as gusts of wind gather up all the trash from the Gilgal and toss it noisily past my front window. Anton has left but I have his number. I wonder if he needs me the way I feel I need him. Now I'm embroiled in some sort of hideous mystery where, if it was a movie, he could just as easily be the bad guy. Obviously this is too strange for the police and I didn't ask Tibby if what Giovanni held in his hand was actually the keys or something else. How could he have looked like Israel? Can devils disguise themselves to suit their agendas and what exactly can children see?

I go through Israel's drawers; rifle through clothes, jockstraps, cockrings, cockroaches, plastic baggies that perhaps once contained silt or other substances. God only knows.

Mary comes by after work with some food for me. It would be sweet of her but there is an ulterior motive. She's concerned about Tibby, she thinks he's overly obsessed with Israel's disappearance. I don't mention the keys but I feel a wave of annoyance. I tell her that I have no control over how concerned he is. It's as though she thinks she can just turn off her involvement with people when things get too much. Perhaps that's what law does to you, perhaps it's single motherhood or maybe it's just one of Joshua's many legacies. She leaves me with a plate of curry and I feel like a meals-on-wheels recipient or a cheap remittance woman. The subtext is clear, stay away from Tibby. I cry again after she goes, I suppose with self-pity but then I think back on how hideously I have betrayed her in the past and am forced to reckon with something like retribution. I turn to face the mirror that hangs over the fireplace in the front room and there I am, thicker than I ever wanted to be, my hair looks lank, my face tired. Of course I say tired but really it's age. I can freshen it up or brighten it with color and cosmetics but the truth is it just doesn't hang together the way it used to. I'm forty-two, no longer the siren I pretended I was when I almost stole that baby from Joshua. I am not, and was never, to be trusted though. I don't think I was ever evil and I wonder what value, if any I'll be without Israel. I put the dinner in the kitchen. I'd choke on it if I tried to eat it. Then I think about all the pills that are in the house.

At the kitchen table I line up the bottles: the uppers, downers and even-as-you-likers. Years of moderated moods and controlled sleeping patterns stretch behind me and in front of me as I think of the fancy footwork I've done to switch pills frequently so as not to become addicted to the especially notorious ones. "Steady as she goes," I mutter quietly and reward myself with a Xanax and a slug of the whiskey Mary also gave me. An emptiness so vast opens inside me that I try to fill it with another whiskey and another. I put on Dead Can Dance wondering if it's true, and light candles all about the house for Israel, for me, for a child never born. I sing snippets of things that seem to be right—"Stormy Weather," "Court and Spark" and "The Mockingbird Song." And on I go in my madness, creating fanciful floral designs using the different colored pills. The orange and mauve capsules, the blues, the greens.

Like the cosy doll families I made as a little girl. Valium and the diazepams are the mothers, Prozac and the fluoxetines are the fathers. I lay out all my babies in their familiy trees: Under Valium the Buspar and Tofranil, Under Prozac the Faverin and Luvox. Then there are the aunts and uncles, the dopamine connection with Merital and Zyban, the sleepy cousins like Remeron and Bolvidon and the mad relatives and bastard children; Inosital, lithium and sweet, forgetful Imiprimane. All the zany steps on my dizzy hedonic treadmill.

They're all pastels now, soft, conservative designer colors that hint at contemporary décor, tranquility, relaxation and freedom. Not the fiery reds, toxic blues or go-get-'em greens I remember from years ago. Their names have changed too now. Feminine, healthy words like Paxil, Cipramil, Survector, with just a hint of

Izzy and Eve

Latin serenity inferred by hefty pharmaceutical imprimaturs. Gone are the gutsy names: Mogadon, Quaalude, Rohypnol; the sort of imperial titles that drag queens might designate for themselves. Gone, gone, gone along with decades of users, dizzy debutantes, worried wives: all the pretty, faded creatures who could put up with anything but what was going through their heads. "Bye girls," I say cheerily as they tap-dance their way like Ziegfeld's Follies into historic amnesia and existential ennui. Martyred matrons and broken beauties who'll be hoping for more strength, more fortitude, greater desirability next time around. (If there is a next time and please God there isn't!) I close my eyes to see them dolling up in the dressing room between lives. Each one fighting for longer lashes, perter breasts, a slimmer waist or a more winning smile. Each vying to be the Cleopatra, Marilyn, Jackie O or Madonna of her day.

Pills, pills. They are fashion items too, not unlike the gourmet jelly bean, I think as I switch them around in order to try different color combinations. Passports to the desired contemporary psyche, invitations to all tomorrow's parties. *Dolls* as Jacqueline Susann called them. I even decide, then and there, to create some jewelry in resins: rings, earrings, bracelets, belly button droplets, anklets—whole complete matching sets of pastel-colored capsules resembling popular prescription drugs. This would be a thoroughly modern and innovative departure for me. Not appropriate perhaps at Gothic Mist but Carlo Monenzo would love that sort of stuff. I could try Doll Face or Polyester Girl—they'd totally buy a range like that. And after all—you are only what you've got to sell—aren't you?

I swallow a Survector, a drug that on more than one occasion has given me spontaneous orgasms, and consider my designs. I cackle to myself. If I can still manage to think of such things I couldn't be that mad. I'm still reptilian enough to be contemplating my own survival in the midst of this dreadful nightmare. I drink more because there's nothing else for it. I put the pills back in their respective bottles, careful not to lose any but consoling myself that I've done well not to take them all tonight. One supersonic lethal dose could so easily take me there. Home, to visit Israel and all the new friends he's sure to have made. I think of visiting Curtis but I'm too drunk now. And messy. I do try to avoid being the sort of middle-aged woman who sits drunk in bars and lures men into conversation. But hey, I slip up from time to time. Part of me would like to do it and why should I be excluded from the life of the city just because I'm no spring chicken. FUCK THAT! Sure, I've gone down that road a few times before. Who hasn't? Mary maybe, fucking ice queen Mary. But with all the things going through my head right now, it would get ugly. Drunk at forty-two, the best I'll get is some boozy stalwart who endures an hour of maudlin conversation but only to one end. One crazed, ugly, penetrative end. I could say to Curtis, "Don't let me pick up tonight, sweetie," but all he'd say is "When pussy's hungry, she gotta eat," which is not entirely true. I can't expect him or anyone else to be my chaperone. "I'm a big girl now," I sing to myself. "So take the ribbons from my hair."

The wind has picked up outside. I can't find the draft excluders. Too much effort. I wander up to Israel's room and look through his things again, the drawings, the pornographic videos, the rubbish piled on top of a computer he hardly ever used, the powdery drug bags, the empty jars of Viagra, the eyedrops, the aftershave bottles, the lube sachets and the condoms (years past their use-by dates). I doubt he ever bothered with them anyway. Why would he? If you don't like the heat get out of the kitchen, that's what he always said. No Lord, no master. I rummage through the scraps of paper with forgotten phone numbers, the rings he never wears anymore, the stained T-shirts, the loose change in different currencies, the check stubs, the poppers, the hash pipe and all the other curious detritus men like him keep at arm's reach. I marvel at how different a man's (even a fag's) boudoir is from a woman's. I yank hard at his desk drawer until it pulls loose from the desk, scattering the contents on the floor. Then, just as I'm about to collapse into the frenzy of my madness, I notice beneath the drawer there is an envelope. I pull it out to find it contains four plastic sachets of brown crystals. They glint in the candlelight and look very much like the sugar crystals people used to serve with coffee. I also notice a red-bound document that is the power of attorney I'd been searching for and a will that left everything we jointly owned to me.

I open one sachet, lick my finger and without thinking, taste the crystals. They're definitely not sugar but dissolve quickly on my tongue as if they are. Their taste is similar to a bitter herb, a Vietnamese mint or a peppery oregano. I wonder as it passes into my system if it is silt, and if it is, whether I'll be lost to it again as I had been the previous night. I begin to regret what I've done. I look at the clock. Midnight. I've been lost in my crazed state for four hours. I consider phoning Anton just as the very thing begins to ring. I jump. It's him.

"You all right?"

"Yes, I'm peachy, fine and dandy," I lie.

"Have you been drinking?"

"Always Anton, always."

I tell him what I've found but don't mention that I've tried some.

"Sounds like the stuff to me. I'll come over tomorrow."

"That would be great, I like your company."

I hang up, thinking I've probably said too much. Once again the emptiness fills me. I take in the room; it looks as though a burglar has ransacked it. I feel far too drunk and strange to attempt to clean it up. Thunder booms outside, which is strange this late in the season, then I think I hear a knock on the front door, a feeble, half-audible knock. The sort that Tibby might make if he weren't tucked safe in his bed. I descend the stairs precariously because my perception is shifting again. I wonder if I should even answer it. What if it is Anton or even Israel? A strange, inner clarity edged with an ominous fear guides me to the door. As I open it, my heart descends into a chamber of unmitigated darkness.

He glistens from the rain, at once like a slick Italian model from expensive European style magazines and a spivvy, greasy, mafia hit man. He wears the same long leather coat I'd seen him wear before, he brandishes a heavy gold ring, the type that was popular thirty years ago. He smiles at me in a conquering, licentious way and whispers, "I've seen Israel."

"Where?" I ask, my grip on events and reality beginning to slip ever further from my grasp.

"If you let me in I can show you."

I think about the Devil, about vampires. Don't they say you have to invite them in? Unless you're fool enough to invite them, they can do you no harm. Isn't that what they say?

Already his foot is dripping over the threshold like an unfolding prophecy, the drips appear like tiny diamonds scattered on the carpet, they look so precious I'm tempted to gather them. He towers above me, this creature who is haunting our lives, who lured innocent little Tibby down that alley, this monster who works those dank toilets like a troll. His face seems to change with every slight movement of his head, filthy, depraved, evil, grotesque then magnificent, stallion-like, a statuesque *bello*, Italianate God. Is his thick black hair dripping with oil or is it shimmering from the rain? I can't decide. His other foot is now inside and he shakes his mane the way a thoroughbred horse or a regal hunting dog might; the spray of tiny wet diamonds seems to paint every wall. The door closes behind him. Now I am his prisoner.

"Israel's inside you lady. You want, I show you."

He's taking me by the hand and I'm speechless at his invasion. His first breath smells foul; his second, honeyed, spiced like the sheik's. Suddenly I yearn for the sheik. His touch, his dominance. The filthy things he'd whisper to me—things he'd never say to his wives.

"Are you wet little girl? I touch you inside so you make a special noise for me—I like you make that noise." The sheik's hands would run beneath my dress, the cool metal of his rings and the hot flesh of his fingers making me weak to his touch. "Such breasts you have, Evangeline—no wife of mine has these and down here—oh yes— you're already moist for your prince. He likes that, you serve him well and he will reward you with his treasures." And with that his mouth would cover me. His tongue would search for the gifts I kept inside and he would never do *this* to his wives because they would lose respect for him. And even though I have no true respect for him, his terrible politics and archaic traditions, I allow myself to be overcome by his search and when he finds the sweet, sticky clump of rose-flavored Turkish delight I have already planted for him, he shudders with appreciation, perhaps even with passion.

But now as I look up and smell again that foul, more immediate breath I realize this is not the sheik. Now above me, in my own room, is Giovanni, shirtless and as aromatic as the toilet cubicle of a bar in Stonemasons Walk.

"I show you the secrets inside you, I show you Israel if you let me in."

His huge hands have already lifted my dress, his rough fingers are pushing down between my legs and I gasp with shame because he's discovered how wet I am in spite of my fear. I look about for the sheik, wasn't he just here? I could swear he was. Didn't he work me into this state of consensual culpability? Sweet God in Heaven.

"You want be as dirty as Israel. He dirty as HELL!"

I don't want to be as dirty as Israel, I'm not even sure how *dirty* that is but somehow I've reached my own bedroom with this crea- ture, this envoy of darkness who I am terrified of, yet about to be entered by. His fingers fill me while his palm presses down on my pubic hair. With his other hand he undoes the fly on his tight ragged jeans. With an obscene flourish, a monstrous serpent is unleashed from within, thick and long with an enormous, gruesome, drooping hood of foreskin. He holds it proudly like a baton, his hand barely covering half of the length. Then, as if he were a conjurer producing a bunch of feather dusters or silk flowers, he pulls back on the foreskin to reveal the gleaming, stinking head. I am not resisting him; I'm still half looking for the sheik. Wasn't he the one who organized this dramatic, terrifying change in the entertainment? The rich cheesy flora of the exposed glans reaches my nostrils, dizzying me, and I'm appalled but even so it acts like some sort of ether or tincture, a poultice to anesthetize me. It gleams like a rare metal, mercury perhaps, as I prepare to engage in something more akin to gynecological surgery than intimate congress. That I should be engaging with such a thing at all, appalls me. Though I am not resisting. I can't.

He whisks my pants off in a maneuver so deft I'm at a loss to work out how precisely he did it. For a moment I see him as a magician for hire, the type who performs at children's parties but I'm no little girl and this is no party. No puffy dresses or candy apples here. My heart is racing like crazy, I'm sure it's the drug and he manipulates me internally like a fisherman gutting a trout. My cunt feels like an abattoir beast, ready for slaughter.

"This easy for you lady, you done this plenty before."

He winks with grotesque familiarity, then with unlikely animal grace, he plows that huge stinking appendage of his into me. I breathe in like it's my last, wondering if it might be. His breath is wafting over me, becoming strangely reminiscent of someone more pleasant. His moves inside me are powerful and invasive yet I'm unusually detached and with his motions, I'm travelling across mountains and plains to a desert where I see a figure carrying another figure—staggering over the sand. I feel I'm flying above them. I dive down like a witch on a broom. "I-S-R-A-E-L!" I cry as I swoop just overhead. He

Izzy and Eve

looks up surprised to see me there. "You're dreaming," he cries. I take another swoop at him but now I'm flying with my arms outstretched. I don't seem able to land. As I get closer I see the body in his arms, a beautiful serene corpse, *Marat Assassinated*, Jesus in the fourteenth station of the cross, all of humanity at the end of its mortal coil. And I see the glowing tattoo, the Maltese cross, and I know that it's Jordan and Israel is carrying him home.

ISRAEL

There are no towns, or houses or inns or horses anymore. The sun is hot but it never burns and whenever I thirst, a spring bursts forth. I long for Jordan to speak again but he's been silent for an age. I lay him beside the spring and take its cool water in my mouth. I open his parched lips then let it trickle upon his tongue. He pulls me to him with a frailty that breaks my heart and I kiss him gently and feed him water until he'll swallow no more. The excess runs like warm lava from the deep well of his mouth. "You're as light as a feather and your sins are gone. When will the strength in your limbs return?" His answer never comes.

I look to the distance, and for a moment I think I see Evangeline gazing back. I hear a name and it could be mine. I look down at my companion and think how we have travelled far. I wonder if he remembers how far. It matters little and I care even less. I feed him more water, kissing him deeply. I think I taste rose water. I think I could disappear inside him and we could be as one. I think there is an ecstasy at the end of our journey that neither of us could have imagined and Jordan is my key to Zion. I love him so much though he's never been mine. He's a child. He's a savior. He's the emperor who came dressed as a beggar to my door.

EVANGELINE

It's as it was twenty years ago. I wake up as groggily as I did after being administered that heroin by those thugs. I'm in bed but a freezing wind howls through the house. I check to see if it is coming through Israel's window but that's sealed. A gust blows up the stairs so I go down to find the front door wide open. I look at the clock on the stereo which, miraculously, is still there. It's six a.m., the sky outside is beginning to lighten. I slam the door and inspect the pool of water that has welled up on the doorstep, then I sit down as the insane terror of the previous night dawns on me. What had I done? How could I have done it and why had he come here, that dark demon of sleaze? I'm still in my dress, my pants upstairs tangled in the bed sheets. I wish that Giovanni did not exist, I feel as if I could kill him with my own bare hands. I begin to cry because I honestly feel I've lost my mind. I wonder what terrible infection I might have contracted from that…thing. I run the bath, take a sedative then proceed to pass out in the bath. When I wake, I clean myself with a vigor that is painful and drift off again. When I wake again the water is cold and tinged with pink because I've made myself bleed. I turn on the shower and get warm again, hoping to God I haven't got pneumonia.

As soon as the hour seems reasonable, I call Anton, horrified to think I will have to confide in him what has happened to me. I tell him I need to get out of the house, that something awful happened to me that I can't explain over the phone. "I've some rather disturbing news myself," he mutters in a barely audible whisper. He gives me the address, which I'm stunned to note is in the Cartesian Condominiums, the very development that nearly cost me my life. How any Haseeshi could justify living there is beyond me. Still, there are issues afoot of more import than that and I've begun to feel a gradual descending calm since I took my medication.

I throw out the dress I'd had on and put on a plain woollen winter one. I grab some boots and a coat. I ring the locksmith to get him in to change the locks. Giovanni may have copies of the keys. The last thing I want is another midnight rendezvous with him. Some of the previous night still remains vivid but I can't remember anything after seeing Israel. I put on my favorite ring, a conical-shaped number with a pearl on top. It's pointedness makes it feel vaguely like a weapon and I'd like to feel armed with something today.

The quickest route from the Gilgal to the Cartesian Precinct is via Stonemasons Walk though I'm loath to go that way in case I encounter Giovanni once more. If I carried a gun I would shoot him. As I get closer to Anchors Aweigh, I notice it is cordoned off with crime tape. At a small day bar called Trashed, groups of tireless party people sit gossiping, watching the comings and goings of police. Curiosity gets the better of me and I go in to ask some guys what happened.

"Murder most foul my dear, nothing out of the ordinary," says one guy whose eyes are as big as dishpans.

"Who, when?" I ask.

"They're not sayin' love. We were at Tempt last night, never go to Anchors, us," offers another.

I walk past the scene slowly as clusters of people confer out of my earshot. A photographer emerges with someone else from the constabulary who has an air of officialdom; he appears somewhat shaken and I am able to catch only a fragment of what is being said.

"…around eleven last night."

"And it wasn't reported until midnight?"

"The door was locked. From the inside. That's all we're prepared to say at this stage."

"Jesus…you'd think the smell would have been enough," says the photographer as he slips into a waiting car.

I hasten towards Anton's, another quarter of a mile. He buzzes me in. His apartment is on the fourteenth floor; the door is open when I arrive.

"Never leave your door open again, Anton."

Neal Drinnan

"Why?"

I look out over the Latin District, Stonemasons Walk and beyond to Gethsemane Park. I don't cry but I feel inconsolably miserable. I simultaneously marvel at and repulse myself with the levels of depression I can sometimes endure. Now I feel as if full-scale, medieval madness is adding itself to an already unsustainable mental profile.

"Because I had an unimaginably horrific encounter with Giovanni last night. He…he raped me…I think."

"You think! Jesus! When?"

"After midnight, that's when you rang. Probably closer to one. I was drunk and I'd accidently tasted some more of that silt that I found in the bottom of Israel's desk with his will. Bizarre, don't you think? And that's not the end of it…" I tell him how I'd seen Israel with Jordan in my drugged, astral-travelling state, "and, on my way over here I find they've cordoned off Anchors Aweigh because there was a murder there last night. Can you believe?"

Anton's looking at me like either he's mad or I am. Right now I'm more inclined to believe the latter.

"I know about the murder. I went down there myself after I'd phoned you. Couldn't sleep. It's become like a sanctuary for me, that joint. That stupid, useless shrine blazing away with candles and prayers. When I arrived it was already surrounded by cops. You know who was murdered, Evangeline?"

I shake my head. As if it couldn't possibly be of any concern to me.

"Giovanni."

A chill shot up my spine.

"Not just murdered. Butchered—in his favorite cubicle."

I let this latest installment sink in. I nod involuntarily. "Killed before midnight," I mutter.

"His cubicle was sealed. There was no way anyone could have got in, there's only a couple of inches gap under the door. It was the spreading slick of blood that finally brought it to the attention of the management. Perhaps I shouldn't tell you any more?"

"No, go on. It's sickening, I won't lie, but I'm up to my neck in it."

"He'd been strangled by the chain that flushes the cistern. The initials of everyone who is on the missing board were carved into him and his penis was…cut off—which in Giovanni's case is a good bit of him."

"I know," I volunteer. I'm struggling to reckon with this new development but I perk up momentarily. Sometimes it happens like that, some valve or substance in my brain just releases a lifesaving dose of a much-needed chemical. Amen.

"Well, one thing is for sure. Either the clock at home is wrong, I've completely lost my marbles at last—or the whole episode was brought on by that bit of silt I tasted. It doesn't explain why my front door was open when I woke this morning. But hell, why expect rational explanations for any of this?"

Anton paces the lounge. I wander into the kitchen and put the kettle on. The time is ripe for that sort of cliché. I notice some of the finishes in the apartments are not aging well. There's already been subsidence in both towers and the papers have been full of residential lawsuits over the past fifteen years. It's almost as if the development has been cursed from the very start though the company who built them is notorious for its shoddy craftsmanship. *Overpriced condos today. Slums tomorrow* someone had scrawled over the car park entrance below.

I make a plunger of coffee and take it into the lounge.

"How do you justify living in these apartments, Anton?"

He looks at me blankly. "What do you mean?"

"Well, this was Haseeshi land, surely you remember the kerfuffle?"

"Oh, I didn't live here then. I lived in Di Lido, but yeah, I know the story. Well, I'm Haseeshi so if anyone's entitled… It's Jordan's apartment anyhow. His parents bought it off the plan for next to nothing. His father's business was involved somehow, the legal side or something."

"What's Jordan's surname?"

"Tait."

"Jesus...I was one of his staff twenty years ago." I proceed to give Anton a potted history of what happened.

"Well, they're dead now. They have been for over ten years."

"How?"

"A pleasure craft accident, they were nearly seventy. It was all a bit suspicious. A blocked fuselage or something caused a fire. His partner was on the boat, so were a couple of clients. Everyone else survived. Jordan wasn't close to his parents. We never talked about them. He said they were real conservative, very racist, but he was happy to inherit this condo. It was just an investment property for them."

"Morty Simkiss."

"What?"

"That was the partner's name. I only ever saw him a few times. I was far too lowly to have any dealings with him. He was a big brothel owner back then I've since discovered, before they'd been legalized. Simkiss was only in the business so he'd have access to plenty of legal advice when his brothels got raided. It's funny, I was always in favor of legalizing them but I've since learnt that the type of men who operate brothels are not the type of men who generally let the law stand in the way of their capital gains anyway. Guys like Simkiss would probably have preferred they stayed illegal. It makes the workers more compliant."

"Well, I moved in here seven years ago and let me tell you there's some bad karma in these old towers. We never talked about family. I guess with one like his, being queer and having a Haseeshi lover would have been...well, definitely beyond the *pale*."

"I've never had a Haseeshi lover," I say almost apologetically.

"Well you might have to soon."

Izzy and Eve

"What do you mean?"

"You want to find them don't you?"

"Israel and Jordan?"

"No, Tait and Simkiss—of course Israel and Jordan. You may have to let me be your guide or companion."

I'm shocked. "And that would mean being my lover?"

"Well it would make things a heck of a lot easier. You saw what happened on silt last night with your own eyes. Do you think you could bear it?"

Bear it? I'm weak at the knees just thinking about it. "So with women, it's not a...problem for you?"

"Not a woman like you. Not for the journey we've got to make." I feel myself flush and realize how disastrously I've always managed my desire—my real desire.

"So you think they're dead and can still be reached? This is too bizarre."

"No one's dead," he says like it's a given. "And perhaps there's still time for us to see them again. I'm afraid for Jordan, he felt so darkly about himself. He was really very good in so many ways yet always seemed so full of fear. Society, religion, guilt...I don't know what made him so hard on himself. Certainly not me."

"I've seen things since Izzy left, things I wouldn't have believed before. He always wanted me to find faith, I've always bah-hum-bugged it. And it seems last night I must have been taken by a corpse or a ghost or a desperately overactive imagination. Whatever it was, at least if he was dead by midnight and I was only fucked by his spectre, I don't suppose you can catch diseases from the spirit world, can you? What's his connection Anton?"

"Well, he must have been the one selling silt. That stinky cubi-cle's his office or was until someone painted the walls with him. He knew who is buying and we know it is users who are disappearing. Someone wants to know who is on the stuff—it may even be the supplier who is bumping off the prime cuts. Or…"

"But why, what for? That's like a parasite destroying its host."

"You tell me, Evangeline; you've been on the silt more than I have. Wouldn't it be easier to cross over in a moment of that sort of extremity? Could you imagine crossing the greatest of barriers on it and no longer caring?"

I think about it. "Maybe," I say. My coffee suddenly tastes so civilized. "I think Israel expected something like this."

"So what are we to do?"

"We'll take it together. If you trust me, that is; we'll have the ride of our lives. If you don't trust me, it could turn nasty. Think about it carefully."

I feel beastly careless really. The world is so out of control. Anton is sitting beside me now and his hand is holding the back of my neck. He caresses me gently while I look at a photo of him and Jordan entwined on the couch. I imagine them together, I imagine Israel and Jordan together and some wild and animal part of me imagines us all together. I often wonder what makes the idea of two men together exciting for me—am I a gay man trapped in a woman's body? But then I think of the thousands of men who get off on lesbian porn and no one thinks that particularly shocking, except perhaps lesbians themselves.

Anton surprises me with how gentle he is. His hand reaches across to my forehead, gently brushing aside a bang that covers my eye.

"We've got ourselves in quite a mess, haven't we poppet?"

That word again. "Ha, Israel used to call me poppet sometimes. Lately even in dreams."

"Do you dream about him a lot?"

"Constantly at the moment. Even when he's not in my dreams, it seems as if they are designed or directed by him."

"With Jordan it's the same. He's always crying out to me, in the midst of some sort of peril. He cries out as if I could save him. I never can. I'm always just out of the frame somehow which is strange because that is how I often felt even when he was here. I miss him very much but at least you're in the picture."

"Not exactly your average holiday snap is it?" I ask as my hand reaches out to him and I hold his stubbly square chin for the first time. He moves faster, his hand on my knee, rubbing it softly but unmistakably pushing the hem of my dress up.

I look at him inquisitively. "So you are really quite into this type of old-fashioned straight sex?"

"Oooh yeah, there's nothing old fashioned about how I like it though. This was the part of my life Jordan never quite understood. Do you find me attractive?"

"Yes, absolutely...but I don't want..."

"Ssshhh. We're going to try and find our boys, aren't we?"

"Yes."

"And we lost them to appetite and depravity, didn't we?"

"Yes."

"And if we're to follow them in using silt, perhaps we should get to know our way around each other."

Something purrs inside me as his hand unzips the back of my dress. I still feel hot and raw between my legs from where I'd scrubbed. I don't have much trust in the desire of men who I think are gay but I've shown even less trust in the desire of men I know to be straight so where does that leave me? I've always lived in the zone where the lines became blurred so why get scared now that the real adventure has begun? I know there are plenty of women who spend half their lives trying to get gay men in the sack, just as there are loads of fags obsessed with seducing straight men. I feel Anton's smooth chest, the swollen-looking nipples shot through with iron rods, and my fingers follow the skunk line of hair from his navel down into the noticeably engorged tropical realms beneath his fly.

He's already hard for me. My dress slides down the length of my body. The lining crackles with static as I kneel before him, this beautiful golden man, my own special prime cut, and I think about how those whores on the videos at work behave. I'm more quiet than them of course but I'm an actress too, especially with the sheik. With Anton who knows? Perhaps I can drop my guard a little. Perhaps I can make it real. I think this is the end in itself. That our sex will be enough of a revelation for the day—but as he leads me to the bedroom, he begins to speak: "Do you want to see...no, it'd probably freak you out."

"What?" I say, thinking how this is the first time I've been naked with a man in broad daylight for years.

"Do you want to see Jordan and me together?"

"What do you mean?"

He picks up a remote control and motions to a television on the dresser at the end of the bed.

"We made tapes.... I guess of late I've been watching them to a morbid degree."

"Who can blame you? Turn it on." I toss my hair back. I concentrate on being a woman of the world—which, after all, I certainly fucking well am now! I'm wondering if it might be too much for him to watch the video while we're having sex, but I want to see it myself.

"As long as you're not filming *us*," I beg plaintively.

The video begins to play on the large screen. Anton's hair is longer, perhaps this is a few years old. I watch them together, they are tongue kissing with a very showy passion. It looks delicious. Jordan is pale against Anton's golden, coffee skin. "You're beautiful," I hear Anton mutter in a manner that seems both studied and earnest. "Take me to Dionahkesh," Jordan whispers with a smile. The shot widens and I see the two of them lying length to length on this same bed, though the sheets in the film are black. (Beside me, Anton explains that you get too much glare from white sheets.)

Izzy and Eve

Anton is slightly taller than his lover. He runs both his hands down Jordan's back, his thumbs tracking the spine and moving down into the cleft of his buttocks. "Let's get you nice and opened up," I hear Anton say just as that same thumb presses on my clit. I can't tell whether he's just said it to me or on the video and he gasps because he's discovered my secret. My clit, I've been told, is considerably larger than most. It's my trump card. I'm watching Jordan from the rear now. Anton's fingers are working into a glistening pink hole darkening to a blurred black oblivion at the center. A black hole in which Israel too may have been lost. Anton pokes him quite roughly with three fingers and I hear Jordan's breath catch but still he backs up for more. What I'm seeing is a study of the border between pleasure and pain. I'm feeling wickedly hot myself, ultrasensitive because of my douche and scrub. I'm shocked yet delighted to find myself in such a riotously depraved situation. The camera moves again and Anton is holding his cock, ready to insert it into his lover. Men always say the cum shot is the money shot but for my money, the penetration shot is easily the best. Especially so when I'm being entered myself in sync with the movie. I'm lying flat on my stomach so I lift my hips to make it a little more easy for him while resting my chin in my hands like a child watching television. The camera captures both their faces: Jordan's seems so young and wholesome, his teeth truly as white as they are in the still photos I've seen. I shudder with a small orgasm and I know if I'm lucky that will be the first of a gradually rising crescendo. My vision blurs a little; I can only put that down to the residual silt in my system.

"You happy?" I hear it twice, once from behind, once from on screen and uncannily Jordan and I answer in unison, "For now, yes."

He turns his lover over in a practiced maneuver that allows him to stay inside. They kiss again and I tremble more. Anton has Jordan's legs up now and he's working a lot harder. The tenderness is gone from Anton's face as Jordan strives to meet the thrusts with a teeth-grinding hunger of his own. I feel all of us mounting towards something so I try to allow Anton a deeper penetration. I see his face in the mirrored wardrobes, it has lost its gentleness but I don't feel threatened. I'm in that doglike position that can seem ugly, more masculine than feminine, but I'm suddenly lost to all notions of gender. Men in men in women: it's a scandal. And on the screen I hear Jordan say, "Feed me Anton, *feed me*," and with that Anton pulls his long brown cock from Jordan and carries it to his mouth bursting forth with a volume of seed unlike anything I've ever seen. Jordan laps it up like a puppy as I feel Anton shuddering with his latest emission into me.

"Jesus," I cry, my heart racing, my body flashing. "Is that a party trick of yours?"

"If I don't get you pregnant, Evangeline, no one will."

I collapse, whimpering, laughing, crying. "The sperm would have to be able to untie knots," I murmur breathlessly.

I look again at the TV, the show's over but the cameraman catches himself in the same wardrobe mirror. "*Wunderbar*," I hear him say—and recognize Torsten in the moment before the screen goes blank.

"That's Torsten!" I scream. "He and his boyfriend were into some weird stuff with Israel. Did you both know him?"

"Jordan obviously did. He hired him to do the video. That's what this…Torsten does for a living."

"Huh, that's just *one* of the things. Their house on the Escarpment is like a postindustrial torture chamber."

We lie looking at each other for a minute, then laugh.

"Animals," I say gruffly, then ask rather more gently, "How long since you've had sex with a woman?"

"Oh, a year perhaps. I used to be an escort you see. A lot of rich women in the wealthy precincts love to have a taste of Haseeshi and they'll pay for it while their husbands are at work trying to find ways

of getting rid of us—'I always think half-castes are so beautiful,' " he
says, mimicking one of these women.

"So you were an escort for women, but not men?"

"What do you think I am, a slut?" We laugh, then he adds, "I did-
n't want to get myself a reputation in Stonemasons Walk did I?"

"Certainly not one like Giovanni's. So what, or who do you like
most...sexually, I mean?"

"Huh... I like Love. Spiritual love, sexual love, filial love, platonic love. The Eskimos have a book full of words for *snow* while we get
stuck with this one puny word that is supposed to encapsulate so
many forms of expression."

"People kill for love," I murmur.

"Well if they do, it's not love. Unless perhaps it's euthanasia.
Anything bad that happens in the name of love can't be love because
love doesn't ask or want or resent."

"You sound like one of those books in the esoterica section of a
bookshop."

"Good. I can live with that. Of course I can mix lust with love as
you've seen. I'm still an animal too. I loved the way Jordan hungered
for me, though I guess in the end he was hungering for more than I
could offer. I'm starting to love you too, maybe because it seems like
fate, maybe because it's what I do. Perhaps we need to love each
other in a totally new way. Love is not what those rich couples in the
suburbs have. That much I've learned. Their love is founded on fortunes. I couldn't keep working as a call boy. The racism and politics
fucked with my head way too much. Some of those starved blonde
socialites with their Haseeshi art collections and their breast
implants—uuurrggh—enough to drive you gay! Besides, look at me.
I'm forty-three with a face like a hatchet. Pretty soon I'd have to do
seventy-year-olds."

"You've got a beautiful face," I say, gently stroking his cheek.
"The second most beautiful I've ever seen."

Neal Drinnan

"I don't know where Mary got the money to do all those renovations. She's only just started work," grumbled Evangeline from behind a magazine.

"She probably borrowed it. Why don't you just ask her for God's sake? If it matters to you so much."

"It'd be *rude* wouldn't it?"

"No ruder than humping her boyfriend out in your sweaty workshop. Jesus, Evangeline!"

"Israel! What sort of talk is that! We're neither of us saints, Lord knows. She never talks about her family. It's as if she was found floating in a basket on a stream."

"Well why don't you ask her, Eve? It's obviously causing you great consternation."

"Izzy, you know me, I'm not nosey; I'm not that *type*."

"She grew up in the precincts like all the rest of us's all I know. How interesting could it be?"

"Well she's on her own with that baby now, poor lamb. If she had family, a mother or someone, you'd think they'd be around to help. I'll watch him for her but I'm not doing diapers. I draw the line there. Besides, now that I'm barren as a dustbowl and corrupt as the proverbial Jezebel, I'm likely to turn into a pillar of salt if I go thinking back on Joshua."

Evangeline was bored with everything and, I imagined, consumed by guilt. Joshua had run off, and, well, we'd all had our fingers in that pie. Mary had retreated from us so who knows what had been said between her and Joshua in the final days. We'd heard the doors banging, the thumping footsteps up and down the stairs. The howling. I suppose it's hard to face anyone when you know they've heard something as primal and desperate as Mary's pleading in the days leading up to Josh's departure.

"She thinks I'm a slut," said Eve as she regarded the state of her cuticles disapprovingly.

"There's this bloke, comes into the brothel every week, single father. He likes Magdelaine but I've even done him myself once 'cause he's kinda sweet. He always brings his eight-year-old boy in and slings us an extra twenty bucks to look after him. The girls would do it for free because he's such a little cutie. He brings in his Leggo and toys and stuff and we take him out back to the kitchen where we gossip and smoke because if he was playing in the waiting room it might put some of the punters off. Remind them of their own wives and kids. Anyway, he tells his son that he's got a business meeting with the nice lady and up he goes. He's always done in an hour..."

"Does this story have a point, Evangeline?"

"Sure it does. When I was with him I asked him why he brought his son in all the time. He said he had no one else to look after him and the boy loves having the pretty ladies fuss and pamper him. He reckons the boy will grow up with fond memories of whores...."

"And never have sex with any other type of girl?"

"*No*, just not be all fucked up about women and sex, thinking they're either whores or Madonnas like most men. He hasn't the time with his work and boy to manage another relationship; says the last girlfriend he had was cruel to the boy and the boy comes first."

"Sounds like it's the father who does that," I snigger.

"Well anyway, all the girls are quite smitten by this guy and none more than Magdelaine herself, who asked him out and he said yes...."

"And they all lived happily ever after."

"Let's not overdo it. But let's see how open-minded Mary is about things as wee Tibby grows up. Faggots and whores for godparents? I don't think so."

"If Mary's bitter towards us, we've only ourselves to blame. We're still enjoying our days of wine and roses while she's on to her years of blood and guts."

"I absolve myself of any responsibility. Joshua was a cad and a bore. Not worth the trouble if you ask me."

"Mary *didn't* ask you, did she?"

"Mary doesn't want to know, Izzy. Joshua plowed more fields than just these ones!"

Curtis, now there was some fun that Evangeline never interfered with. She liked Curtis because it was lust and liquor at first sight with him and me, and the drinks were on the house for her. What could a girl with a taste for the top-shelf liquor and crude barroom banter do but jus' sit back and enjoy the hospitality?

"Here comes a no-good honky lookin' for some chocolate-flavored luuurve. Everything they say about a black man is true Israel and I's gonna break your white ass in two."

Curtis was one-third Motown, one-third *Shaft* and the other third drag queen and I don't think we ever slept together sober. All his bravado about being a top fell away just as soon as I got him in the sack: "Watch where you stick that thing you dirty-assed motherfucker. You put that in there people gonna question my masculinity."

"We couldn't have that," I'd say as I pushed into him with little or no resistance. "Ain't no one in the world mess my hole so good as you Is-ray-el," he said once in a rare moment of intimacy that came unaccompanied by rousing bravado.

Mary never went out much at all after she had the baby, while we tended to virtually live at Bar None and stumble home when it closed, doubtlessly waking her as we fumbled around for fifteen minutes trying to get the key in the lock. We probably spoke too loudly in our inebriated state. We doubtlessly said things that were less than kind about our friend. My needs were simple then and Evangeline was happy that I was around—but Stonemasons Walk, that still had a pull to it like gravity.

After a while, when we'd finished at Bar None and Curtis and I were getting over our "thang," I'd have to wander further afield. The bourbon lit my eyes, adding further allure to those dens of darkness. Being lost to all the pleasures and perils of the night sometimes felt more like being found.

There were those with lovers of course, good old boys who drank at Crouch or Anchors with their partners of years, but I'd bypassed that. So it seemed had thousands of others. We clung to the shadows, intrepidly making filthy and dangerous pacts with each other that lasted sometimes hours. Sometimes moments. Moments in which you could live completely in the instant. If that's what the Buddhists mean, I'm all for it.

The slide from "you could be the man of my dreams" to "you'll do" is gradual though not quite as dismal as you might think. You can accrue a lot of intimate and meaningful relationships over the years. You can sleep with the same person many times over a decade. But the decades go faster than you think.

One minute you're in an expensive apartment with a fine if shallow catch, the next you find yourself leaving a drunk and impotent man weeping in his bed only to be frisked on the way out by the roommate who'd seen this all too many times and needed to make sure you hadn't stolen anything.

You become immune, even inured to humiliation and rather than annihilated by it, you become exhilarated at the freedom of it. Or at least I did on those evenings. The crushing lows, the ghastly post-encounter ruminations came later. When things wore off. I was no longer a reasonable contender for any sort of cosy, conventional loving union of two. So a good job it was that neither Evangeline nor myself were seeking those unions. I could nod at those good old boys whose transgressions probably never extended beyond a drunken threesome once in a while and they could smile back at me like I was some sort of lost cause but I didn't feel lost. I was flying above the clouds, wading beneath contempt.

Neal Drinnan

"Avarice, Bestiality, Carnality, Drugs!" The woman on the mailbox has worked them into a litany from *A* through *Z*. She's failed to find one for *Z* though animal liberationists might cite zoos. For *X* she says Triple-*X* Movies. "Step right up! Tick your boxes! Sinners you are and sinners you'll be," she cries, revolving in a rapture of piety and obsession. Or is it? "Where are your children tonight?" she shouts at a flustered shopper. "Workaholism and alcoholism are destroying our families you know!" she cautions another one. It's almost as if she, like me, loves being caught up in this filthy carbuncle, this festering flower with its magnificent and hazardous blooms. If there were a symphony to be played for it all, she'd need an orchestra bigger than Grand Central Station to perform with and still there are notes I've struck that she'd never have heard or seen as she bears witness to the city's shame.

"Sin is life's test," she announces with a demure bow to no one in particular.

And on we all dance like merry fools. The DJs, whores and junkies, all. The discount shoppers in the Gilgal, the goodly folk with kids and mortgages in the precincts. The letches, the thieves and the filthmongers from pornographic peepshows and crack dens. And I try to tell Evangeline that it all has its reason. That every puzzling, glorious, seething episode has a purpose in the scheme of things and that I've made an ally of my depravity because I had no choice. But of course without any faith, without a vision beyond this world, I don't suppose anything can ever make any sense. I can forgive my own trespasses but can she forgive hers?

EVANGELINE

We walk back to my house and as we pass along the Stonemasons Walk shopkeepers gossip and shake their heads, each looking ghoulishly towards the Anchors: "It'll do nothing for business." "I blame the Haseeshi with their drugs and voodoo." Snatches of conversations fill our ears while a meat wagon unloads a dripping carcass in front of a butcher's shop where it's business as usual. I look at it and picture Giovanni.

"Let's go into Trashed," I say. "See what word on the street is."

Anton shrugs as we go up to the bar. Apart from the gawkers at the front, the rest of the people are talking as if nothing untoward has happened. In one corner, a couple of queer Goths are singing *there'll be blood on the cleaver tonight*—it drifts over to my ears and I see them pretending to chop at each other with imaginary weapons. There are times when the city bubbles with an obscene *schadenfreude* at the violence it fosters. We both order a Bloody Mary, not to be glib but because it's all we can bear to drink. The barman, a typically buffed and carnal beauty covered in curious Oriental tattoos, chats with Anton in a familiar way while I take a table. I can't hear what they're saying over the din of a freshly remixed version of "The Jackal." "Everything old is new again," I recall from my dream.

The barman waves Anton away and grimaces—"You don't wanna know, buddy. It'd seriously fuck your head up."

When he arrives at the table, he tells me that the grand puzzle, the question on everyone's lips, is how someone could have got out from the cubicle after doing what they had done. The walls to the cubicles are the old-fashioned tiled sort, floor to ceiling, not like the modern cheap Formica modesty screens that barely offer you any privacy at all. I suppose it is obvious why Giovanni chose it as his place of business. "The management must have turned a blind eye to his dealings because people knew they could score in there. They need the trade after all their misfortunes. It makes economic sense even if Giovanni wasn't the most savory of characters. You can bet someone was getting a cut though."

"Yeah, Giovanni. Literally," I say. "But I thought you said he had sex in there with people *for* drugs, not that he actually sold them himself."

"My mistake," says Anton. "I don't use drugs so I wouldn't know what he got up to in there. He could have been doing shoe shines for all I knew."

"But why the interest in us? Me?"

"Well, we'll have to assume your little escapade was more to do with the shift from silt than any reality."

"But Tibby, the keys?"

"Giovanni would have known Israel, Jordan too I guess. Jordan had a whole life I never asked him about. That's the only explanation. Toilet-boy's communication with you was getting us closer. Obviously we're not supposed to know about...something."

"And you think that by getting closer to this, using silt ourselves, we'll find out what we want to know?"

He shrugs. "I'm not suggesting that what we'll find out is necessarily something we'll want to know," he mumbles as the last of the red from his glass vanishes between his brown lips.

"I think we should pay Torsten and Gustav a visit."

"Why?" he asks, slightly perturbed.

"They never make any sense on the phone for a start. They're not far away."

"I don't really know them, Evangeline. We just found an ad in a queer mag, we were feeling kinky and wanted to make some home movies. It was only Torsten who came around. I never met Gustav—couldn't even have told you Torsten's name. Those videos were made five years ago."

"And Jordan's allowed himself to be sidetracked somewhere along the way since. There could easily be a connection."

I search in my bag for their card but can't seem to find it. It doesn't matter because I know where their house is.

ISRAEL

I find a little reed flute and begin to play it. Never thought I could.

Izzy and Eve

No one ever taught me. I'm thinking like a character in a movie. Don't know which one, about a girl I once knew. *A woman sure can be a friend of mine,* I think and it plays on my flute. I think how a world of songs is at my fingertips though I no longer remember who sang or wrote them. It's as though we all did.

I've been across a desert... how did that one go? *When you walk through a storm—don't cry out loud—man who is born of woman has but a short time to live and his days are full of woe—when you know the notes to sing...* A cavalcade of lines pass through my head and it feels as though they all belong to Jordan and me. *Wake up you sleepyhead, put on some clothes shake up your bed,* I play but he doesn't seem to hear me. My hands are going over Jordan and my fingertips create ripples of light. I wonder if he's made from quartz crystal, minerals and matter, or electricity and vibration.

I'm lonesome, I'm blue, I'm longing for you.
I came upon a crystal stream
or was it merely just a dream?
I burned a candle through the night
I whispered things would be all right.

He stirs, his breath scented by wildflowers and the sour grasses I sucked upon as a child. I am still a child. His breath is that of an infant's not even tainted by milk.

"Where'd they go?" he mutters.

"Who?"

"The men, the men who hurt us."

"No one hurt us."

"Oh but I'm broken, Sir. I thought you would have forsaken me by now."

"I won't do that and already we've travelled far. The desert is behind us and your body is mended. Why not stand on your own?"

"I'll try Lord if you can no longer carry me."

"But I can if you need me to. Your legs could quicken our journey but the hour is of no concern."

"Could you hold me again?"

"Of course."

"I've lost someone."

"You'll find them."

"I've strayed too far I fear."

"Fear not."

And so we rest a while longer in a strangely lit night by a gentle stream where harm is no spectre and dreams are becoming clearer.

EVANGELINE

I feel like a teenager. It's absurd really, wandering around town with a new man whose interest in me, however bizarre, is at least compelling. I don't cling to him in any way. People have such strong opinions about women who attach themselves to gay men. Not that I give a toss for what people think anymore. We arrive back at my place. Mary's putting Tibby in the car. She nods but looks at me like I'm some sort of nightclub casualty dragging home a stray. Tibby's not looking at us and I feel a pang at how he's been implicated in all this but it's beyond me now. On the wall opposite, his chalk marks have washed away. Chalk Mark in a Rainstorm *isn't that a Joni Mitchell album*? I think. My mind becomes infused with stray lines from half-forgotten songs; *Don't pay the ferryman, it felt good to be out of the rain.* For a minute I forget how I came to be with Anton at all. That's drugs for you. I feel a surge of pure need mix with a quiver of fear. I feel hot from the vodka in the Bloody Mary then a minor surge of shame at the outrageous sexual encounter I experienced with Anton earlier. He seems completely unperturbed by the whole thing. He is sifting through CDs, then notices all the vinyl. "You keep all this stuff."

"It's Israel's," I say, putting on the kettle.

"Quite the raver wasn't he?"

"He used to DJ, back before everyone got CD players. I think he did it because it served him so well in the shag department."

"Did you and he used to fuck?" Anton can shift disarmingly between topics without the slightest change in tone.

"Yes and no."

"Either you did or you didn't."

I carry the cups in. "Well we did, then we didn't, so *yes* and *no*."

"So what happened?"

"His homosexuality was…something of a disturbance in the field—that's what shrinks call it I think. Pity the girls who fall for fags," I say sarcastically as I hand Anton his coffee. "It only happened a handful of times. It was before we moved in here so I wouldn't like to tell you how long ago that was." I stare at the collage of photos Israel had put together and mounted on the wall. He'd pasted up pictures from the different parties and gatherings we'd had over the years and interspersed them with his own cartoons. My caricature had never changed in twenty years, always the same wild mop of hair, pouting rosebud lips and hiked-up breasts. His own cartoon-self was rather more butch than I would have drawn him. That's artistic license for you. The captions are bawdy and vulgar; Magdelaine holding up a bright pink ice lolly with *What you gonna do with that then?* scrawled below. Me and the girls from the brothel on the sofa raising our daiquiris to the caption, *Whores for one and one for whore'll.* There are a few panoramic shots from parties. They all seem so long ago, some date back maybe eighteen years. I can't remember the names of the people but suddenly Anton says, "Look." I move closer and there in a lineup of at least ten radiant faces, each one well and truly sporting the kiss of Bacchus, is Curtis beside someone remarkably like Giovanni. A proud, handsome Giovanni.

"My God," I say, "I can't remember him ever being here. Israel must have known him for a long time. It's frightening."

"He wasn't always like…he's been lately you know."

"Well obviously I suppose. Who is?" I take a closer look.

"He used to be a top model, *Vogue*, *GQ*, *Esquire*. He was signed to an important European designer for a while, spent half his time abroad."

"How the mighty have fallen," I say, thinking how his story is worthy of my scrapbook. "How old was he?"

"Maybe thirty-eight or nine. He's been wearing that same coat for years. Certainly hasn't modelled for ten. The Latin District is full of stories like that."

"Don't I know it. But why I would have received such a visitation around the time he was being murdered is beyond me."

Anton shrugs and stands up. "We should go to the Escarpment if we're going to do it."

"All right," I say, just as the locksmith arrives to install a new lock, and we wait while he does his work—though it now seems like too little, too late. *What else, barring murder, could happen to me now?* I wonder, locking the door behind me. If there are any more dead guys who want to fuck me, they'll have to get past one mother of a bolt.

We take the trolley car because neither of us can be bothered walking. At Torsten's, just as last time, there are no signs of life from the front of the house. I ring the bell and the dog barks like it's choking on something. I don't dare guess what.

Eventually Torsten opens the door, dressed in a bathrobe. He looks annoyed but still ushers us into the front room.

"Do you remember Anton?"

He shakes his head as he checks Anton over superciliously.

"You made a couple of videos for my partner and me a few years back."

"I make many videos for many people. I cannot remember all the faces but Haseeshi—not many videos for them. Maybe I do remember: you live in the tower?"

"That's right."

"Haseeshi in the tower!" he chuckles at the irony of it and I look to see if Anton is offended. He seems to be keeping a poker face.

"If anyone's entitled to be living in the towers it's the Haseeshi," Anton throws in.

"Beats the Causeway." Anton lets this more offensive quip ride. "Videos, I don't do this anymore."

"Torsten and Gustav are busy with other...enterprises now," I say as the dog sniffs around me again. "Where is Gustav," I ask, "polishing the silver?"

Torsten looks crestfallen. "Gustav is gone now."

"What, disappeared too?"

"No, he is gone back to Germany. We are fighting and he is saying I am all the time looking at other men..." I'm just thinking Torsten's about to cry when he leaves the room for a moment.

"Jesus," I whisper to Anton. "These two operate a virtual S/M dungeon and a home porn empire. They used to just about tear Izzy in two and were always phoning for him, and now they break up because Torsten looked at other men! I thought that was the whole point. Mind you, Gustav never struck me as the sharpest tool in the shed."

Torsten has returned with a clump of tissues. He seems to have composed himself. "I am making coffee, you want I can pour you a cup."

This sudden shift towards hospitality takes us both by surprise.

"Why not," I say mesmerized by each fresh development. We follow him to the kitchen for the coffee, the dog close at our heels. I ask if I can show Anton the basement and he shrugs miserably as he pours. I lead Anton to the winding staircase and down, but when we reach the basement I see that instead of the surgical implements and leather apparatus, it is now filled with flowers in buckets, green fronds, ribbons, twisted willow switches and dried foliage. There are Styrofoam wreaths, trumpet lilies, birds of paradise but not a

Neal Drinnan

sign of the implements I'd witnessed before. The *House Rules* sign however is still on the wall. I turn, gob-smacked, and we climb back to the kitchen. "What on earth's going on down there?" I ask as he hands me a cup.

"It is my work, I am a florist."

"You weren't a florist a week ago."

"I have always been a florist; now with Gustav...gone I can continue my work here instead of in somebody else's shop."

"What about the videos?"

"For a time, this was good money for me. Now I am wanting life more simple."

"And what about silt?" I ask hastily.

"What do you ask me about silt for?"

"Weren't you and Gustav into taking it?"

"We never touch this stuff. Is very dangerous, yah? All these men who vanish, they take this I think."

"Did you know Giovanni?"

"I know who he is. I have had dealings with him before many years ago, I do not know this man though. I think he is quite strange," He points to his head and twirls his finger while I'm thinking that Torsten was not exactly going to win the Steady Eddie Man of the Year Award himself.

"What sort of dealings?"

"This I cannot say, all my clients are assured of total discretion."

"Is he the person Israel was getting silt from?"

"Possibly. I never ask Israel about this. Gustav and I do not approve." With that he shakes his head and looks very self-righteous.

"But you knew he was on it?" I'm starting to sound like Nancy Drew.

"Not really. The danger with silt is that no one can tell."

"That's true enough," ventures Anton.

"But how can someone be so affected by a drug and no one be

able to tell?" I'm stumped by this one.

Anton looks at me and presses his lips together.

"That's why they call it the shift. It *shifts* a lot of things. Not just within but without."

"Giovanni has been murdered," I blurt.

"Well he's dead anyway," offers Anton. I look at him, perplexed. "He couldn't have done *that* to himself," I say, but then I figure if a postmodern torture chamber could become an upmarket florist in the space of a week, then why the hell not? Torsten no longer looks at all formidable with his hangdog expression and towelling bathrobe and here's me sitting in a spotless state-of-the-art kitchen filled with Scandinavian appliances, drinking coffee with a jilted German eccentric and a disarmingly attractive Haseeshi ex-prostitute who's already fucked me and may very well be an irreversible homosexual, and we're looking for two people who appear to have vanished into thin air.

"Will we head back to yours then?" Anton asks when he finishes his coffee. We leave Torsten to his own bereavement, and begin the walk home.

"So will we go for the shift tonight?" asks Anton as we wait for the trolley car. I suddenly remember that I have to work. "Where?" I tell him. "So you're a prostitute too?"

"Hardly, I make jewelry." I brandish my ring at him.

"Nice," he says.

"But some of my best friends are."

"Do they use silt?"

"No, I can't imagine it's the sort of thing you'd want to *do* strangers on, if my deluded account of recent events is anything to go by. They're not supposed to use anything but you can hardly blame them if they blow some coke or down a Valium and a neat vodka before they come to work can you? I certainly do...or I mean...would."

"Or a Viagra," he says.

"You'd know more about that I'm sure though Israel assured me that women dig it too. How he'd know *that* is anybody's guess."

"I've never had any problems in that department. Me Haseeshi!" he cried with tribal valor. "We stay hard all night."

"You're certainly a mystery," I say as we board the trolley car. It hauls us up the Escarpment and I can feel the weight of its progress in every joint of my body.

I don't invite him in this time. I tell him I'll see him tomorrow and give myself a couple of hours to get ready. As he kisses me on both cheeks, something occurs to me.

"I haven't asked you what you do Anton, now that you've...retired."

"Not much at the moment. Just drive a cab three nights a week."

I curl up on Israel's bed, talk to him wherever he is, and drift into a strange slumber.

I come to a clearing in the woods. The vivid green grass has the imprint of a body in it and the forest seems much less treacherous than it had when I'd fled that evil gingerbread cottage. I lay myself down in the imprint of the body—not Israel's, I can feel that much. A stream gurgles close by so I splash some water on my face. It revives me greatly but warning bells are ringing and they shake me from my reverie. They are in fact the sound of the phone. I reach for the cordless on the bed beside me. "Hullo."

"Is that Evangeline?"

"Speaking."

"Evangeline, I hope you'll forgive the intrusion but I'd be awfully grateful if I could meet with you sometime to talk about Israel."

"What do you know about him?" I ask, still in the grip of slumber and filled with suspicion.

"Well, nothing specifically but I'm attached to the University of Vorstock, psychological unit. Parapsychology is my specific area and I've undertaken a good deal of research on these dreadful disappearances. I saw the poster at Anchors Aweigh. My name is Dr. Orson Alexandria."

I remember what Anton had said about a student who'd been studying the case. I wonder if this is the same man. He sounds older, and I've begun to take Anton's initial appraisal of events less as gospel. After all, his initial theory on Giovanni was somewhat wide of the mark. I decide to meet with this Orson anyway. He says he happens to be in my "neck of the woods" this very evening. I don't want him in the house so I agree to meet him at Bar None at seven p.m. At least I know Curtis will be there. Seven still gives me an hour before work. "Ask the barman for me when you arrive. He'll point me out," I tell him.

I arrived fifteen minutes early and ordered a whiskey sour. I wore a knee-length cheung sam in pale blue and black. Slutty enough for the brothel but smart enough for the bar.

"Looks to me like the sheik's in town," sang Curtis as I pulled a twenty from my purse.

"God, he's the last thing I'd need right now. I'm meeting some weirdo parapsychologist here tonight. Curtis, can you remember a guy called Giovanni? He was a model. There's a picture of you at our place with your arm around him. It's at least ten years old." I smile mischievously. "Back when you were still good looking." He splashed me with ice. "Girl, you remember that far back and you game enough to admit it, you more fool than I thought you were."

"Honey, I'm the original Earth Mother. Show me some R-E-S-P-E-C-T."

"Giovanni, I knew that dude. Mr. Armani we called him. To hear him talk, he was goin' here, goin' there—the original male supermodel if you believed all his talk. Course, end o' the day we weren't good enough for him. No ma'am, not with Milan and Paris on his itinerary. Talk is, he dead." Curtis blew himself a kiss in the reflection from a martini glass he'd just polished.

Neal Drinnan

I lit a Sobranie and crossed my legs. I was feeling extremely cinema noir. My constant anxiety was giving way to the unsettling new role that seemed to have provided me with an unexpected kick start.

"No more is he going to ride through Paris, in a sports car, with the warm wind in his hair." I plucked an olive from the dish on the bar. "Chopped to pieces in his own private cubicle at Anchors." I blew a cloud of smoke that hung over the frozen margarita machine. "Selling silt and sucking cock seems to be where his promising career landed him."

"Bad news that silt, them kids gonna die if they keep takin' that stuff."

"Well Curtis, it seems they *are* dying and they're none of them kids. They're all old battle-axes like us. Old enough to know better. They take it and they disappear. Israel, Jordan—the whole Goddam Middle East if you look at the notice board in Anchors."

"It's some weird shit that silt crap. Don't you be takin' that, Evangeline!"

I stubbed out my fag. "Jus' what kinda girl do you take me for, Curtis?"

I noticed a man in a sports jacket arrive. He looked somewhere between forty and death. It's hard to tell with those academic types. He glanced around the room then began to walk over to the bar. I picked up my purse, spun off the stool and met him halfway. "What are you drinking, Orson—a glass of red?"

"Very perceptive...Evangeline. A good guess."

"I have an *uncanny* sense about these things. I work in hospitality."

"The Merlot and another whiskey sour, Curtis sweetie. We'll have them over here."

I slid into the booth and he sat opposite.

"So I suppose you've heard the latest?" I asked him.

"What's that?"

"The murder, last night, Giovanni?"

"Oh yes, but it wasn't murder, no no no, not at all."

"What? You think he choked on a fish bone?"

"No, it appears all the injuries he sustained were…self-inflicted."

"You mean he cut off his own…?"

"It seems so. I've talked at length with the detective in charge of the investigation and he was even so good as to let me visit Giovanni's room as they call it. Not a pleasant experience I must say."

"The police are actually calling it *that* too?"

"He was not unknown to the police. They are very concerned about the increase in silt usage amongst the gay community."

"Oh I bet they are. They were just bending over backwards to help me when I told them about Israel's disappearance. So if it wasn't murder, why'd he do it?"

"Well, my theory is that he was under orders to…eliminate himself. It seems users of the drug are dangerously open to suggestion."

"But orders from who?"

"Whoever is supplying the silt."

"And why would they want to get rid of him like that?"

"Because Giovanni was…leaking. He was giving the game away."

"Yes but what *game* and to whom?" I'd no sooner let the words escape my mouth than some sort of chilling adrenalin anomaly galloped up my spine. I had my answer. It was me. Jesus H. Christ, it had been me all along. My cool was lost for a moment as the truth dawned and he would have had to be a fool not to have seen it.

"You've not taken it yourself have you, Evangeline?" I shook my head, not daring to admit.

"I've a dossier the size of a small family car on all this business and if you take my advice you'll mind the company you keep. The government didn't ban the Haseeshi from using it and try to eliminate it completely without good reason. Now if you'll excuse me, my wife is expecting me for supper, it's roast duckling tonight. Best not be late or there'll be squawks." He laughed at his dreadful joke and pushed a very official-looking card across the table at me. "Perhaps you'd care to visit me in my office at Vorstock University, I think you'd be interested in some of my research on this matter." Then he was up, his drink almost untouched and me left with the check. And a good-fucking-night to you too, Mr Alexandria.

ISRAEL

Evangeline's mood has been all over the shop lately. At first she resisted medication because I suppose with manic depression or borderline personalities, the highs tend to justify the lows. Tonight Tibby's crawling about on the floor and she seems pleasantly distracted by his antics.

"Come and sit on Aunty Eve's knee," she says in the most maternal of tones. You're just about good enough to eat aren't you—when you don't have a load on board your diaper."

She's been pinning pendants onto a velvet board, getting ready for the next morning's market and I remind her to keep the pins away from the baby.

"What are you reading?" she asks and I tell her it's this quasi-Buddhist doctrine that is really interesting.

"So just when Joshua's taken flight and I thought it was finally safe to discuss politics again, you're off to cloud-cuckoo-land too. Bring back Dr. Dick, I say." She's dangling an Indian-styled piece over Tibby and he's playing with it like a kitten plays with wool. "You're gonna look just like your Pappy young Tibby—where did you get a name like that from anyway, a cartoon or some cereal box superhero?"

"I think it's cute. He can't say Toby yet, just Tibby."

"Cute for a puppy or a lamb perhaps. So what pearls of wisdom does that tome have to offer?"

"You really want to know?"

"Why the hell not?"

I explain to her how the author maintains that our ability to ultimately reject the world, to no longer want for its illusions, is as close as we can get to Nirvana in our lives.

"Some Nirvana," she grumbles.

"To the man with vision the world is as it is, to the man without vision the world is as it is. So essentially if we can dismiss the world as not being good enough for us, we can accept that we are moving closer to the next level. It's okay to say this world is not good enough—this guy reckons it's essential that you do. Christian doctrine has all that shit about us not being worthy enough to gather crumbs from under God's table. Endless sermons loaded with self-oppressing nonsense—whereas this says we should say: no, I've had enough, the world of the ego is impossible, fragile and explosive. It's okay to say, I'm beyond this and I want to return to the eternal continuum. We're not expected to grovel, we're expected to be as God. Of course he then maintains that when we tire of that cozy eternal consciousness, as we surely will, then before we know it we're back in the fray for more chaos and drama. But it's a great notion."

"So basically, the greatest moment of our life is when we're so fed up with it we want to die? Great stuff. I think I might just slash my wrists right now and spare myself another forty years."

"Well, I suppose it only works for those who've had enough of the mortal struggle—who are looking for something else. Who *know* there is more out there."

"And how can you *know* that for God's sake?"

"You just can, that's all." Evangeline has picked up Tibby and he's feeling her tits. She's talking to him, mimicking me. *"You just can Tibby, that's all—*Jesus, he's been off the tit for nearly a year and he still wants a suck."

I look over at her. "If he's anything like his father he'll be wanting to suck on plenty more of them in years to come."

"I need some new bras and some new beliefs," mutters Eve as

she settles him back down on the rug and he picks up his plastic rattle. "The Mormons think they can convert you to the faith after you've died. Can you believe the gall of them? They believe that Native American Indians were also once Mormons but somehow 'lost their way.' Their entire religious history rests on this ghastly wagon train trip across the Midwest. As for the polygamy, I would-n't have so much of a problem dealing with that if it applied to women too. Salt Lake City! The name says it all. Because you're not supposed to engage in any drinking, illicit sex acts or even a cup of coffee, the whole society lives on a sugar high from the endless array of fast-food outlets. For a community of fundamentalists, it's the most Godless place." Evangeline seldom speaks of her religious history. "But you might like it, little Tibby, because it's full of ice cream and donut shops and clean pretty ladies who don't show too much cleavage."

"Oh I think he'd want some cleavage," I add, looking up from my book. "Perhaps you make your own hereafter, and those folk in Salt Lake City will find themselves somewhere just like that or on an eternal wagon train trip across prairies; the Catholics will be in some vast Vatican filled with incense, gilt and guilt; the Jews by some Wailing Wall or some eternal Miami Beach and you'll be working the bars and cafes of some endless Cannes or Monte Carlo coastline while I lure strange lost souls into dark warm places."

Evangeline finishes her work and puts Tibby in his playpen. "But we'd be allowed to meet up for coffee or a cocktail from time to time?"

"Of course, at a venue of our mutual choosing...."

"And mutual design."

"Exactly. Kind of Gothic but with a *je ne sais quoi* contemporary chic to it. Good food and even better cocktails."

"Or just scotch and bourbon neat. *That'd be neat, Tibby, wouldn't it? Really neat."*

"Eve, if life's what you make it, why shouldn't the afterlife be as well?"

EVANGELINE

I'm furious at that man for walking out on me like that, roast duckling or no. I left feeling like a stupid schoolgirl and there was something condescending about him that reminded me of Mr. Tait. I'm flummoxed now; "Mind the company you keep," indeed! Whores, fags, boozehounds and druggies. *Mea culpa!* Of course implicit in that comment were the Haseeshi. He's unnerved me there. It's freezing as I walk down to the brothel; stupidly I didn't bring a coat. As I get to 755 I stop in my tracks. There's a bloody limo out the front, which means the sheik is in town. That Curtis is uncanny. Fortunately I've two whiskey sours on board and while I don't feel like sex especially, they may just have been the jump start I need. I pull out the useless little mirror in my purse and try to apply some more lipstick as carefully as I can. There's an ancient bottle of perfume in my bag and I give myself a quick spray with it, hoping it hasn't gone off. I catch my breath then make my entrance.

"Ah, here she is," says Mai, all big toothy smiles. "We're just coming, Abdulah." She turns to me and under her breath says, "Where the fuck have you been? I've been calling you at home—you know what he's like."

"Calm down, Mai. Leave him to me."

I enter the waiting room and there he is. "Abdulah!"

"Evangeline, ma chère."

I shove my bag into Mai's hand as his eyes wander to the Turkish delight. I avoid the girls' stares as I try to pick one out as discreetly as possible. He takes my hand as I mouth over my shoulder, "The Al-Ghaydah room?" Mai nods. What a busy woman I've become. What a perfect whore.

Neal Drinnan

"Frère Jacques, frère Jacques, dormez vous?"

Jordan stirs. "What?" He looks up and smiles. "I was dreaming."

"Yes, for a lifetime."

"Am I awake now?"

"I don't know. Are you?"

"Sin is life's trophy."

"Or its topiary."

"What do you mean?"

"Well, you keep trying to cut it back don't you? Work it into some sort of manageable shape. In the end it doesn't seem to make much difference—it keeps sprouting new branches."

"You carried me so far. I'd have been lost without you."

"Oh, I don't know, someone else would have picked you up, sinful trophy that you are."

"I thought you might have been the promised land."

"You'd be the first."

"Sophistry has been my undoing before. Where are we now? It can't be much further."

A wide river passes at our side, the sky above is blue but does not scald us and in the distance pyramids rise from golden sands. Jordan's been walking on his own for a while now but in the distance I see another casualty. A dark, wounded figure by the bank of the river. "Let's walk ahead," I say, unsure whether the sun has cast a mirage before us, but quickly we see it is one like us. His wounds are glowing in a crisscross of hieroglyphics. Just as with Jordan, molten light shines from within. I take water from the river to splash upon him but he barely stirs and we sit by his broken body where a light fantastic is cast from the groin.

"Do we know him?" asks Jordan.

"I think so," I say.

Izzy and Eve

"Will we take him? I could help now I'm growing stronger," he says with a gutsy pride that reminds me of a child I once knew. "That would be grand," I say and kiss him again. He smiles like an angel and I wonder if that's not what he might soon be.

EVANGELINE

"Once more," he whispers and I say, "Three times a charm." Though in all honesty I feel hot and raw. Three men in one day is a new record for me though I'm sure it wouldn't have been for Israel. One of my secrets, and I certainly don't tell the girls, is that I'm the sheik's choice because quite apart from the trick with Turkish delight, I allow him unprotected sex. It's a folly perhaps but my follies in the sexual department are my own business and they're few enough these days. Most men would rather have you go down on them than fuck you if it means using a condom. Their erections dwindle at the first sniff of rubber. Sure, they probably think you're a total slut for not making them wear one but my experience is that they don't need any encouragement for that and within the fucked-up universe I seem to have had most of my sexual encounters in a little disrespect can go a long way.

I don't doubt he has women all over the world as well as a number of wives. How many, I don't ask. Israel always thought it was some mad infatuation on my part that flew in the face of all my sexual politics but really it started off over ten years ago, and it was about money and jewels. A *lot* of money. He must be pushing sixty now and his appeal is less about how fine he looks than it is about the confidence a man like that has. A man whose wealth seems never to have dwindled and whose power has seldom been challenged.

He thinks I'm impressed with his sexual vitality but he sweats and huffs enough these days that I wonder if he might not give himself a heart attack. As he labors towards his third orgasm, in itself a miracle at his time of life, I think of Egypt or the mosques calling the likes of him to prayer. I never went to Egypt with Israel. He always joked that because of his name, none of the Islamic states would acknowledge his existence, and me, I've never had any wish to venture into regimes that oppress women. So I have sinned against my own rhetoric. But this one fact so far remains a secret just between Abdulah and me. Even between us it is unspoken. "If a tree falls in the forest and no one is around to hear it, does it make any sound?" whispers Israel from afar. "Shut up," I tell him. "I'm working!"

When it's over, he says he must go but before he does he gives me a bag full of stones. From these I'll make several pieces that will be worth a packet. And I'll give him a couple as gifts for his wives. They'll be beautiful pieces and perhaps they'll go some way to repay those women for the miseries of purdah.

He leaves me to shower and fix myself up. I notice three hours have passed. Mai will be niggling because she'll have been on the desk all night and while he'll pay twice the fee, she'll have earned half her usual loot by covering reception. "It happens once in a blue moon," I'll say. A blue moon on a golden Nile. Sin is life's trophy, I remember Israel saying as I push the velvet bag of stones into my bra, trying not to let it mar the line of the dress. Those Oriental tarts who wore dresses like this didn't leave themselves much room for a tip. I wipe a speck of lipstick from my teeth and wonder why I feel so good in spite of everything. Despite the terrible fear that my life could be in danger again.

Part IV

The Kaba

Tobias is sprawled across the floor in the lounge, his shock of auburn hair now streaked with blue-black. On his left ring finger is one of Israel's chunkiest rings that I gave him a couple of years ago. His mother hates it. Curled on the floor is Morgana, a brooding, lumpy girl who seems to have become his shadow this past six months. She's already eighteen and frighteningly world weary for one so young. A thick silver stud pierces her tongue and clicking it against her teeth seems to be the only thing that brings her any real pleasure. She's flicking through my photographs carelessly with her mold-green fingernails and a casual sneer.

Tobias is in a band now called Orphans' Seed: a demo CD plays in the background and an eerie instrument interrupts the guitar riff.

"Hear that Evangeline? Don't you reckon it's awesome! Oh man, that sound is *sooo* awesome, like that sound *IS* the estuaries at night with those foghorns, don't you think? Can't you hear it?"

"I suppose it is awesome, it's certainly haunting," I say, trying not to convey the dull, middle-aged truth that nothing is really ever as awesome as it is when you are seventeen. It's good or bad, interesting or boring. But who could deny the young man his enthusiasm?

Mary doesn't approve of Morgana and I can't say I'm particularly keen on her myself. Mary doesn't like her because she thinks she is Tobias's girlfriend, which says a little about how removed from reality she is these days. Girls like Morgana don't have *boyfriends*, they latch on to boys like Tibby: confused, dreamy, art-school type boys who anyone with any insight can tell are not going to have *girl-friends* at all. Still, it's not for me to lay the cards on the table for anyone. Each revelation in its own good time, I say.

Morgana is going to be a filmmaker but at the moment she runs the coat check at a nightclub in the Latin District called Sour Puss and I can just see her there, clicking her tongue over thrift store rags that cost more to check than they did to buy.

"You should come down—it goes off on Fridays and there are a few, like, older people who come in. You wouldn't feel like a freak or anything. I could get you in for free."

"Gee thanks," I say, "but I think my nightclub days are done, Morgana."

I'm trying to get back to the point of the visit which is a film clip for a track that Orphans' Seed are doing and the only reason they are here is because Toby has written a song about Israel. Morgana will be directing the film clip, and, if I understand this correctly, she will be playing some version of me. She's already shown me the rushes of what they've done on Tibby's digital camera. It is a bit hard to make out but it features Morgana made up like a corpse, clad in rags and crawling through the gutters of the Causeway on a very foggy night. Her expression reminds me of those seen in silent films from the early part of last century and I'm more than a little annoyed by her appropriation of my story, to say nothing of how I feel about my depiction.

"Morgana, my character looks like a rabid dog! I never wore makeup like that, my stockings weren't torn to shreds and I caught cabs or walked, not crawled through those streets on my hands and knees."

"I know, it's…stylized. We want to make it speak to a new genera-tion. Those silt deaths are deeply etched in the city's psyche," she says to me as if this answers everything.

"Deaths, were they?" I mutter quizzically.

"Sure they were deaths. You think a whole bunch of guys flew to the Bermuda Triangle for an orgy or something?"

"Morgana!" chides Tobias. He's sensitive to my feelings even after all these years. He's fiddling with his rings but looks up at her, flicking the hair from his eyes. "Evangeline was nearly killed too!"

"From silt Evangeline?" she says, desperate for more of the story.

"Yes and no," I say just as Tobias bursts into song.

He was nobody's father
but hey if you'd rather
he was nobody's father but mine.
Why should dreams ever taper
like his pencils on paper?
You'll never lock him into time.

Tobias's voice is really quite good but perhaps more importantly, he has an earnest confidence that makes me think he'll go somewhere with it. Me, I'm lucky I still have him as much as I do. Mary sold the house about five years ago and moved into the Escarpment with a straight-laced lawyer she married in a grim little ceremony last fall, but Toby always finds excuses to stay at our place. Anton likes him and I'm glad he still needs me. He's not too keen on his stepfather and Mary's been needlessly cautious to ensure I don't get to know him too well.

"What do you mean yes and no?" Morgana wants knowledge like she wants Tobias. She'll be just as nice as she needs to be to get what she wants but then she'll fuck me off straightaway. On the other hand, the story belongs to Tobias as well and in part it is his story too, but I want him to get the most out of it that he can, not throw it away on this drama queen.

"So did you take that silt stuff, Evangeline? In history they always said that's what really fucked the Haseeshi up."

"They say a lot of things in history. History is as much about interpretation as the incidents themselves. It never fucked the Haseeshi up at all Morgana. They understood it all along. I thought you'd be more discerning than that."

"But wasn't there some creepy Haseeshi dealer who turned himself inside out in a toilet cubicle or something? What about him and the shift, what's that?"

"So many questions and so much misinformation." I look at her. "What happens if you build something on silt?"

She's confused. "What do you mean?"

"Literally, what happens?" Morgana doesn't answer. Tobias tilts his head towards her.

"It shifts."

She's confused. She doesn't get it and this pleases me. I take the photo album from her. "And really, Morgana, that's all you need to know my dear."

ISRAEL

This is me, I'm at the bar in Anchors and Samuel serves me.

"What are you like you big fag?"

"Sammy, you *know* exactly what I'm like."

"And we reserve the right not to serve any patrons we deem too inebriated!"

"Too inebriated for what? A blow job from Giovanni?" He slides my drink over.

"I'd never stoop that low," he whispers mordantly.

"No comment," I murmur into my bourbon. I can see the flicker of the candles at the rear of the bar, there are a few sombre men in what appears to me to be traditional Amish or Orthodox Jewish garb discussing the disappearances. I can't trust my eyesight now but their voices come to me over the din of a song about fucking someone whose name you've forgotten. Their whispers have old words in them, *sin, thou, whithersoever, ways of the flesh, corrupted, sons of God.* The drug is in my system so it is likely none of what I'm seeing and hearing is literal and since when have rabbis or elders come in here? *Your children are lost and whither shall you find them,* I cry, but no one pays any heed.

I feel like going and telling them that they won't find their missing loved ones, that they'd have to move Heaven and Earth but who am I to say that? If they'd loved them more to begin with they might never have wandered into the wilderness at all. Hope is all you have if you don't have faith but try telling that to Evangeline! I am a wreck and I catch my reflection in the grubby smoked glass behind the bar. Samuel is pulling beers while taking intermittent drags from a cigarette resting in the ashtray. Liquor, cigarettes, drugs: I could annihilate myself on all those things. *Hell,* I have done that. I'd hoped my faith would save me, help me bring more to the world but the stark truth seems to be that the world has failed me. It's got its own agenda and I'm no longer part of that. A trumpet sounds and on one level I am saved, I know I shall endure. But not here and not in this form. Giovanni lurks like a sinister ferryman in those dark toilets where more drugs have been blasted, snorted, swallowed and shelved than you could even guess at. In there—where cocks have been sucked, asses fucked, adventures extended and curtailed—he waits. All of this in a quest for something *else*, something *more; anything* but another day of the same. Most of them won't touch silt. Giovanni keeps it for his special customers and for my sins; I've become one of those. Lucky me! He straddles consciousness like a drunken outlaw on a stolen horse, galloping between one world and another and I'll be fucked if I know how he does it. It's monstrous.

The bar is filled with men, faces I've known for years. Tarnished

Izzy and Eve

by the grind of it all or noble and resplendent in their maturity. Some fine, others like ravaged angels in need of some spit and polish. They've been doing this as long as me; like me, they love it, they hate it. They have no choice because every night spent at home is an opportunity lost, a conversation not had and here no one will judge them or tell them they drink too much or that they are pathological in some way.

I have been luckier than many of them, I've Evangeline and there are few partners in the world to rival her. But even platonic relationships shift. There were years of going places with her but now I choose places she won't go or can't go and I'm not sure why because I love her still. I choose to be on my own, forging quick bonds with stray dogs, savage beasts and unlikely sprites.

"They put water in the beer here," says the guy sitting next to me but a shift is happening and I'm unable to engage with him. I think about people who put water into beer but that leads me to thinking about the broader issues of man's inhumanity to man.

And whoosh, in CinemaScope it all stretches before me, *Baraka* inside me, all of human history: the bloody, hacking murderous tale of us all, the screaming Haseeshi mothers watching the settlers drown their babies in the estuary, the leagues of nations guarding similar atrocities like bald eagles on their eggs, the fires in the Middle East, the suicide bombers and their surprised victims, the music of grief over Africa, the desperation and exhaustion of a million refugees and the glistening lump of bleeding gore that is violence and greed, and the illicit joy these commonplace things represent to many an ordinary man. I shudder because I know that violence is a part of the condition, it is a serpent coiled deep within mankind and much of mankind loves it. I see the serpent's tongue flicker in the eye of the stranger beside me.

And I feel for a moment like Evangeline, saddened and transfixed by that nature show on television: "Everything devours everything, the strong slay the weak and on it goes...." And I wonder as I have so many times before, if sin is life's triumph and whether I should stay, as so many have before, to try to correct it. But I'm a lazy man and all the faith in the world can't fill me with the love or patience of the great prophets. No, the price I must pay for my most valued possession, faith, is that the world in all its rags and riches has become a charred offering, a grieving mass of lost endeavor and a carnival of blood and guts. And all the cars and condos, boys and bars cannot fill the void. For I am a bottomless pit.

"Are you going into the Shift," says the man beside me, the man with water in his beer and serpents in his eyes and I'm surprised he can tell.

"I am," I say. "How could you tell?"

"Well, a lot of guys come here for a drink first. No one goes there before midnight." And I smile because he's talking about the bar around the way and he smiles back and I think I see Jesus in him for a moment or one of the other gurus who drop by from time to time when events start to get like this. And then all the horrors come flooding back and I know I'm not meant to carry the burden of it all but I'm full of chemicals, loaded with toxins so things are bound to morph into God help me.

"On the way to Heaven, you *have* to visit Hell." I look at the man who seems to have said this in the same voice a Jewish aunt might use to say, "If you're on your way to Miami, you just *have* to visit Orlando."

"Hell is other people," he whispers a few octaves lower, then slams the beer on the bar.

"What?"

"I said, hell of a lot of other people going."

"Oh." And it's true people are moving like spectral beings to the door.

"I swear to Christ there's Goddam water in this beer!" he shouts.

"Temper, temper," admonishes Samuel with a fiery wave of the hand. And I see the flames leap from the ends of his fingers. I feel I am drowning in the beer glass. Then I find myself at the bottom of the ocean. I see Jordan fighting for breath while the candles at the back of the bar seem to flicker, flaring up like Roman torches. "Brilliant theatre," I gasp and I know someone will have to save him. To right this earthly snare.

EVANGELINE

University of Vorstock is situated to the west, in the Vorstock Mountains nearly an hour from the city if the traffic isn't too bad. The university has always been considered our most august academic institution but in the past decade it's taken just about anyone who can buy his way in. That's the only way tertiary education survives nowadays. On a clear day, the view of the city's towers and estuary is good but today it's hampered by smog and fluffy, icy snow clouds. The original buildings are over two hundred years old but the architecture imitates an even earlier period. I must say it is in keeping with my recent Bavarian fantasies. As we pull into the car park and search for a space, a man jumps in the back.

"Cartesian Precinct," he barks.

"Excuse me!" I say, shocked by the intrusion and forgetting Anton drives a cab after all.

"You're getting out aren't you?"

"Sorry sir, this cab is not for hire," explains Anton with reticence.

"Damn..." The man holds out one hundred dollars. "That's on top of the fare."

Anton looks at me beseechingly. "Perhaps I can pick you up in two hours?"

"Fine," I say and off they go.

I wander through the quadrangle, the agora, to a Gothic pile of a cathedral with flying buttresses and moss-covered pillars. On the notice board at the front is a gaily painted poster proclaiming *Jesus is Coming* to which various witticisms have been added such as *well I hope he's wearing a condom.* I get closer and read someone's stream-of-consciousness scrawl: *in metaphysics the figurative and the literal are both conundrums, the spirit world remains eternally impartial and inactive in the face of the material world and ignorance and idiocy are the only true states of grace…*in answer to which someone else has dashed off *yeah, whatever.*

For a moment I stand in the cold reading some of the other crazed messages and obscene scrawls on the church notice board. Beneath the proclamation are some lines of poetry in strong cursive script:

Look up to heaven, and bless his darling boy.
If e'er these precepts quelled the passions' strife,
If e'er they smoothed the rugged walks of life,
If e'er they pointed forth the blissful way
That guides the spirit to eternal day…

"Wordsworth." I jump, not realizing someone is breathing down my neck. I'd heard no one approaching. "*Despondency Corrected* I believe." I turn to see a man of the cloth, a Haseeshi man of the cloth no less.

"Sometimes you have to seek inspiration from places other than the Bible. I've always had a passion for the Romantics and let's be honest, this church has no real congregation; just expensive weddings, funerals and christenings for the wealthier graduates."

I don't really know what to say to him but his smile is definitely engaging, sexy even. I return it with one of my own.

"I'm not sure I like the sound of it, *eternal day.* I think I prefer the night. The delineation is too simplistic. Good equals day, Evil equals night. White good, black bad; you're Haseeshi for God's sake, I wouldn't have thought you'd fall for that." He laughs at my bluntness.

"Well, I know this is a university and all, but I try never to get weighed down in the semantics of it all."

"No? *Jesus is Coming!* What's that about? Alienate all the Jews, Muslims, Buddhists and why not the Haseeshi while you're at it."

"That belongs to the Youth for Christ group who use the sacristy on Mondays. I'm told they get quite silly on cups of herbal tea and naive piety. Nothing to do with me I'm afraid."

"I don't understand why a Haseeshi would serve mainstream Christianity—after all it's done nothing for your people. You have a wonderful tradition of spirituality. Every bit as rich as all that high church nonsense. I of course am a confirmed agnostic." I'm beginning to babble. I'm not sure why but I forge on without thinking, "Weren't you initiated as a boy? Have you ever had silt?"

He laughs. "Silt. Why do you ask that?"

"Because I'd like to know your thoughts on it, I'd like to know what you think it is."

"It's a very dangerous drug is what it is," he grumbles, maintaining a hint of irony with his practiced paternal severity.

"All right, that might do for your freshmen, but you're talking to Mother Earth here and before I go chasing down Dr. Orson Alexander to find out exactly what he's up to, I intend to do some research for myself. I believe I've...lost someone to it you see."

He smiles a little; his teeth are stained as if he chewed betel nuts or cocoa beans. "You can't lose someone to silt. They can only lose themselves."

"Are we back to semantics? To the figurative and the literal?"

"Possibly. No one knows what silt is."

"Well someone must, tribal elders? It's not as if it fell off the back of a truck, is it?"

"In the Haseeshi language, *zilta* means truth. *Zilt*, its abbreviation, means sin, or at least that's how the whites have translated it—but it really means 'being as God.' This of course was taken as heresy by early settlers, who, in their puritanical and self-righteous way thought this an outrageous presumption for humans in general to make. Doubly so when it came from heathens like us. I'm sure you've heard the communion service, "and though we are not worthy to gather the crumbs from beneath the Lord's table…blah blah blah."

"So why on earth are you here?"

He smiled. "Why on earth indeed?" I'm stunned momentarily as the web of intrigue is woven ever more tightly about me. He continues.

"To the Haseeshi, that idea was anathema. The Haseeshi never saw themselves as apart from God to begin with. They had no notion of sin, or the fall in the biblical sense and if there was a God, they and all those before them were part of it. Separating God from the self *was* the fall. We saw our own evolution as the evolution *of* God and that was never going to be acceptable to the reigning Judeo-Christian principles of the new governing tribe, was it?"

"I don't suppose so."

"And it does seem rather absurd to base religion and lifestyle on some text written so long ago, don't you think?"

"Well of course… You are preaching to the unconvertible, you know."

"Good, I like to work with a contemporary philosophical psyche. So it confounds me why we think it's okay for the laws of the physical world to require constant updating, but not those of religion. God by His very nature must be much more modern and with-it than us! Right at the cutting edge of morality and discourse I would have thought, yet our religious stalwarts still have him sloshing about in a primordial swamp using archaic language to baffle us further, and all the theologians can do is quibble over a virgin birth, a nasty crucifixion and transubstantiation. Not very satisfactory is it?"

"It never has been for me," I mutter. I'm shocked and fascinated.

Izzy and Eve

The clouds are engulfing us as we stand talking. The church itself, now completely shrouded in mist, is even more like something out of an Arthurian legend, like Avalon. I can smell snow for the first time. It always snows in the Vorstocks before it reaches the city and while I contemplate the wisdom offered by this man who came out of nowhere, I feel the cold seep right through my thick woollen coat. Luckily, the fur on the collar is warm.

"I believe there is hot coffee in the vestry if you'd like to join me?"

"I couldn't think of anything better. I'm Evangeline," I say, offering my hand.

"And I'm Damian."

"Quite the omen you are too."

"Perhaps, though I've yet to master the three-sixty-degree turn of the head."

"It's probably for the best. It might unsettle me."

We walk through the church, its light medieval and thick with dust. I follow him with ears tingling from the cold and I see an old woman kneeling to pray. I think I hear her saying, "I loved you then but love you more." As I pass I mutter to myself, "...as winter knocks upon your door."

"Did you say something?" asks Damian.

"Umm, no," I say, but I'm wondering where I'd heard that line. I'm following threads and scraps and filigree things. Israel is closer than I thought. I can feel him in the ice, in the rain, and a chill passes through me because I can almost sense his warm hand on my back, pushing me towards the vestry. Towards another man with a head full of thoughts and beliefs that I must wade through like a lake, never knowing when I might slip into hidden, perilous depths.

ISRAEL

Could I have told it was the last time I'd see him as I was pinned by those dark eyes in the rearview mirror? Who can say—but as I looked, I saw Jordan in that driver's eyes, or he did in mine. Jordan hung in the air like vapor. Things were shifting again. I wondered how he could stay on the road, see ahead if he was looking behind at me the whole time. The blades of the windshield wipers sliced through the rain like a barber's cutthroat through four-day whiskers while some cheap Haseeshi sun-song poured out of the radio like thick sweet syrup. Sickly sweet, maybe too sweet and the heat was up so high I could smell myself, the secret terrible parts of myself. The worst of me, the best of me, my essence running out, cheap like a superseded model of car. And out the windows, lost, terrible people loitered desperately outside shopfronts, their faces appearing to be handwritten shopping lists of what they needed before the winter set in. I could read their thoughts: *How can I make someone love me before the nights grow cold? Will there be something better before I grow too old? How did fortune fail me so? Who reaped the crop I tried to sow? Why are there dreams I can't let go? Is there some bread inside this bin? What is the price of all my sins?* And I snatched these thoughts from more than one of those rat-faced vagrants. "Sinners you are and sinners you'd be again if the opportunity arose."

"Is that so?" said the driver. I had spoken aloud.

"Oh yes, for I have gone over Jordan. I have been over there."

He smiled—at least I thought it was a smile—but my vision was fractured. It could even have been a snarl but I dared not think it that.

"We've all been over Jordan." He averted his eyes for the first time to the road. "We've all been over Jordan. And someone's going to have to carry him home."

EVANGELINE

Snow whipped me with a vengeance as I made my way to the psychology department, some distance from the church. Students gathered in clusters awaiting the end of the blizzard but I forged on,

Izzy and Eve

my collar gathering flakes, my breath soothing me with its coffee-scented warmth. Three weeks ago I was in sleeveless tops—now this! Damian had recommended a list of texts to look at in the library. He suggested these would help me understand the Haseeshi mythology more, if not silt itself, because according to him, silt is not something you can easily pin down. "It's like mythology or mercury or faith itself. You can know of it, you can possess it, but you can't make anyone else find its secrets until they are ready. Its truth will differ from soul to soul."

I told Damian a little about Israel, and how his notion of faith came from no particular book and no specific experience. I even said that his sense of certainty about these things infuriated and confounded me at times.

He was not surprised. "And so it has been throughout history: Jesus, Ghandi, Mohammed, Buddha, the Dalai Lamas, just to name the A-list." I laughed to myself when I thought of Israel dragging his filthy ass home after twenty-four hours of sex, drugs and God knows what. But then I thought about seeing him with Jordan. About all that had happened and about how I was believing things now that were so beyond this world that they had to be glimpses of a greater truth or proof that I was truly, madly and deeply fucked up.

"The path is different for everyone," he offered. "Drugs will take some people directly to Heaven, others to Hell. Some, to both over time. Your body is your temple and how you choose to worship amongst your own congregation is entirely up to you. One thing I am sure of is that this is the only Hell we'll have to visit. Those who think God has something worse in store for them have a very dim view of God, a dearth of faith. They must think God is a real asshole."

Well I do sometimes wonder, I thought as I drained the last of the coffee from my cup.

Orson Alexander's office was a cliché—leather chairs, books, dirty coffee mugs. From our conversation, it seemed history and psychology had done more to confound him than enlighten him. Huge amounts of private money had been waged on this foundering institution in recent years so that it might carry on educating after the government lost interest in education. Ancient colleges like The Trinity and New Merton now have their names prefaced by multinational companies: Globaltel & Rochedale, CorpINC, Pfizer, Buy-o-tech. All the old signage replaced by new with appropriate, paid-for logos. The language syllabuses, the history and literature had given way to business stream courses funded by vast multinational petrochemical, pharmaceutical and biotechnical corporations. I'd seen some of the books that were being read by students: *How to Prosper from Third World Debt, Arise in the Downsize, Green Future Lean Future.* There was no romance to any of it anymore. No existentialism, no mystery and certainly no Age of Aquarius. Just expensive courses with income and debt prospects calculated for each student upon intake. It was naive and pointless for me to object to the changes—perhaps my reaction was just a sign of my age. Israel had said he had been expecting a positive shift in ideologies, said he'd been waiting for that but instead things had got worse. I was prepared, in my cynical way, to believe that "worse" was actually truth. I didn't like to think that, but humanitarianism and sophistry had been my undoing before. His faith hadn't changed the world at all, merely fashioned some sort of elaborate escape. The bastard.

What a doctor of parapsychology could possibly have to offer me remained to be seen. As did the source of his funding.

"These are strange and dynamic times, Evangeline."

"The best of times and the worst of times?" I quipped to match his tedious theatrics. "They are dull, conservative times, Dr. Alexander. They are mean-spirited, self-serving, depressing and given the hopes of the past, I have to say they are a massive disappointment but you didn't ask me here to get all sentimental about history's broken promises, did you?"

"We're both busy people and you'll be wanting to get back to your Gilgal. I'm sure you have work to do." He cocked one eyebrow.

"Yes, but not before I have a look in the library. I just met the priest. Very inspiring!"

"Old Father O'Shea—you don't mind a bit of fire and brimstone then?"

"He didn't strike me as the fire and brimstone type. O'Shea? Isn't that a very Irish name for a Haseeshi?"

"There's nothing Haseeshi about Father O'Shea, I can promise you. He's been the chaplain here for forty years."

"No, the man I was speaking to could barely have been forty."

"Hah, I might have suggested it was the caretaker—now *he* was Haseeshi, but he's been gone a couple of months now."

"Gone?"

"Gone, like all of them I'm afraid. Poof!"

I ignored the inference. "What did he look like?"

"Fortyish, nice enough fellow. Can't say our paths crossed often but he was quite well educated. Actually he studied here part-time. The Romantic poets I think, something very Anglophilic I seem to recall."

I shivered, imagining him receding into the mist from whence he came, back to wherever they all seem to have gone. "I'm surprised they still include poetry in any of the syllabuses."

"Or *syllabi*, to use the Latin. Which is definitely off the menu these days."

I was sure Damian had worn a clerical collar of some sort but thinking back I realized he'd never said he was a priest.

"The Haseeshi have a long history of magic. Most of it based in their mythology and the poor wretches have had a devil of a time keeping it alive. But silt, well, that has been their one powerful edge over imperialism. Their trump card if you like. Pure chaos. Their culture was never really worldly enough to endure the rigors of modern capitalism and as we both know, capitalism isn't going to go away, of that much we can be sure. *Any man who isn't a socialist at twenty hasn't got a heart and any man who is still one at forty, hasn't got a brain....*"

"That's all well and good. God knows you're not alone in your philosophy but none of this is about parapsychology, psychology, Israel or even silt, so what have I come here to discuss with you?"

"I'm concerned by who might be involved with all these disappearances. With Giovanni Ricci gone we've been left somewhat in the dark and your Anton, well we are concerned that he may have had an axe to grind."

I flinched at the metaphor. "Why, for goodness sake—because he's Haseeshi? And who the fuck is *we*?"

"I've been working with the police on this. It's all got a bit much for them as I'm sure you can imagine." As if to prove it he turned his computer screen to face me. There, in a macabre and constantly changing slide show were the faces of dozens of missing people, each of them smiling: almost as if *missing* was a good thing to be, as if it was an island in the tropics or a jazz music festival in the provinces. *Foul play suspected, suspicious circumstances*, and various other dire captions headed these tales of woe. As I touched the screen, the liquid crystal display rippled and almost engulfed my finger and I was charged with a sensation that could only be described as a shift. I was transfixed as I watched the parade of missing people. Not one of them looked as if they'd want to vanish from this realm of senses but vanish they had. Between their jobs and the car park, between bars and bathrooms, between home life and another life no one else knew about. Israel always said people vanished between cracks in the pavement but until now, I don't think I ever realized the extent.

"I don't know whether you know this, Evangeline, but Jordan's family had rather fallen afoul of the Haseeshi community with some of their developments...."

"Yes, I know all that. They died in mysterious circumstances...."

"Not really. Money, graft, murder and profit. Nothing mysterious about it. The city has operated on the same rules for hundreds of years and they knew the rules. No, perhaps if I tell you a story, Evangeline, it will help you understand things a little better because I suspect you're floundering somewhat with all of this. We'll need to go back about fifteen years. You see we don't believe silt has been produced here for some time. It has been coming in from abroad and if you can lend me your ear it may help you to make more sense of it too....

"In days of yore when all was green, there was a magnificent young Italian man called Giovanni Ricci whose green eyes and abundant black hair launched him on a modelling career that was the envy of his contemporaries—a career that if he'd had his wits about him, could have made him a considerable amount of money. Sadly wits and smarts are not necessarily synonymous with magnificence and here began Giovanni's downfall. He came from a strict Catholic family and as you probably know, he was a homosexual—not the preferred genetic outcome for a family as respectable as the Riccis. Fortunately for him, his work on the catwalk afforded him much time away from this oppressive Latin regime, plenty of time in Europe generally and a good deal of time in Paris where he came to know a very wealthy Arab sheik with whom I believe you have, yourself, had...*dealings*...."

My jaw dropped.

"I see bells are ringing. Well, the sheik is a man of vast resources and apparently, quite mercurial and eclectic in his sexual tastes. As a young Italian boy whose own father had never taken a passionate interest in him, Giovanni found it easy to become rather enamored with this exotic stranger who showered him with money and gifts. He was a lover *and* a father figure. Soon he was installed in an expensive apartment whenever he was in Paris so the sheik could access him as easily as possible. And access him he did!

"The sheik may have had a soft spot for *amoré* but he also had bigger fish to fry—ulterior motives—and while his libido is legendary to say the least, he is first and foremost a businessman. Wealth such as his does not maintain itself on candlelit suppers. His oil wells had dwindled and he'd become the casualty of several Machiavellian political and military maneuvers in his own country. But there is one commodity I dare say there will always be a need for in the Middle East: weapons. As you know, our own proud country has an artillery stock that could cheerfully blow us all to kingdom come several times if need be and we're not above selling outdated components of our arsenal to tin-pot regimes when our own coffers need topping up. Trading arms requires a good deal of discretion and more than a little ignorance on someone's part. A young, vacuous, narcissistic model in an Armani suit was the last person anyone would expect to be ferrying currency and paperwork between here and the continent.

"Now I don't know exactly how well you *know* this sheik but our research has shown you to have had dealings with him for some time. In my analysis of him, I'd say that he is something of a megalomaniac. During his years at university here, he did not follow the usual streams of study but majored in pharmacology. His area of interest has always been in organic hallucinogens and their traditional cultural applications. Silt, for obvious reasons, is one of the most fascinating hallucinogenic substances in the world. He saw it was potentially another area of commerce for him but more importantly, he was fascinated by how it might be used psychologically and to his advantage. In the course of his studies he ventured out into the prairies with Haseeshi guides to sample the real thing and doubtless took it back to laboratories in Europe in order to have a bevy of researchers work on synthesizing it.

"What he found through his research was that under its influence, users were very gullible and vulnerable. He realized if he was able to create total euphoria for someone the first time they used it, they would trust him again and he could create whatever havoc he liked when he administered it later on. He saw it as potentially giving him strategic political and personal advantages. This is where Giovanni got himself into trouble. His Catholic guilt made him an easy target and whatever spectacular pyrotechnics he had experienced the first time he was given silt by your sheik would leave him vulnerable to further doses...."

"He's not *my* sheik!"

"Let's hope not. I trust you've not been one of his silt guinea pigs because when users have experienced the highs the drug can inspire, and then begin to experience the lows, they tend to keep using to try to get back the high. It is during this period that users...get into trouble. This was certainly the case with our Mr. Ricci. However, he had one card up his sleeve that the sheik had not contemplated. That was a video he had made of himself and Abdulah in flagrante delicto. He'd had someone film the two together, in secret, during one of the sheik's visits. As you would understand, for one who had as many political and marital ties as he did, it would not do for that video to have fallen into the wrong hands. Any hands at all for that matter. As Giovanni's drug habit worsened, the one thing he was able to negotiate with his former lover was a continuous supply of the substance—enough for him to sell to other users as well. Silt was only one of the substances he used. Certainly one of the less addictive, but he got himself into a shocking mess on drugs over the past decade. For a time he held it together though his career was over. He worked in bars but couldn't keep his hands out of the till, then prostitution, but through all this he was the one who had access to silt. He knew its mysteries and terrors. It was his vocation and, I fear, his damnation. It allowed him to enter places and dimensions usually denied to men. It was destroying him but he became skilled, to some extent, at managing it.

"And then there was Jordan, who looked like another easy ride for Giovanni Ricci—who, given his druthers, always preferred to be kept by someone else. You could say he loved the clothes but loathed the laundry. Jordan had good looks, money in the bank, and solid family but he also had a lover he would not dispense with. Giovanni had learnt the rules of silt. He knew them almost better than anyone and he had the power to make things turn nasty quickly for people who fell under his influence, if he chose. He could shift in and out of their experiences. He could ride them to Hell and back.

"This is where he has come to fascinate me, this psychic ability to infiltrate other people and other worlds merely by imbibing a substance. He was jealous and guilty himself, so he worked long and hard at punishing those who'd betrayed him, or those he *imagined* had betrayed him. In the end I'm sure it was hard to tell the difference. The sheik—he was far too strong and intelligent for Giovanni. But Jordan, he was not so strong. Giovanni mined that weakness for all it was worth."

"But how do you know all this?"

"It's my theory. The result of many hours' work. Have you a better one?"

I looked from his window at the snow and sleet in full fly now. "I'd need to think on all this for a while. I know nothing about silt, not its composition or even its price."

"In that sense it is a bit like a fabled charm. For everyone the price is different."

"You think it's a fairy tale? The good will be rewarded because their hearts are pure?"

"*And the clean person shall sprinkle upon the unclean on the third day, and on the seventh day he shall purify himself and wash his clothes, and bathe himself in water, and shall be clean at even. But the man who shall be unclean, and shall not purify himself, that soul shall be cut off from the congregation, because he hath defiled the sanctuary of the LORD: And it shall be a perpetual statute unto them, that he that sprinkleth the water of separation shall be unclean until even. And whatsoever the unclean person toucheth shall be unclean; and the soul that toucheth it shall be unclean until even....*"

"Sprinkleth, toucheth, whatsoever, whosoever, yadda yadda yadda. If you're trying to scripturalize all this shit you're wasting your time. What is that anyway—Exodus?"

"Numbers 19:19."

I fixed him with a stern gaze. "I can tell you myself that if you go into the shift, you could meet any of these guys, but according to Anton, not for long. So perhaps the sheik is the real villain here. He's certainly been fucking with people's heads for years."

"Yours?"

I shrugged and fiddled with a paper clip, not sure how much I should tell him. If this was some sort of battle between Good and Evil, the lines were not clearly drawn. Besides, I thought I'd be with Israel on this—most behavioral morality is a construct anyway. I never hurt anyone, or so I tell myself. "I'm not what you'd call Little Miss Average when it comes to sexual morality, Orson. I've had my fingers burnt and I've probably burnt a few myself. I don't beat myself up over it."

"Don't you?" He looked unconvinced. "That's admirable and shows a keen sense of economy."

"I don't know about economy. I survive. Israel was the one who challenged it all and God knows where he is. He was always searching for a link between this world and the next. I guess he found it. It seems you can't sit on the fence for too long before you fall onto the other side."

"But the idea that it can be proved is what fascinates me." He was beginning to get all twitchy and conspiratorial with me.

"Well honey, why don't you take some silt and see for yourself?"

"I'm not a religious man you understand, but I am fearful it is some sort of trespass...an accursed place like Jericho was before they shouted down the walls."

"I'm not big on my biblical history Orson, but I'd say that's exactly what Israel was doing. God forbid that I should be one of his prophets, but I do live in the Gilgal and we've got plenty of good-hearted harlots there so who's to say they don't do their part in guarding the city from evil? Any one of them could certainly write you a thesis on double standards. Israel's been shouting down morality and all its paradoxes for years. He maintained the Bible was the most stifling impediment to spiritual growth in the history of man. I myself just find it an archaic bore; why anyone in the modern world would base his life on it I couldn't guess. One thing I'm starting to believe though, is that Israel saw Zion and it's not like anything we thought. He was bored with the world. Can't say I blame him."

It became clear as we talked that Orson wanted me at the front line. He was a voyeur, just as I suspected, imagining me on my hands and knees, me in the brothel. Me as a dominatrix at the very gates of Hell. And the day had taught me much. It had given me an idea for an experiment so absurd it would have made me laugh if I wasn't also aware of how high the stakes were. I listened as he told me at length of the sheik's crimes, of the vanishing acts, of Giovanni's frightening escapades between this world and the next. Then I went to the library for a little research and by the time Anton returned, I had devised my Waterloo, my spell. My Goddess moment. When the time came, I would be ready.

ISRAEL

I remember a story like this: a jolly bunch of travellers marching down a yellow brick road. I look at my two companions, their teeth white, their footing sturdy now. They smile so wholesomely that I'm reminded of the men who peddled the word of God on street corners in a Gothic dream I'd had. I laugh at the idea of selling God and of God being as pure and fractious as they supposed. It's crazy the ideas you have in your sleep. There was a girl in the dream. I miss her a lot but something tells me she will be at my journey's end.

"She'll join you by and by," says Jordan. "I think she's happy now."

"I think you're right," I say, because it's true.

"Or as happy as anyone can be in a dream. In Hell."

We all laugh, and no one louder than Giovanni whose spectacular mane of black hair falls about him as if it was grace. His green eyes glisten like crystals and if it were possible, here, to envy him, then envy I would.

"*Bello* Israel, such times we had!" he shouts. "*Israel è perfettissimo*," and the windows to his soul tell me it is so as his enormous hand playfully ruffles my own hair sending a vibrato of harmony right down my back.

Jordan's already planning how things will be when we get there, though I'm sure there's no need. He's so pleased with his recovery that there's a bounce in every step he takes. He's like a child. I suppose we all are—there's not a mark on one of us, not a scar or blemish because no one can really hurt you in a dream.

But still I have visions from time to time of an auburn-crested child who sings haunting songs about a city of terror, of foggy estuaries and missing heroes. And that honey-haired woman in heavy coats with fur collars and rings she brandishes like weapons to protect a heart that someone might too easily break.

I don't make plans—my faith has carried me this far and the journey is every bit as important as the destination. Best of all, I am no longer constrained by time. Now when I draw, it becomes real; if I dance, it makes sense. I look to the others, all our feet are marching in step. "Where's the war?" I laugh. "Where it's always been," answers Jordan. "And where it shall always stay."

Neal Drinnan

"There's something I should tell you but I don't know how you'll take it," he whispers so quietly I'm not sure if it's a dream. I feel the cold beyond the bedclothes, it's like a knife at my throat but beneath them the air is dense with our warmth, his smell and my own. Such a precious and intimate space we've made through the night. I dread the thought of dragging myself from bed to turn on the heat. I move myself closer to Anton. I can feel his hardness against me. He's always hard. I'm impressed.

"Don't tell me, let me guess. You're...queer?"

"No, this is serious."

"More serious than that? I dread to think."

"It's about Israel. I saw him."

"When?" I urge, propelling myself onto my side, at once wide-awake.

"The night he disappeared. He was in my cab. He was saying weird stuff. He said he'd been over Jordan and I knew at once that he was the one who'd been making Jordan crazy. I knew as soon as I looked into his eyes that he was the one I'd been losing Jordan to. I can't explain it. It was like I could see Jordan inside his eyes. It was the strangest thing. You know what I said?"

"What?" I'm almost lost for words but I'm not afraid.

"I said, 'Someone will have to carry him home.' "

"And what did he say?"

"He never said another word. He gazed away from me and here comes the strangest part. The one thing I'm still totally at a loss to explain."

"What?" my voice drops several octaves. It must sound like gravel.

"Well...I stopped for some traffic lights. It couldn't have been more than five seconds I didn't have him in my sights. I'd been watching him in the rearview because it was like I knew him. I was trying to place him. He'd been at Gutz, that's where I picked him up.

Izzy and Eve

Right outside the front, and he smelt like...sex. I was excited by that. Anyway when I put my foot on the gas, I looked in the mirror again and he wasn't there. He was gone, the smell was gone. I had to stop for a coffee to figure it out; I was really shaken because he couldn't have opened the door or got out without me noticing. It was impossible, then when I looked at the meter, it wasn't on. I swear I'd started it when he got in. He vanished into thin air. They all vanished into thin air."

"Why didn't you...?"

"You know why, Evangeline. Because you would have thought I'd killed him and you know...by saying what I said about carrying Jordan home...I felt...like maybe I had." Anton starts to whimper quietly but instead of running from him I pull him closer because I know what he's said is true. I have faith in him.

ISRAEL

Giovanni has found shoes, the finest pair, and threads to cover him from head to foot. Jordan has wrapped some cloth about his waist at a fetching angle. But I am naked still and feel no shame. We have sailed upon the river and Giovanni gathers jewels from the sands, rings of gold and luminous stones. Jordan thinks we should build a home and finds much land that is good, east facing, west facing with steady streams close by. I urge them on for I know in the distance is our journey's end. Pride has returned to Giovanni, ambition to Jordan. "Many could live here," Jordan proclaims with hearty bluster. "Our brothers and sisters would come in time and we could build more rooms for them, turrets with views over the valley, gardens in which to stroll. Can't you see it Israel, how grand it all could be?"

"I can see it," I assure him, "but I have grander visions yet."

"Beautiful men and women would gather there," yells Giovanni. "We would laugh, drink and make love all through the night. It won't get cold in the winter unless we want it to and we could wear the finest garments cut from the best cloth. We will host the most sumptuous parties. People will come from all over. We'll be famous, forever."

"We could," I say. "We could do anything we choose but forever is a long time. If you trust me and keep to this path, I think you will find we're already bound for the best party, and that our houses and clothes, our food, wine and love await us."

EVANGELINE

Yes I'm nervous. Who wouldn't be? I know what an awesome adversary he is now that I've waded through Orson's bizarre dossier. I've never been scared of him before but I have my mission clearly in my mind. It was obvious, and when Rahab phoned me from the brothel, it was like I'd been expecting the call. I knew it would come tonight. I'm wearing a diaphanous black number with gold threads running through it, my makeup heavier than usual, vulgar almost. Tonight I really want to wow him because tonight will be special. The most special night of his life. He just doesn't know it yet.

I've prepared the Turkish delight myself this time. It's something I've been working on perfecting for a long while but I never get the quantity of rose water and gelatine quite right. This time I have. I've triumphed. I feel like the wicked queen in *Snow White* with her basket of shiny red, toxic apples. I sometimes wonder if the icing sugar might not give me a nasty yeast infection but so far, so good. Tonight however, with the special ingredients I've used, I don't want to put it inside until I'm undressed. Ready. I can't afford for it to be in there too long in case it dissolves into me. That is the risk. My betrayal must be flawless.

He's impressed, I can tell when I walk in, he looks younger himself and I wonder if he's had work done since the last time we were together. He certainly has over the years I've known him.

"You are a timeless beauty, Evangeline," he whispers as I lead him up the stairs.

"And you are the only man in the world I want to go to Heaven with tonight, Abdulah…," I coquettishly whisper in his ear. "When Rahab phoned…I was wet as soon as we spoke, as soon as I knew you were waiting. Do you think me a terrible harlot? Am I wicked to say such a thing?"

"You are the only woman I would forgive such thoughts. You are like my *best* wife. The one the others would hate and their hatred would make me love you more." I smile with a feigned modesty, with an artifice I hope doesn't appear grotesque. I open the door to the Al-Ghaydah room, pulling from my bag the three fine pieces of jewelry I have made for him on the pretext that he will take them to his wives. They are exquisite even if I do say so myself. I could cackle at the treachery of it all but I don't.

"Abdulah, at least your wives can wear my rings. Do they love them? Do they unsettle the house?"

"Oh yes, they wait for them breathlessly. They will fight like *cats* if I'm not careful who I give them to."

Ah yes, I say to myself. *Men are the reason women hate each other.* He grabs me roughly, frightening me for a moment. I look at the savagery in his eyes and wonder if he hasn't guessed at my plan. His hand works its brutish way beneath my dress. I hadn't lied when I said the phone call made me wet. It was true though not for the reasons I told him. This excitement is different. It's like something I've never known. I could die, or vanish tonight, if anything went wrong.

He slips the dress down my back and I stand naked but for an absurd little sex-shop bra that supports my breasts but barely covers my nipples. I'm wearing matching lace pants and suspender belt with all the traditional trimmings: hooks, eyes and black satin suspenders. My shoes are outrageous. They're so high my calves nearly go into spasm when I walk in them but I want the performance to be full scale. I don't expect there to be any encores. I stand before him; for once I'm almost his height. He looks at me that way he does, a salacious little boy crossed with a lethal delinquent. I know exactly what he wants but he can't see me put it in or it will spoil his "surprise." This ritual reminds me of the way my grand-mother hid coins in our Christmas puddings; she put them there annually but they were always a thrill to discover. I am his Christmas pudding. He is my Easter sacrifice.

I brush his lips with mine leaving a scarlet stain. I touch them with my finger to quiet him as I vanish into the bathroom. My heart is beating wildly, my thoughts so close to the surface I can't believe he doesn't see a motive glistening in my eyes. What if he does? Would I have the skills to beat him?

My pants are not crotchless. I find those too vulgar even for whoring. I'm a good girl really. I pull the piece from a tissue in my bag and dry myself off a little with another tissue before I insert it. This is one time when moisture really could ruin a girl's day and I hope against hope we're going to get straight down to business.

When I return, he is still dressed. I will have to undress him but only after he's had me naked before him awhile. That's the deal, he needs to feel served, superior, Godlike. I climb onto the bed, posi-tioning myself in front of him. I feel quite shameless but must attempt a degree of coyness. With the sheik—too bold and he could turn, too coy and I might lose him. I touch myself softly; hard, bright nails on the softest folds of flesh. That both textures can be of the same organic origin is a marvel in itself. He licks my nipples then lowers himself before me. My legs form a V into which his head can bob, a fragrant isthmus or special vortex for him to snuf-fle like a hog for his truffle. I push myself forward a little because I don't want that confection in there for long. Already I'm perceiving little sensory changes though it could be just my imagination. His tongue and teeth are burrowing deeper, I picture a beaver or a chip-munk—some terrible gnawing rodent that could destroy an entire house or undermine a city if it is not kept in check.

Then at last he's got it. I feel him pulling back out of me but instead of seizing the whole chunk, he bites it in half. Half is still inside. A chill passes through me. What if he has guessed, and how quickly will it seep into my bloodstream down there?

"There's more, sweetie," I whimper. "Not hungry today, Abdulah?"

"Peckish," he says, eventually diving back for the other half. I sigh audibly, and too soon because no sooner has he got it in his mouth than he's trying to spit it into mine. He seldom kisses me so this comes as a surprise. It's only the second half, but even so there is a shitload of silt in it. I want as little in my system as I can get away with.

I try to kiss it back to him but he keeps forcing it into my mouth. I begin to panic a little. Is my accepting something that has been inside me supposed to be the gesture of an uninhibited libertine or an act of shocking humiliation? With the sheik it's hard to tell. Does he adore women or despise us?

I straddle him and dominate him. I can taste the silt in my mouth. Surely if I can, he will. I grab the cup of mint tea from the bedside and the honey spoon beside it and lean forward, threatening to drip honey on his shirt. In a moment of involuntary self-defence, I slip the remaining Turkish delight back into his mouth, dribbling honey in after it. With so much going on he's forced to swallow it, forced to pretend for a second that he's enjoying himself when in fact I have overpowered him. He doesn't like that.

He's tearing off his shirt now. He always wears Western clothes in Western countries. Again he grabs me roughly, his fingers pushing inside. Hurting. Now I could use some more wetness but he's not letting me go to the bathroom where I might be able to quickly douche out any residue from that silt and freshen myself up a little to receive him. No matter how vile men are, there are few who will question your reasons for visiting the bathroom. That much I've learned. He's more aggressive now and I'm a little scared—too dry, too wet, just right. *Goldilocks,* I think as he starts pushing his cock into me. It's a rude shock, he's not usually like this.

"I'm angry for you," he mumbles. I can't tell whether he said angry or hungry. It feels like anger though. I don't care, I'm the martyr, the heroine, the messiah. I'm on a mission from God! Who'd have thought I'd end up with the task of dispatching the sheik, of challenging him at the sport of his own invention? The new polo for the nouveau elite or the desperately depraved. This is one instance where luxury may surprise but won't disappoint. I slow him down a little because I can't afford for this to all happen too fast. Already my perception has shifted somewhat. The colors are brighter. *He* looks more powerful, more dangerous—sinister. I wonder for a second if he might not be God, or Satan. Both. That's silt for you. There is going to come a moment when he realizes what has happened. That is the moment I most fear, the minute or so when he is still worldly enough to comprehend my betrayal. I hope—or do I pray?—that this comes far enough into the shift that our battle will be fought there, with him at a distinct disadvantage. Gently I take his wrists and hold them above him, still straddling him, still taking his rough thrusts deep inside me. I reach for the manacles that hang from the bedpost to see if he'll let me fasten them to his wrists.

"We've never done it like *this* before," I whisper and he doesn't say yes but he doesn't say no either so I lock one of them in place. I reward his compliance with an extra grind of my pelvis. He smiles then grimaces. It's hideous.

I had shown Orson the silt I found in Israel's desk. I opened the bolt of satin I'd hidden it in and displayed the sachet of crystals as if they were rare jewels. He'd come over one evening to meet Anton. At first I wasn't going to tell him what I had planned but that changed after we all drank some wine. I knew the twisted, filthy nature of my quest would be too much for him to resist being in on. It probably made him cum in his corduroy slacks.

Orson thought, just from looking at the crystals in the bag, that there was at least enough for four standard doses. He's an expert in theory at least. Anton and I had decided we didn't want to take any more ourselves. Ever. And the best thing I could do was to beat the sheik at his own game. A frightening and dangerous endgame. I devised several strategies: the first was to dissolve the silt into the Turkish delight mixture, but that was no good because he'd only eat one piece anyway. Then I decided to carefully insert it into a clump that I'd had to cut in half and stick back together. Because silt has a salty, bitter, slightly metallic taste, I put pistachio nuts in the mixture also. It was the taste that was my greatest fear and I knew that when the time came, when next we met, it would be a duel to the finish. One that I would only win if I could stay clear headed. I had learned from Orson that the sheik took nothing lying down (well almost nothing), that he would stop at nothing. That it was easier for a camel to pass through the eye of a penis than it would be to get him to relinquish his worldly empire.

ISRAEL

Giovanni's mood has darkened like the sky. I hadn't thought it would be possible here. Lightning tears through the clouds like a knife through flesh.

"We should have built a house," says Jordan, who points to the sky like it's a good argument.

"This is trouble, I just know it," says Giovanni, turning his collar against a wind that has picked up out of nowhere.

"There's a house up ahead," I say. "Won't that shelter us from the storm?" Giovanni is agitated. He's turning the rings on his fingers. "It will take more than that house to shelter us from this storm, my friend."

Still we go in. The house is a little cute for my liking. Like gingerbread. "Did you build this?" I ask Jordan.

He smiles enigmatically. "Maybe I did, maybe I didn't."

The lounge is warm; a fire crackles in the hearth while a TV flickers in the corner. I can't quite make out what is on the screen but I seem to recognize the show. Canned laughter breaks through the silence. There's a woman and a man. In my dream it would have been dirty. Jordan takes a chair. "We've gotta watch this!"

Yes folks it's time for everyone's favorite show, Kingdom Come. *And here's one girl who doesn't know if she's too wet or too dry, it's Goldilocks— she's in the hot seat tonight. And our question tonight is, can she BEAR it?* shouts the TV voice-over as more canned laughter issues forth. *Gol-di-locks, Gol-di-locks,* chants an unseen studio audience as the woman cracks her whip and circles the restrained man.

And our other contestant is the Big Bad Wolf. He's certainly going to be sweating tonight, oh my wordy Lordy yes. It seems poor old Wolf just doesn't know if he's coming or going so let's y'all just sit back and see what tricks Goldilocks has up her pretty little sleeve, shall we?

Giovanni flops onto a cushion, a flicker of concern mixes with his excitement. It's as if we're about to watch the soccer final or the running of the bulls. "Have we seen this show?" I ask them.

Giovanni shakes his head. "No, but I've been waiting a long time for it to come out."

"What's she got in there?" says Jordan, peering at the fleshy close-up on the screen.

"*Ave Maria, piena di grazie. Signore è contè!*" shouts Giovanni as she displays the trophy.

"And check out those heels!" I add as we prepare for the game.

EVANGELINE

He's taking me like a savage now as I'm fighting against strange shifts. I can't get his other wrist cuffed either. It bothers me. I keep thinking there are others here. I think I see Jordan, Israel, and then Giovanni seems to loom above me for a moment. For a second I wonder whether the sheik and Giovanni are the same person but of course they can't be. Can they? I've already been down that road. Israel talked of guardian angels. He believed in that sort of crap. He said when he was doing outrageously dangerous sexual things with total strangers or sociopaths, sometimes there would appear to be someone else there with him. He'd forget there were only two people and he'd think he was in a three-way. He said that was his guardian angel. It was a man. Now I feel the same except mine appear to be the three of them. Are they watching me, or holding me? I can't tell. I'm bucking like a bronco, finally I'm actually getting properly wet though I'm still terrified, and I look into his eyes, which are wild and crazy now. A gentleman he is not. He roars like a beast, like THE beast, and thrusts deeper.

"I know what you've done, you bitch. You Jezebel." His free hand strikes hard on the side of my face. The left side. It's where they've always hit me. My skin sings with the memory of a dozen men as hot blood rushes to my cheek. He roars more, then hits me again. I feel like I'm watching a werewolf in a film, the torture of metamorphosis searing his face. Contorting it. He fights like crazy, holding me to him with his free arm, but he keeps fucking me as if he's a machine or a robotic dog, preprogrammed. As if this is some archaic behavioral script that all men must act out. A primal directive that whatever happens, he must leave one more measure of his seed. What corner of the world has been spared his wretched spray? It's grotesque, frightening, but I must say, spectacular. He calls out someone's name. I'm not sure whether it's mine or Giovanni's, they sound quite similar when uttered in extremis. And he explodes in me with such supernatural force I half slide off the bed and come loose from him also. The veins in his forehead pulse dangerously. I wonder if he'll have a stroke. His eyes are fixed somewhere else. I pull myself from the bed while he thrashes. This is the moment when I must do my real work. Become the ultimate dominatrix: not only She who must be obeyed but She who must be transcended. He groans like a monster, like he's possessed. I stalk around the bed, my legs killing me on these heels but I need the height. I *insist* on the drama of them. Israel would be proud.

"Sheik Abdulah Kazzir you have been a disgrace to your land, to your people, to humanity and to Allah himself: There is but one God and you must submit and that one God is in front of you and She is not happy. She's in a banishing mood!" I pull out a piece of parchment from my bag with the list I had prepared earlier, the arms sales documented in Orson's files.

ISRAEL

"That chick, she's gonna win for sure!" Jordan yells, thumping his fists excitedly on the floor. She's about to read something out. We try to make it out but the reception gets crackly.

"Don't be so sure," admonishes Giovanni. "I've seen this wolf play before. He plays dirty."

"And you would never have done anything like that, would you Giovanni?" He smiles guiltily but admits nothing.

Five hundred Stinger missiles, the infrared, heat-seeking, high-explosive warheads with significant counter-measure immunity.

Two MI-24 Hind Gunships used in three conflicts, none of which your country played any part in but which you profited from extensively nonetheless.

Four Anti-Tank Launcher RPG-7s directly responsible for fourteen-hundred military casualties, three hundred civilian attacks, and, when seized by your opponents, the killing of one hundred and eighty-nine of your own country's civilians in direct counterattacks.

"Go girl. She sure is telling him now! God only knows what she's talking about." Jordan shakes his head in disbelief. I say, "I think there was a war somewhere."

"He's gonna be one Goddammed pussy-whipped motherfucker after this," giggles Giovanni.

EVANGELINE

He's writhing less, his rage is still frightening but he seems more focussed and miraculously he hasn't figured out that he could release his own wrist from the manacle if he wanted to… He seems to have lost his usual wits, possibly even his mind. Maybe God is on my side in this war. I've pulled a whip from the drawer; now I take a deep breath and crack it. Annie Getcha Gun!

"But enough about war, I'm not interested in your anger towards Christians or the hatred between Arabs, Jews and Americanos. You'd kill each other twice if you could. Y'all just have a passion for violence and a taste for blood that I don't share so you can stew in your own juice and pride for all I care." I raise the whip again like a cowgirl. I catch my reflection in the full-length mirror. I'm shocked. I look twenty again, my breasts pert, stomach flat. Must be the silt. *Exercise caution.* It could turn at any time, I think.

"You're a crazy whore, Evangeline. Sluts like you are why we need to protect our women. I could have you beheaded."

"You and whose army? Besides, I wouldn't be much fun then, would I? We're old *mates* you and me. What is it—ten, maybe fifteen years we've known each other? Some great times, some beautiful jewelry, some exquisite drugs and *hell*, I'm not interested in the decades of horror you've put your country through or the fires we light on your doorstep to warm our greasy hands by. What do I care about oil pumping senselessly into the ocean? I don't even drive a fucking car! It's all just sport, a bit of fun. Crazy stuff… No Abdulah, I'd like to think we had become friends and that one day you might have shared some of your friends with me, but you kept 'em to yourself didn't you? Stashed away in a pension on the *Rue de*

Cirque or locked in a stinking cubicle in Stonemasons Walk. I think I'm a kind woman, a decent woman—though looking at me tonight you might beg to differ—but I am a *business*woman Abdulah and it's as a businesswoman I'm going to deal with you now."

I circle him briefly, weighing my speech, cradling the whip, feeling a dizzying high.

"I don't know what your Koran says nor how monstrously it's been perverted by power-mongers and fundamentalists over the years but if it's anything like the Bible or the book of Mormon I'd be giving it a very wide berth. I also think you've probably been pretty lenient on yourself in the sin department too. Arms dealing, drug pushing, adultery, all just beer and skittles when you think about it. Far be it from me to cast the first stone, but I know there is one thing a man of your faith and stature must never do or be. One thing that is a true abomination in the eyes of God—Islamic and Christian alike. Something so wicked it's a wonder He hasn't already smote you or borne upon you a plague or whatever the fuck He does when He's really pissed because you must never, *ever* be as a woman with another man…it says it in the Bible, it says it in the Koran."

He bellows like a wounded steer.

"I have never done this!" he cries like a lunatic.

"No? I think you have. I know you have! You can tell me, sugar, your old friend Evangeline. I know what you've been up to with Giovanni. He had it filmed for Chrissake! It's! Public! Record!"

His face grimaces with an inner pain, a regret I'd never imagined him capable of showing.

"*He* was with me as a woman, I was *not* the woman!"

"Butcha were—it certainly looks that way in the film! Abdulah, what would Allah say? Naughty, naughty, naughty. What would your wives say, your sons, your father and mother? What would the Secretary of State say I wonder when he sees what a big old *woman* you were?"

He's beginning to shake. He's having a conversation with someone or something I can't see—Giovanni maybe—Allah perhaps? Who can say? There is much he needs to reckon with.

"I showed the film to the Imam at the mosque, I thought he'd be able to tell me how evil you had been but he returned it wrapped in brown paper and has never said another word to me." (This is a lie of course but if I'm to play on his fear, his erroneous zones, this seems the sort of shit that would most likely freak him out.) "So you tell me Abdulah honey, why you would try to get all those homosexuals on silt when you're no better than any of them yourself? What's that about?"

"I don't care about these homos, they can do what they like. It's not for me to judge. It was Giovanni, always wanting more from me. More for himself, more to sell. He blackmailed me."

"And what about the shift. Do you like it?"

He's muttering. Sweating like Jesus on the cross.

"No I don't like it."

"Guilty conscience perhaps?"

He says nothing, just rocks like a baby on the bed. A sixty-year-old pathetic baby, and I am pleased. Not because I'm vindictive—I'm not that type—but because for once I can see that a man like him can be reduced to such a childlike state. All my life I've wondered at the strength and cruelty men could sustain. For once I'm reducing one back to what he really is. A little naughty boy who at the end of the day has hurt himself more than anyone.

"Let me go, let me go," he moans.

"All in good time. I think you're still far too agitated," I say, but then I realize he's not talking to me. He's talking to someone else while swatting demons with his free hand. He's drifted away from me completely. He's not fighting me anymore. He has bigger fish to fry.

"I tell you what, Abdulah. I'm itching for a pee so I'm going to vanish into the bathroom. While I'm away, if you have any sense of decency, if you are even half a man, you'll vanish too."

And fuck me if he didn't do just that!

There was no sound. No doors banging, no creaking floorboards. Just an empty bed with a manacle swinging miserably from side to side. The rings I had given him were still by the bed, as were his clothes; the door was still locked from the inside. He had disappeared. I had done it!

I fixed myself up, stuffed his shoes and clothes in a plastic bag that I hid under my coat and carried downstairs. Rahab was at the front desk.

"So he's well and truly done judging from the racket you two were making?"

I fluttered my lashes coquettishly. "Yeah, I went to the en suite in the room. When I came out he'd left. Must have been something I said. Did he pay?"

"No. I didn't even see him come down. I was folding towels out in back there."

"Huh," I laughed. "Fancy the sheik doing a runner."

"Honey, we've got his credit card number, it's in the system."

I opened up my purse, put on some more lipstick. I felt a little giddy but I needed a drink at Bar None, nonetheless. I tottered out of 755 past the waiting limo. The driver chewed on a toothpick, all the while watching me from behind mirrored sunglasses, despite the fact that it was after dark. What would he do when his master didn't return? What would Rahab say, what would I say, and just how much trouble would there be? "People don't just disappear," I muttered to myself. But then I heard Israel whispering to me from places far away. "They do, Evangeline. People vanish all the time." I imagined him in our lounge, with a drawing of us all. One by one he rubbed us out with his eraser. Our grinning, idiotic cartoon mugs, unbecoming. The paper returned to white. Polar bears in a snowstorm.

Izzy and Eve

The image on the screen vanishes. We've all been laughing so much, even Giovanni managed a few chuckles as we watched the woman taunt the funny man who thought he was an abomination. People dream up some truly bizarre things. Outside the sun is up again, the rain has stopped. Jordan goes to the window and I hear him say, "Uh-oh."

"What?"

"Another casualty."

We open the door and there, stretched before us, is a brown Arab boy, his skin only slightly soiled, his head glowing softly. Giovanni takes his head in his lap, entranced by the figure's beauty. He sips some water then dribbles it into the stranger's mouth.

"Let me go, let me go," he whimpers.

"It's all right. No one is going to hurt you," says Giovanni. "We'll look after you here."

His eyes open, then dart suspiciously from face to face. His body is folding into itself as though he fears something from us.

"There's nothing to fear," pipes Jordan. "I was like you too, wasn't I Israel? I thought Israel was God."

We all titter except for the new boy who asks, "Are you?"

"That's how naive you can be when you first arrive. But hey, we don't have that far to go and you'll be up and about in no time at all," whispers Jordan.

"No *time* at all!" I say as we all laugh again. With the sun up once more, everything looks fine but I'm starting to think about night-clubs and taverns, dancing and music. We can't be that far now. The new boy stirs; he seems to have stopped his panicking for a moment.

"We're hoping that soon we'll find a town with some bars and music. What do you think?"

He smiles a little then casts his eyes along the road ahead.

"I don't mind," he says. "I'll follow you but I don't drink and I've never learned to dance."

Giovanni shouts, "Then I will show you how!" As if in anticipation, he stands, readies himself and tries a few moves as we prepare for the journey ahead.

EVANGELINE

The Cloisters hasn't changed a lot since the days when Israel used to DJ here. It's a series of vast underground chambers with very interesting acoustics. It is reputed to be the place where the Catholic priests kept all their wine when the country was first settled. All very Gothic, perfect for Tobias's band. Morgana is already projecting images onto the stone walls: ripples of water across the estuary, ghostly bodies floating by, images of strange angels and feisty demons captured in a tiled toilet cubicle. All this mixed with a low Haseeshi mourning chant and contemporary drumbeat. Mist billows out from beneath the stage and wafts about our feet as interpretive dancers in bondage gear weave through the crowd making grotesque faces at audience members. I'll say one thing for Morgana, she can certainly organize a show.

Anton and I must be the oldest people here—well at least until Mary shows up.

"I couldn't get Calvin to come," she says to me as I kiss her cheek. "It's all a bit too off the wall for him. What do you think of Morgana's slide show?"

"The slide show is fine, I'm just a little nervous about seeing myself portrayed as a Goth crawling around on my hands and knees in men-only sex venues. But hey, this whole thing is bigger than us now. Right?"

Silt is just another one of those myths to Morgana like the Bermuda Triangle, spontaneous combustion or the Loch Ness monster. "What really happened is neither here nor there," I say, and Mary smiles, perhaps at the symbolism of my comment. Her hair is in a neat bob that she still keeps that gray-blonde color favored by so many middle-aged women from the respectable precincts. She is wearing one of my brooch designs from twenty years ago. It still looks good. Her outfit is as hip as I've seen her dare to dress in years. Tobias now wears a fistful of Israel's rings. He looks quite the warlord with his hair long and ratty. He's sporting tattoos that I've seen but his mother hasn't. He's added a long leather coat like Giovanni used to wear to his ensemble, a hefty line of kohl under his eyes and a black T-shirt with white cursive script proclaiming the words to the song, "Going Over Jordan." I've seen several people wearing these since the woman, whose name it turns out was Marta Lushenka, was brutally raped and murdered last year. I shiver again at the thought of it. Who would do such a thing? I kept all the articles and wept: *An Angel Falls*, *Let the Devil In*, *What Grisly Gilgal Horror This*? Thirty of them had raped her. Savage unrepentant youths from the precincts had come to "right her earthly snare," as some journalist had written. Of course all the biblical parallels had been made to Sodom and Gomorrah. The tabloids had a field day. Her killers left her body on the mailbox in a crucifixion-like pose, and it has been said the police found her smiling. I've designed a statue that the council has yet to approve.

The house lights fade, Anton makes creepy noises in my ear and projections of water ripple all around us. A foghorn booms out of sight while an overture played on electric guitars bursts into life. A latex screen is torn open to reveal Orphan's Seed.

Taking chances
shadow dancers
give me something more tonight.
I'm just playing
you're not staying
let me see a different light...

And there it was. The mystery of silt (or an approximation thereof) in a pyrotechnic rock concert that was really not bad at all.

"I don't quite know what to make of it all," says Mary, who is cautiously sipping her second red wine because she has to drive.

"Make of it what you will," I say downing my fourth scotch.

"The truth varies from soul to soul," ventures Anton.

Tobias meanders over wearing a tentatively triumphant smile. "Wadja think?"

"I'm very proud of you, darling," Mary says with a hug. "*Bravo.*"

"Brilliant," I add with a kiss while Anton slaps him on the back and ruffles his hair.

Anton wants to go out and drink with his pals at Anchors. Mary and I walk to a cafe nearby. It's a warm night so we sit outside watching a new fire-eater and an old mime artist interact in front of a few dumbstruck tourists.

"Anton's very quiet, isn't he?" Mary spoons the froth from her decaf into her mouth.

"Mostly. I think he's quite wise. Isn't that the mark of true enlightenment—silence, serenity? Listening but not talking?"

Mary considers it for a moment. "Well, that's what they say. Men make all their noise when they're young. We wait until we're middle-aged biddies or old crones before we start rattling the cage."

"I've always been doing that, more than ever these days. I never imagined life without Israel but it has been full of surprises. It's nearly ten years now."

"I know, doesn't the time fly?" Mary pauses in her small talk. "Does he, Anton...does he still see men?"

"That's where he's gone tonight, Anchors, to see his friends." I wave to Torsten, who is hauling some huge floral catastrophe into a nearby restaurant.

"No, I mean does he still go *with* men?"

I laugh. "Why wouldn't he; I think he's still got it, don't you?"

"Of course but you and he...it doesn't bother you?"

"Mary, I'll let you in on a secret that I'm sure you've worked out for yourself. When you get to be in a monogamous union that is more than five years old, you tend to find there is not much sex going on. It's a trap. You marry in passion, devote yourself for a life-time, then both partners end up doing without. You and I live in different worlds. We've made different worlds. Anton's a dream for me, he never disappoints me or lets me down. To tell you the truth, I think he's getting a bit over all that anyway. He's very spiritual lately and you know me, always something of a maverick in the moral department—a bit of a slut," I add in a whisper.

She pauses but doesn't look at me. "I used to despise you after Josh left. Funny isn't it? I used to think about what you did and how he left and I could have murdered you."

"I didn't even realize you knew."

"Oh I knew all right. But over the years I've thought, what if you had done what you did and he hadn't left? Now I think, God, what if you hadn't done what you did and he'd stayed! So I suppose I'm grateful now."

"I'd love to say it was a humanitarian gesture designed to brighten your future but I'd be lying. I did it because I believed in nothing or thought nothing mattered or perhaps it was my utter cynicism with regard to men."

"Do you still think that way?"

"I still think nothing *matters* in the metaphysical sense but I believe in something now. That what matters is, the poison you put out ends up right back in your own system. That we are all connected— as Israel always said, and I never believed. That he was there with me all those years to show me faith. Don't get me wrong, he was primarily out to serve himself. I was never under any illusions about that, but he was my soul mate. He promised me faith. It's the only thing he ever promised in fact and he delivered. I understand now

how one person can *know* something that others would call a belief.
I also realize how religion succeeds in separating individuals from
faith. How evil religion can be."

"Hmm, I certainly never saw you as one to proselytize on matters
esoteric."

I laugh. "Me neither. I'm glad, though, that there is still some
mystery to life. That one person's unsolved murder is another person's sacred escape. That this world is an illusion—a dream—and
the real adventure awaits us all."

"You believe that?"

"I do now! You've got to be greedy. I want it all and however good
the coffee is here, it couldn't be enough, surely?"

She watches a young couple embrace passionately and shrugs.

"What's enough anyway? I've never had it."

"I think Israel had. I guess Enough is Enough."

ISRAEL

Up ahead is a skyline. Perhaps it is the Emerald City or the Holy Grail—
but yet another figure looms ahead, a shimmering mirage in the gathering dusk. A blonde girl. She's leaning up against a milestone, sipping
a green milkshake from a plastic bag. She looks very bored.

"Who's she?" asks Jordan.

"She's pretty," adds Giovanni. "It's been a while since we saw any
girls and I like what I see." As we approach she straightens her skirt
and adopts a more sophisticated pose.

"Jesus. You took your time, didn't you?"

"*Time*?" I say.

"I've been standing here for, like, eternity sipping this Goddam
milkshake. It's foul."

Jordan takes it from her and drinks some. "Tastes all right to me."

"Yeah well you drink it then. Fucking thing never runs out!"

Abdulah laughs, at what exactly, I'm not sure.

"So are we the first to come by?" I inquire.

"Sort of. Some angels and shit came by before but they didn't look like my scene if you know what I mean, and there's this crazy bitch with a shopping cart somewhere. She keeps ramming me."

Jordan giggles mischievously. "You'll go to Hell if you keep talking like that."

"Sweetheart, I've been to Hell, believe me—I could paint you a picture if you want. Right now I'm looking to party a bit, maybe drink something else besides this Goddam milkshake. You guys know anywhere we can go?"

"I've got a few ideas," I tell her as she spies something behind me.

"Uh-oh, Christ, here she comes again."

In the distance we see the figure of another woman hurtling towards us with a shopping cart. She looks distressed and one of the wheels keeps veering to the side. The milkshake girl gives her the evil eye as she approaches.

"What do you say each time she rams you?" I ask.

"I tell her to shove off, of course. I dunno why she doesn't dump the thing. One of the wheels is totally fucked and it's not like there's anything to buy anyway. I tried to give her this," she waves the milkshake at the approaching woman the way a toreador waves his cape. "She's not interested."

"I don't like green milkshakes either, is it lime or mint?" asks Giovanni.

"This isn't about you, Giovanni," cautions Jordan.

"Next time she rams you, apologize to her," I suggest.

"No way. That bitch can push her cart to Hell as far as I'm concerned. Why should I apologize when it's her doing the ramming?"

"Just trust me on this one, will you?"

The milkshake girl snarls and braces herself for the impact as the cart collides with her.

"So-rr-y," she mutters a little ungraciously to the woman, whose expression suggests she is decidedly elsewhere.

"What did you say?" asks the woman.

"Sorry!"

The woman brushes the thick brown hair from her face. She seems to see us all for the first time. She looks around while composing herself.

"No, it's my fault, I'm sorry. Goodness. I'm so clumsy. Did I hurt you?"

We all laugh including the milkshake girl.

"Hardly," she says dumping her milkshake disdainfully into the baby seat. "You wanna get that thing seen to. That wheel's completely rogered."

The woman smiles at last. "Oh I know, but isn't it always the way with these carts! I still haven't picked up what I need."

"I can fix this," shouts Abdulah. "Then we can all be on our way."

The shopping cart woman grins in gratitude as he fiddles confidently with the wheel.

"I'm going to have to get back," she says. "I just nipped out you see."

"We all did," I tell her. "But if you stick with us we'll see you home. Trust me."

She looks to her wrist but there is nothing there. She shrugs. "Why not?"

"And I'll push the cart," offers Giovanni.

"Can I get in?" asks Lydia, the milkshake girl. "You can take me for a spin. *FAST*."

And in she climbs and off we go as the lights of the city begin to come on.

"We'll be there in no time," I shout triumphantly and Abdulah hooks arms with the shopping cart lady who has yet to introduce herself. Giovanni pushes the girl in the cart, who squeals with delight, kicking her feet in the air, and Jordan and I lead the cavalcade, ever ready for new recruits.

Epilogue

There is a tear in the latex, a tiny fissure that at the right moment anyone and everyone can slip beyond. Into a shimmering Sahara white or a mesmerizing patent-leather black where the habitués of darkness can find what they'd always been seeking. Or where vessels of light can truly shine.

The sheen of metal or the glistening of the strap. Here Evangeline glides easily through the fair, her hair flaxen, her reflection momentarily that of a Japanimation. Refrains from the best pieces of music she's ever heard have been at last, finally, once and for all, mixed into a medley so agreeable, the sound is itself an opiate. And around her people who had been lost amidst their obsessions and weaknesses take a refined pleasure in all the excesses that seemed once to be their ruin. Souls of incalculable beauty collide and merge without casualty and each recovers from its encounter with astounding grace. Is it a cocktail party, a dance party or a classical ball? *Yes,* she thinks, it's all these and more. She's Cinderella, she's Madame Lash, she's Elvira Queen of the Night. Here the glass is neither half full nor half empty and she can walk at whate'er speed she chooses without a slosh or a spill. It is not whiskey or vodka or even gin in her glass but it's as fine a drink as she's ever sipped and as she searches for the face she's longed to see, she begins to greet those she's never met: Giles de Rais, *Enchanté—how very wicked you were,* and how obvious he should have chosen Gaultier; Ms. Austen, *A delight,* and in Dior. *Herr Hitler, you devil—you had us all fooled for a moment there and in Armani, who would have guessed. Auf deine Gesundheit, meine Liebe! Möge sie ewig währen,* he whispered but she wasn't stopping to chat. And through the mirrored château she promenades, one minute in leather, the next in silk and in a moment of luxuriant realization she understands that a glass slipper can be of great comfort to a girl. She can walk with ease and pride on the most polished of marble without fear they might shatter. *Monsieur Blahnik, a pleasure indeed.* And on she strides to encounter a chorus of flattery from Cher (who'd made it after all), Madonna and Helena Bonham-Carter. *Your rings, Evangeline, we could never have done without them,* they gush like a gaggle of Louisa May Alcott creations in Versace and Prada. *It was nothing,* she says with a dismissive wave as she forges on, now in slip-ons made of silk. Past the clusters of rabbis, gaggles of thieves and the Mormons and Seventh Days, laughing like jackals at their former naivete. Past the priests and their cupids and the woman from the mailbox now singing Gershwin with Ella Fitzgerald. The corridor stretches forever but still she's not tired, her armpits remain dry and her hair moves like liquid. At last the promises of those shampoo ads have come true. *I never thought it would all be so exquisitely shallow,* she says, to which a devastatingly handsome bearded man (Rasputin, she suspected) says, *It needn't be my dear,* as he directs her to a marbled staircase going down. *As you can see the bubbles always rise to the top.*

She takes the staircase, which puts her in mind of a Viennese opera house and she laughs as her haste causes her to leave a slipper behind. Barefoot is good. Barefoot is easy as she enters a different domain, rich with the fragrance of leather and pipe smoke. Here she nods and they nod back, Da Vinci, De Beauvoir, Greer, Michelangelo, Einstein—all those she could ever hope to recognize appear on her trek. Her dress, she is pleased to notice, is now just a simple black shift with a solitary string of pearls. Strata after strata she traverses until at last she reaches what has to be the darkest part. Beautiful whores loiter timelessly by quaint European houses illuminated from within by a familiar red glow. Men dressed as women, women dressed as men: gender has yet to define itself and Evangeline herself is changing as she walks into something she'd sometimes dreamed of becoming—a man who liked men—and as she rounds a corner, there is another man loitering beneath a flashing bar sign. She hardens in her trousers, and with a puff of smoke the figure mutters quietly, *You wanna fool around?*

And Vangio, which is who Eve has become, has always wanted to fool around. She wants this shadowy figure more than anyone she's ever encountered. The impossibly sexual physique, the great baton outlined in the trousers and the razor-cut black sideburns deeply etched into his cheeks. And the man grabs roughly at Vangio, who is a Northern Italian blond with a handsomely sized uncut cock and a swarthy sweep of five o'clock shadow, and with a knowing laugh urges Vangio not to waste time.

With no one but them now in the comfort of a lane, the trash cans turn into cushions and the buzzing neon into a Brian Eno and Harold Budd soundtrack. Vangio takes this boy with all his strength and vigor and the boy is not about to hold him back. Vangio feels engulfed by sensation, by this man, and knows that this could go on forever. And they kiss and fondle and drift on the breeze and an hour passes or maybe it's a year. There are no clocks in this part of the world because this is not part of the world. And they drift on a cloud and somewhere, perhaps over Bavaria, Evangeline turns to face her boy lover and in the glare of a sudden moonbeam she identifies the man. He leans on one elbow and fingers a lock of her hair and with the wry and cheeky smile she's always loved best says, "So here we all are then." And Evangeline composes herself, looks from Israel to Jordan to Anton who it seems had been there all the while and realizes it's true. Evangeline mutters, "Well just don't say 'I told you so.' That I couldn't stand." And Israel says, "Everything old is new again poppet. I suppose the end is really just the beginning." And he flops onto the cloud and Eve says, "I know, it is Heaven, isn't it?"

Acknowledgments

This book was completed with the assistance of a residency at Varuna Writer's Centre granted by the Eleanor Dark Foundation and a Hobart city writer's residency granted by the Tasmanian Writer's Centre and the Hobart City Council. Thanks also to my ever supportive lover Tim Mansour; and to Brad Shiach, Bronwyn Lea, Justine Ettler, David Hughes, Adrian Lim, Clinton Sands, Marc Staudacher, Marshall Moore, Glenn Carlson, Janelle Boroday, and Robert Borotkanics for their technical, residential, clinical and psychological contributions.

Neal Drinnan (www.nealdrinnan.com) was born in Melbourne, Australia, sometime in the last century. At seventeen he abandoned his education and suburban family home for the lure of life's more ephemeral things. He has worked in publishing for many years and been a frequent contributor to many magazines and newspapers. He is the author of three previous novels—*Glove Puppet, Pussy's Bow,* and *Quill*—as well as *The Rough Guide to Gay and Lesbian Australia.*